Praise for these three sensational authors!

HELEN BIANCHIN

"Helen Bianchin [creates stories that are]
elegant, graceful, intense, passionate,
enchanting and sensuous."
—*thebestreviews.com*

REBECCA WINTERS

"Rebecca Winters captures the essence of true love
and makes it come alive for her reader."
—*thebestreviews.com*

LUCY GORDON

"Ms. Gordon crafts a sweet emotional story that will
stay with you long after the last page is turned!"
—*thebestreviews.com*

Helen Bianchin worked as a legal secretary in her native New Zealand, then spent two years traveling and working in various parts of Australia. She met and married her Italian-born husband in the tobacco farming town of Mareeba where she cooked for seasonal workers and helped out on the farm. Three years of hailstorms and crop losses resulted in a lifestyle change, and Helen returned to New Zealand with her husband and their daughter, where they added two sons to their family. Encouraged by a friend who enjoyed numerous anecdotes of Helen's life as a tobacco farmer's wife, the tentative idea of writing romance novels emerged. Six years after her first book was published, Helen and her family returned to Australia to settle in southeast Queensland, where they currently reside.

Rebecca Winters lives in Salt Lake City, Utah. When she was seventeen, she went to boarding school in Lausanne, Switzerland, where she learned to speak French and met girls from all over the world. Upon returning to the U.S., Rebecca developed her love of languages when she earned her B.A. in secondary education, history, French and Spanish from the University of Utah and did postgraduate work in Arabic. For the past fifteen years she has taught junior-high and high-school French and history, and says she got into serious writing almost by accident. She has won the National Readers' Choice Award, the *Romantic Times* Reviewers' Choice Award, and has been named Utah Writer of the Year. Rebecca has written over fifty novels for Harlequin.

Lucy Gordon was born in England, where she still lives with her Italian husband. She began writing by working on a British women's magazine. As a features writer she gained a wide variety of experience. Lucy now claims to be an expert on one particular subject—Italian men. According to Lucy, they are the most romantic men in the world. After thirteen years in the magazine business, Lucy decided that it was now or never if she was ever going to write that novel. So she wrote *Legacy of Fire* for Silhouette Special Edition, followed by *Enchantment in Venice*. Then Lucy did something crazy—she gave up her job. Since then she has concentrated entirely on writing romances and has had over sixty-five books published.

Coming Home

HELEN BIANCHIN
REBECCA WINTERS
LUCY GORDON

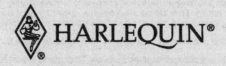

HARLEQUIN®

TORONTO • NEW YORK • LONDON
AMSTERDAM • PARIS • SYDNEY • HAMBURG
STOCKHOLM • ATHENS • TOKYO • MILAN • MADRID
PRAGUE • WARSAW • BUDAPEST • AUCKLAND

ISBN 0-373-83627-9

COMING HOME

Copyright © 2004 by Harlequin Books S.A.

The publisher acknowledges the copyright holders
of the individual works as follows:

A CHRISTMAS MARRIAGE ULTIMATUM
Copyright © 2004 by Helen Bianchin

A PRINCE FOR CHRISTMAS
Copyright © 2004 by Rebecca Winters

THE MILLIONAIRE'S CHRISTMAS WISH
Copyright © 2004 by Lucy Gordon

www.eHarlequin.com

Printed in U.S.A.

CONTENTS

A CHRISTMAS MARRIAGE ULTIMATUM

Helen Bianchin

CHAPTER ONE

CHANTELLE transferred the last bag of groceries into the boot and closed it, then she returned the shopping trolley to a nearby bay. Minutes later she eased her mother's Lexus out from the car park and joined the flow of traffic heading north.

Handling left-hand drive after a four-year absence didn't pose any problems at all, and she slid her sunglasses down to shade her eyes from the glare of the midsummer sun as she headed towards Sovereign Islands, a top-end luxury residential estate on Queensland's Gold Coast, comprising numerous waterways where boats and cruisers lay moored adjacent waterfront homes.

It was an idyllic setting, and she approved of her parents' move from their frenetic Sydney lifestyle. Mother and stepfather, she mentally corrected, although Jean-Paul had taken on the role of father when she'd been nine years old. Too long ago for her to regard him as anything other than a much-loved parent.

The past few years had wrought several changes, she reflected musingly.

Who would have thought at twenty-four she'd

have thrown up a position as pharmacist in an exclusive Sydney pharmacy, a modern apartment, family, friends…for a small villa owned by her parents in northern France?

Yet four years ago it had seemed the perfect place to escape to following an end to a brief, passionate affair.

A month after her arrival, she'd discovered she was pregnant. So she'd stayed, gaining work in the local *pharmacie*, and had the baby, a beautiful dark-haired, dark-eyed boy she'd named Samuel. It had become a matter of pride to be self-supportive, and her parents visited twice a year.

Now, after a four-year absence, she'd brought Samuel to Australia for him to sample his first southern-hemispheric Christmas.

'No snow,' she'd explained when the jet touched down in Brisbane two days ago, and rejoiced in her son's wonderment at the switch in climates as he embraced his grandparents.

How simplistic life was to a child, Chantelle mused as she traversed the first of three bridges leading to Anouk and Jean-Paul Patric's home on one of seven islands linked to form the suburban Sovereign Islands estate.

Children responded to love and affection, and her son was no exception. Bilingual, he was equally conversant in French and English. Tall for his tender years, thick dark hair, beautiful dark eyes, with a melting smile, he was his father in miniature.

Chantelle shook off the whisper of ice slithering down her spine at the thought of the man who'd fathered her child.

Dimitri Cristopoulis. Undeniably Greek, American educated, tall, dark and attractive, an entrepreneur in his mid-thirties who dealt in the buying and selling of hotels and apartment buildings in several major cities worldwide.

Even now, his image was as vivid as it had been four years ago. Broad sculpted facial features, olive textured skin, dark gleaming eyes, and a mouth to die for.

Sexy, sensual and incredibly lethal, she'd mentally accorded when she'd first caught his gaze in a Sydney city restaurant.

She hadn't been wrong. He was all three, and more…much more. She, who was incredibly selective in sharing her body, had gifted hers willingly after one night.

For one month they'd enjoyed life and each other with a passion that captured her heart. Only to have it torn apart with the arrival of an actress claiming to be his fiancée.

Confrontation involved accusations and argument, and Chantelle had walked away…out of his life, her own, invoking her parents' promise not to divulge information as to her whereabouts. In a bid for a new life, a new identity, she had reverted to her legal birth-name of Chantelle *Leone*.

Now Chantelle turned into the boulevard housing the elegant home her parents had retired to last year from their mansion in Sydney, used the remote modem to open the gates, and garaged the car.

Jean-Paul appeared as she opened the boot, and together they caught up the grocery bags and took them indoors.

'Maman, Maman!'

Chantelle deposited the bags on the kitchen table and opened her arms wide to scoop up her son. 'Hello, *mon ange*. Have you been good for Grandmère?'

'*Excellent,*' Samuel assured as he wrapped his arms around her neck. 'Tonight we're having a party.' He pressed kisses to her cheek. 'Grandmère says I am an important guest.'

'Very important,' she confirmed, hugging him close. He was the most precious person in her life, and she never failed to ensure he knew just how much he was loved. 'After lunch you must have a long nap, hmm? So you will be at your best, and everyone will think you totally adorable.'

'Totally.'

Chantelle chuckled and buried her lips into the curve of his sweet neck. He was developing a delightful sense of humour, and his smile...it bore the promise of having the same devastating effect as the man who'd fathered him.

Which tore at her heartstrings more than she cared to admit. Already, the likeness between child and father was fast becoming apparent. Too apparent, she perceived, making it difficult to dismiss Dimitri Cristopoulis from her mind.

A silent derisive laugh rose and died in her throat. As if that was going to happen any time soon. His image was just as powerful now as it had been four years ago.

Worse, he invaded her dreams…teasing, taunting, enticing in a way that brought her awake heated, restless and *wanting*.

'We'll have an early lunch,' Anouk relayed as she began unloading the grocery bags. 'Then we begin preparations, *oui*?'

It proved to be a busy afternoon, and Chantelle stood with Anouk and Jean-Paul for a final inspection before they retreated upstairs to dress.

The large terrace looked festive with a tracery of coloured lights, lanterns and potted flowers gracing the area. Holly and mistletoe, a tall Christmas tree festooned with decorative ornaments, with wrapped gifts for the guests. Bottles of wine for the men, and handmade chocolates for the women which Anouk and Jean-Paul would hand out at the evening's close.

A kindly protestation not to go over the top fell on deaf ears, for Anouk had merely smiled, patted her daughter's hand, bestowed a fleeting kiss to one cheek, and assured it was just an informal gathering of friends.

Given her mother's penchant for entertaining, and the many formal social events Anouk had hosted in Sydney over the years, Chantelle conceded with musing humour that tonight's soirée fell into *informal* by comparison.

Samuel's delighted enchantment with everything was sufficient reward for the requisite part she was expected to play.

Consequently she selected a stunning black evening trouser suit, draped a long red silk wrap across her shoulders, added minimum jewellery, and went with subtle make-up before leading Samuel downstairs.

Jean-Paul greeted guests in the main foyer, directed them through to the terrace, whereupon Anouk ensured they mixed and mingled seamlessly while hired staff offered liquid refreshment and proffered trays of hors d'oeuvres.

Anouk was a charming hostess, and Chantelle joined her mother as they moved effortlessly from one guest to another, pausing while Anouk exchanged a few words, a smile as she introduced her daughter and grandson.

Everyone seemed pleasant, and Chantelle silently commended her parents' circle of friends.

Samuel was in his element, and determined to illustrate his good manners as he formally offered his hand at each introduction.

He was a hit, she acknowledged with maternal bemusement, exuding the charm of a child twice his age.

Just like his father.

Where did that come from? A hollow laugh rose and died in her throat.

Not a day went by when she wasn't reminded of the man who'd fathered him.

Chantelle was aware of her mother's voice as she effected yet another introduction, and she summoned a smile as she greeted the guest.

'Andreas recently moved to the Coast,' Anouk explained. 'And purchased a mansion in a neighbouring Sovereign Islands boulevard.'

There was something about the man's stance, the way he held his head that drew her attention.

'Your parents very kindly included me in this evening's festivities,' he informed in a voice that held a faint accent that was difficult to place.

Andreas... The name was of Greek origin.

'We have something in common,' he offered. 'My son is also visiting for Christmas. He's in the car finishing a call on his cellphone.'

She envisioned with some scepticism a high-powered entrepreneur digitally available twenty-four by seven, negotiating and closing deals worldwide.

'I'm sure you'll enjoy his visit,' Chantelle conceded politely, aware of a momentary intentness evident as the man's attention focused on her son.

Was it her imagination, or did she glimpse conjecture before it was quickly masked?

Then the moment was gone as Anouk steered her towards a young couple who spent several minutes enthusing about their recent trip to Paris.

Chantelle enjoyed their praise of a city she adored, and they lingered together awhile.

'If you'll excuse us?' Anouk inclined with a warm smile. 'Another guest has arrived.'

The last, surely? Chantelle mused as she followed her mother's line of vision to a tall, broad-framed man whose stance portrayed an animalistic sense of power.

Even from a distance he managed to exude a physical magnetism most men would covet.

The set of his shoulders beneath their superb tailoring held a certain familiarity, and she fought against the rising sense of panic, tempering it with rationale.

How many times had she caught sight of a male figure whose stature bore a close resemblance to that of Samuel's father, only to discover his facial features were those of a stranger?

As it would prove on this occasion, she mentally assured as she saw Andreas move towards him.

Father and son. Had to be, she registered as the two men greeted each other with familial ease.

Seconds later they both turned at Anouk's approach, and Chantelle froze, locked into speechless immobility in recognition of a man she'd hoped never to see again in this lifetime.

Dimitri Cristopoulis.

What was he doing here? Here, specifically in her parents' home?

Dimitri's family resided in New York…didn't they?

He'd never said, and she hadn't asked. She choked back a hollow laugh. Had she even given it a thought?

In seeming slow motion Chantelle witnessed the introduction process, aware of Dimitri's calculating gaze as it encompassed first her, then her son, before settling with ruthless intensity on her own.

'Chantelle.'

The sound of his voice sent shivers scudding the length of her spine. How could so much be conveyed in a single word?

No. The silent scream rose and died in her throat at what she glimpsed in those dark eyes before it was masked.

With mounting consternation she watched as he sank down onto his haunches and extended his hand to her son.

'Samuel.'

The similarity between man and child was indisputable. Her son, but undeniably *his*.

Everything faded to the periphery of her vision, and she was conscious only of Dimitri and Samuel. Her hand closed over her son's shoulder in a protective, reassuring gesture.

'Pleased to meet you,' Samuel offered with childlike politeness.

Dear heaven, this was the culmination of her worst nightmare. Instinct screamed for her to scoop Samuel into her arms...and run as fast and as far away as she could.

Except Dimitri would follow. She could sense it, *knew* it in the depths of her soul. This time there would be no escape...no place she could hide where he wouldn't find her.

Chantelle was dimly aware of her mother's voice, although the words failed to register.

Did anyone guess she was a total mess? Every nerve in her body seemed to shred and sever, changing her into a trembling wreck.

Dimitri rose to his full height, and she caught sight of the veiled anger apparent in those dark eyes an instant before he masked it.

There were questions...several, she sensed he would demand answers to. Yet the most telling one was startlingly obvious.

Fear closed like an icy fist around her heart. He couldn't take Samuel away from her...could he?

Was it her imagination, or did the air fizz with tension? For a wild moment she felt if she so much as moved a muscle, she'd be struck down by its invisible force.

'Maman, may I be excused?' A small voice penetrated the immediate silence, and brought Chantelle's undivided attention.

'Naturellement, petit.' She offered a polite smile, then she turned and led Samuel towards the staircase.

A reprieve. One she badly needed. It would allow her time to recoup her severely shaken composure, and prepare for whatever the evening held in store.

For the next hour she could legitimately use Samuel as a shield. But the time would come when she'd have to face Dimitri alone. What then?

She felt the slight tug of Samuel's hand and realised she retained too tight a hold on it. A self-derisory sound choked in her throat at such carelessness, and she lifted him into her arms, then buried her lips against the sweet curve of his neck.

'Maman, who is that man?'

Bathroom duty complete, he studiously dried his hands, his dark eyes solemn as he posed the query.

Your father. Two simple words which couldn't be uttered without an accompanying explanation to his level of understanding.

'Someone I met a long time ago,' she said gently.

'Before I was born?'

Chantelle bent down and brushed her lips to his forehead. 'Uh-huh.'

'He's very big. Bigger than Grandpère.' Solemn dark eyes locked with hers. 'Do you like him?'

Oh, my. 'Grandpère?' she teased. 'Of course. Grandpère is the best, *non*?'

'*Oui*. And Grandmère,' Samuel added. 'But the man is scary.'

Scary covered a multitude of meanings to a child whose vocabulary was beginning to broaden. 'He would never hurt you.' She could give such reassurance unequivocally.

'No,' Samuel dismissed. 'He had a scary face when he looked at you.'

Out of the mouths of babes. 'Maybe it was because we had a disagreement.' A mild description for the blazing row they'd shared.

Her son absorbed the words, then offered with childlike simplicity, 'Didn't he say sorry?'

'No.' But then, neither had she. 'Shall we go downstairs to the party? Grandmère will wonder where we are.'

To remain absent for too long would be impolite. Besides, she adored her mother and refused to allow Dimitri's presence to mar the evening.

It took considerable effort to act out a part, but act she did…smiling, laughing as she mixed and mingled, conversing with what she hoped was admirable panache.

Exclusive schooling and a year being 'finished'

paid off in spades, and she defied anyone to criticise her performance.

She was supremely conscious of Dimitri's presence, and he made no effort to disguise his interest. It was only by adroit manipulation that she managed to avoid him during the ensuing hour.

Samuel held most of her attention, and it was with a sense of suspended apprehension she signalled it time for him to bid the guests 'good night.'

Preparations for bed and the reading of a story took a while, and she watched as his eyelids began to droop, saw him fight sleep, then succumb to it.

Chantelle switched off the bedlamp, leaving only the glow of a night-light to provide faint illumination. Five minutes, she allowed, enjoying the time to study his face in repose.

He was growing so quickly, developing a sensitive, caring nature she hoped would remain despite the trials life might hold for him.

An errant lock of hair lay against his forehead, and she gently smoothed it back before exiting the room.

As he was a sound sleeper who rarely woke during the night, she was confident he wouldn't stir. However, she intended to check on him at regular intervals, just in case the excitement of travel, a strange house and a party atmosphere disturbed his usual sleep pattern.

A degree of misgiving caused her stomach to

tighten as she re-entered the lounge. Most of the guests had converged on the adjoining terrace, and she caught up a flute of champagne from a proffered tray as she moved outdoors.

The string of electric lanterns provided a colourful glow. The sky had darkened to a deep indigo, and there was a tracery of stars evident, offering the promise of another warm summer's day.

Anouk and Jean-Paul worked the terrace, ensuring their guests were content, replete with food and wine. It was a practised art, and one they'd long perfected.

Chantelle followed their example, pausing to chat to one couple or another, genuinely interested in their chosen career, the merits of the Gold Coast, relaying details of her plans during the length of her stay.

Invitations were offered, and she graciously deferred accepting any without first conferring with her mother.

Dimitri was *there*…a dangerous, primitive force. She was supremely conscious of his attention. The waiting, watching quality evident…like a predator stalking for a kill.

If he wanted her on edge, he was succeeding, she perceived, aware of the cracks beginning to appear in her social façade.

'Chantelle.'

The sound of his deep drawl shredded her nerves.

All evening she'd prepared for this moment. Yet still he'd managed to surprise her.

'Dimitri,' she acknowledged, forgoing the polite smile.

He wasn't standing close enough to invade her personal space, yet all it would take was another step forward.

'We need to talk.'

She arched a deliberate eyebrow. 'I'm not aware we have anything to discuss.'

'No? You want I should spell it out?'

It wasn't easy to maintain a distant, albeit polite façade. 'Please do.'

Dimitri didn't move, yet it appeared as if he had, and she forced herself to stand absolutely still.

'Samuel.'

Chantelle felt fear gnaw at her nerve-ends. 'What about him?'

A muscle bunched at the edge of his jaw. 'The Cristopoulis resemblance is uncanny.'

'Consequently you've put two and two together and come to the conclusion he might be yours?' How could she sound so calm, or inject the slight musing element into her voice, when inside she was shaking?

'You deny the possibility?'

'I'm under no obligation to you, or anyone, to reveal his father's identity.'

'You want me to go the distance with this?'

Dimitri queried in a voice that was dangerously soft. 'Seek legal counsel, access his birth certificate, request DNA?'

Ice slithered the length of her spine. 'Is that a threat?'

'A statement of intention,' he corrected.

'I could deny your request for DNA.' The need to consult a lawyer seemed imperative.

His mouth formed a cynical smile, although there was no humour apparent in those dark eyes. 'Try it.'

Her stomach performed a slow, painful somersault. 'You possess an outsize ego. What makes you think you were my only lover?'

'I was *there*,' Dimitri reminded with deceptive quietness. Leashed savagery lay just beneath the surface of his control, and he gained some satisfaction as soft colour tinged her cheeks.

Was his memory of what they'd shared as startlingly vivid as her own? They'd spent every night together, never seeming to be able to satisfy a mutual hunger for each other.

Possession on every level. An all-consuming passion that had known no bounds.

She had lived for the moment she could be with him, resenting each minute they were apart. The sun had never shone more brightly, nor the senses become so defined. If hearts sang, hers had played a soaring rhapsody in full orchestra.

As for the sex... Intimacy, she corrected, at its most intense...highly sensual, libidinous, *magic*.

'There was no one else for either of us,' Dimitri pursued in a silkily soft voice that speared her heart.

Chantelle drew in a deep breath, then slowly released it. 'Aren't you forgetting Daniella?' Even now, it hurt her to say the actress's name.

A muscle bunched at the edge of his jaw. 'We dealt with that four years ago.'

'No,' she corrected with incredible politeness. 'We had a blazing row over the disparity between *her* account of your relationship, and *yours*.'

'At which time you chose to believe her version, rather than mine.'

Even now, the scene rose up to taunt her...the harsh words, the invective. 'She conveyed telling evidence.'

'Cleverly relayed to achieve the desired outcome,' Dimitri attested. 'Daniella is a scheming manipulator, and an extremely clever actress.'

'So you said at the time,' Chantelle declared bitterly.

'Yet you still walked.'

Her trust in him, what she'd thought they had together, had been destroyed. 'I couldn't stay.' He hadn't tried to stop her. Nor had he called.

To be fair, neither had she.

'Shall we begin again?'

'There is nothing to discuss.'

'We can do it here, now. Or we can share dinner tomorrow night.' He waited a beat. 'Your choice.'

'No.'

One eyebrow slanted. 'You want to play hard-ball?'

'I don't want to *play* at all!'

His features assumed a hard mask. 'I deserve to know if Samuel is my son.'

'What if I tell you he's not?'

His gaze pierced hers, indomitable and frighteningly inflexible. 'I want proof, one way or another.'

Bravado rose to the fore as she held his gaze. 'You don't have the right.'

'Yes, I do. Seven, tomorrow evening. I'll collect you.'

She didn't want him here. In fact, she didn't want to see him *anywhere*, period!

'You want to do this with a degree of civility?' Dimitri queried. 'Or—?'

'I'll meet you.' She named the first restaurant that came to mind. 'Seven.'

Without a further word she moved away from him, seeking another guest...*anyone* with whom she could converse and therefore escape Dimitri Cristopoulis' damning presence.

CHAPTER TWO

'YOU look charming, *chérie*,' Anouk complimented the following evening as Chantelle collected the keys to her mother's car.

'Thank you.' She'd chosen a slim-fitting dress in black with a black lace overlay, short sleeves and a square neckline. Black stiletto-heeled sandals lent her petite frame added height, and she'd swept hair the colour of sable high into a careless knot.

'It's nice of Andreas' son to invite you to dine with him.'

Nice wasn't a description she'd accord Dimitri…or his motives behind the invitation. If Anouk knew the real reason there would be concern, not pleasure, evident.

However, not even her mother knew the identity of Samuel's father. Her parents had been absent from Sydney at the time of Chantelle's affair with Dimitri, and afterwards, when told of her pregnancy, they'd counselled informing the child's father… advice she'd chosen to discount.

She crouched down to give Samuel a hug. 'Be good for Grandmère, hmm?'

'*Oui, Maman.*'

27

Such solemn brown eyes, she mused, kissing each childish cheek in turn.

'Thanks,' she said lightly as Anouk gathered Samuel close. 'I won't be late.'

For the past eighteen hours she'd derived countless reasons why she should opt out of tonight. Only the knowledge Dimitri was capable of forcing a confrontation in her parents' home prevented her from employing any one of them.

It took twenty minutes to reach the glamorous hotel situated on the Spit at Main Beach. Chantelle chose valet parking, and stepped into the marble foyer.

Expansive with glorious oriental rugs, comfortable sofas, it stretched out to a double staircase leading to a lower floor, beyond which lay a wide decorative pool, an island bar and, in the distance, the ocean.

It was spectacular, and a waterfall added to the tropical overtone.

Chantelle admired the view for numerous seconds, then she turned towards the restaurant.

'Punctual, as always.'

The sound of that familiar, faintly accented male voice caused the knot in her stomach to tighten.

Get a grip, she remonstrated silently. She needed to be in control, and nervous tension didn't form part of the evening's agenda.

She turned slightly and met Dimitri's steady gaze.

'It's one of my virtues.'

'Would you prefer a drink in the lounge, or shall we go straight in?'

She even managed a slight smile. Amazing, when the butterflies in her stomach were beating a faint tattoo.

'Why don't we cut the social niceties?' Cool, but neither calm nor collected.

Damn him. He'd always had this effect on her equilibrium. The sight of him sent her pulse racing to a crazy beat. It was the whole male package, his choice of cologne, the freshly laundered clothes... the faint male scent that was uniquely his.

All it took was one look, and her system went out of control. Even now, when she told herself she hated him, heat pooled deep inside, and the pulse at her throat felt as if it jumped beneath her skin.

Could he sense it? *See* it? Dear heaven, she hoped not.

The *maître d'* issued a greeting and led them to their table, where he summoned a drinks waiter, performed an introduction, then graciously retreated.

Dimitri ordered a crisp chardonnay, requested bottled water, and then he settled back comfortably in his chair.

There were a hundred places she'd rather be than *here, now*. Yet what choice did she have? Her parents could cope with anything life threw at them, but Samuel was too young, too vulnerable, and she'd go to the ends of the earth to protect him from harm…physical, mental, emotional.

Take control, an inner voice urged as she reached for her glass and sipped chilled water.

'Let's not pretend this is anything other than what it is,' Chantelle opined coolly, and saw one eyebrow slant in silent query.

'Perhaps we should order?' Dimitri suggested as the waiter presented the menu.

Food? The thought of calmly forking artistically presented morsels in his company killed what little appetite she had.

Nevertheless, it was necessary to order something, and she settled on a starter and skipped the main course.

'Not hungry?'

'Is my appetite an issue?'

His gaze remained steady, and had the effect of unnerving her…which was undoubtedly deliberate.

'Relax.'

Oh, sure, and that was easy, given he inevitably had a bundle of legal tricks up his sleeve ready to heap on her unsuspecting head.

'I'm here at your insistence,' Chantelle reminded. 'Sharing a meal I don't particularly want in the company of someone I'd prefer never to have to see again in this lifetime.'

'Pity.'

Her eyes flashed dark fire. 'What do you mean...*pity*?'

'If Samuel is my son,' Dimitri voiced with dangerous softness, 'you'll have to get used to me being part of your life.'

'The hell I will!'

Something moved in his eyes, and she felt a chill slither down the length of her spine. 'Take it as a given, Chantelle.'

The words were hard, inflexible, and seared her heart. 'You don't have that right.'

The arrival of the waiter brought a welcome break, and she viewed the contents of her plate with misgiving, sure the smallest mouthful would stick in her throat.

'Eat,' Dimitri bade, and she did, managing to do justice to the food. He wasn't to know her taste-buds had gone on strike.

Conversation had never been so difficult to summon, and anything she thought to offer seemed inane.

It irked her unbearably he was able to affect her this way. *Act*, she chastised silently. Adopt a practised façade, and pretend Dimitri Cristopoulis is just a man like any other male.

Oh, sure...chance would be a fine thing! She had only to look at him and every nerve-end tingled into vibrant life.

Four years hadn't made the slightest difference. It

was as if her soul recognised his on some base level and sought recognition.

Damn him. Damn coincidence for putting them both in this part of the world at the same time! Fate was playing a cruel hand, intent on causing emotional havoc before the game was over.

Who would win? a silent imp taunted.

Dimitri replaced his cutlery, then he picked up his wineglass and leaned back in his chair. 'Do you want to begin, or shall I?'

Chantelle lifted a hand in a negligent gesture. 'Oh, please. Be my guest.'

For a few seemingly long seconds he didn't speak, and she could tell nothing from his expression.

'Samuel's birth certificate records June one as the day he was born.'

How could he know that?

Dimitri's mouth moved to form a wry smile. 'I called in a favour.' All he'd had to do was make a few phone calls, and he had the information he needed within hours.

'Nine and a half months after we began our relationship,' he pursued, watching her expressive features through a narrowed gaze. Anger had been just one of the emotions he'd experienced at the confirmation. Resentment had followed with the knowledge she'd chosen not to reveal her pregnancy.

There was also a mixture of pride and joy at the thought he had a child…a son.

As to the child's mother…he'd deal with her. But not easily.

'So,' he continued silkily. 'Shall we move on?'

'Samuel is *mine*,' Chantelle reiterated fiercely. 'I could have had an abortion.' She'd never considered it as an option. Hadn't, even from the onset, thought of a child…Dimitri's child, but indisputably *hers*… as an encumbrance.

'Yet you didn't.'

She remembered the birth, when she'd cursed Dimitri a hundred times…and she thought of the moment the nurse had placed Samuel in her arms. The indescribable joy that transcended all else, and the fierce protectiveness for the tiny life.

'No.'

He wanted to reach across the table and shake her. For denying him the opportunity to be there, to care for her, and to claim the child as his own.

'Tell me,' he pursued silkily. 'Did you ever intend for me to know I had a child?'

'Not if I could help it.'

'Your body, your responsibility?'

'*Yes.*'

'Allowing some other man to take my place? Raise my son as his own? Give him his name?'

Chantelle could sense the anger beneath his control, *feel* it emanate from his body as a tangible entity.

'Samuel is registered as Samuel *Leone*.'

'Something that can easily be changed.'

'To what purpose?' she demanded. Anger rose to the fore, darkening her eyes. 'I live in France, you reside in New York.'

'Samuel is a Cristopoulis. He has a heritage,' Dimitri endorsed with quiet savagery. 'I intend to ensure he claims it.'

'With you?' She was like a runaway train, unable to stop. 'What are you going to do, Dimitri? Engage a nanny during Samuel's visits? Maybe look in on him as he sleeps when you leave your apartment in the morning, and again when you return long after his bedtime?' She picked up her napkin and thrust it on the table. 'Is that your idea of parental visitation rights?' She rose to her feet and gathered her purse. 'Hell will freeze over before I'll allow it.'

He watched her with interest, admiring the fire, the sheer will beneath her fury. A mother defending and protecting her own, he mused.

The waiter chose that moment to deliver the main course, only to stand poised as he sensed the onset of a scene.

Chantelle turned away from the table, only to have her escape forestalled as Dimitri's hand closed over her wrist.

She tried to wrench her hand free, and failed miserably. Fury pitched her voice low. 'Let me go.'

'Sit down.' He waited a few seconds, then cautioned with chilling softness, 'We're not done yet.'

'I'll have the *maître d'* call Security.'

'Go ahead.' His voice was a hateful drawl.

'There's nothing further you can say that I want to hear.'

He didn't move, but something about him changed, hardened. 'If you prefer negotiations to share custody of our son be dealt with through the legal system...so be it.' He released her wrist, and regarded her steadily.

Why did she feel like a butterfly whose wings had been pinned to a wall?

'Sit down, Chantelle. Please,' he added.

'Following the manner in which we parted, anything amicable between us is impossible.'

'Daniella fed you a tissue of lies, which you chose to believe.'

'You walked out,' Chantelle accused.

His gaze speared hers. 'What did you expect?'

'You should have told me about her.' Even now, she could feel the anger surge at the memory of that awful scene.

'Daniella was never in the picture.'

'So you told me at the time. Perhaps you should also have told *her*.'

'I did.'

'That's not what she said.'

'It wouldn't have served her purpose to tell the truth.'

'Her purpose being?'

'To send you running as far away as possible.' He waited a beat. 'She succeeded.'

'And you know that *because*?'

'You'd already left your apartment when I rang. The phone number I had for you was disconnected. Ditto your cellphone.'

Pain spiralled through her body. 'That's easy to say *now*.'

'You'd left the pharmacy,' he continued. 'No one had any idea where you were.'

Anouk and Jean-Paul had been absent, enjoying a European vacation, and Chantelle had begged both employer and work colleagues to disavow any knowledge of her whereabouts. 'I took leave to visit relatives in France,' she revealed. 'Within weeks I was offered a job, so I found lodgings, began work…' She paused fractionally. 'And discovered I was pregnant.'

'With my child.'

There seemed no point in further denial. 'Yes.'

'You refused to consider I might choose to support you?'

'I didn't need your support.'

'Therefore you imagined I had no right to know you'd conceived my child?'

She looked at him carefully. 'Imagined?' A wry smile tugged the edge of her mouth. 'I didn't think there was *anything* left to the imagination, given the way we parted.' Her shoulders lifted in a negligible shrug. 'At that stage neither you nor I wanted anything to do with each other, ever again.'

'And now?'

'What do you mean—*now*?' Her stomach took a dive. 'Nothing has changed.'

One eyebrow slanted. 'No?'

'In three weeks Samuel and I return to France. You'll depart for New York, and we'll probably never see each other again.'

'Wrong.'

'Excuse me?'

'Think again.'

'Samuel doesn't need a father,' Chantelle said fiercely. 'He especially doesn't need *you*.'

'I intend being part of his life,' Dimitri reiterated silkily. 'With or without your permission.'

'Something you'll never have.'

'You'd prefer a legal fight rather than a cordial agreement?'

'I'd prefer,' she managed with a degree of vehemence, 'never to see you again.'

'That's not going to happen,' he asserted in dry, mocking tones. 'By virtue of the interest we have in our son.'

'A son you knew nothing about until twenty-four hours ago!'

'But now I do,' Dimitri said smoothly.

'I won't share Samuel with you.'

'The law courts will have a different view.'

The waiter appeared and presented Dimitri's main course, and she watched as he made no attempt to pick up his cutlery.

Instead, his eyes were dark, almost still as he regarded her.

'I don't want Samuel to be pushed and pulled between two parents who don't like each other,' she said quietly.

'You consider us as enemies?'

Oh, God. 'We're not exactly friends.'

A faint smile tugged the corner of his mouth. 'Yet we were lovers.'

Dear heaven, just thinking about what they'd shared sent pain shafting through her body. She'd lived, breathed for the moment she could see him, be with him. Just the sound of his voice on the phone was enough to send her pulse racing and have heat pool deep within. She'd loved him, *loved*, she cried silently, with all her heart. Her soul. Everything. Only to have it shatter into a thousand pieces.

'That was years ago,' she managed carefully, hoping her voice didn't convey her shredding nerves.

She wanted to ask why he'd tried to make contact after that fateful day.

'Not so many,' he reminded. 'And it feels like yesterday.'

Don't, she wanted to protest. Please don't go there.

'You should eat,' Chantelle encouraged in a bid to change the conversation.

'Concern for my digestive system?'

'Why not admit we've reached a verbal impasse?' she countered. 'We oppose each other on every issue regarding my son.'

'Our son,' he corrected.

'If I hadn't—'

'Visited your parents? If I hadn't chosen this particular year to spend the festive season with Andreas?' His regard was unwavering. 'Yet we did.'

'And now we have to deal with it?' As soon as the query left her lips, the knowledge hit that it was *she* who would have to deal with the changes. Dimitri would insist on playing a part in Samuel's life, and he was powerful enough to enforce his legal right to do so.

His eyes never left hers, and she struggled to diminish the impact he had on her senses.

'Perhaps we should take advantage of fate, and redress the day we walked out of each other's life.'

A cold fist closed round her heart. 'Rehashing the past won't achieve anything.'

'It might, however, give credence to our reactions.'

She didn't want to do this. It evoked too many painful memories.

'You're not curious as to why I tried to contact you after I returned to New York?'

'Guilt?'

He recalled that day with disturbing clarity, aware it ranked high among those numbered as the worst in his life.

To Chantelle's credit, she had no idea, and he took in her expressive features, the slight tilt of her chin, the pain in those beautiful dark eyes.

'An hour before I arrived at your apartment I'd had a call from New York to say my mother was in hospital on life support following an horrific car accident.' The food on his plate remained untouched. 'I'd spent time organising a flight, delegating work to colleagues. Leaving was the hardest thing I had to do. There were words I wanted to say,' he continued. 'Except I didn't have the time or the opportunity.'

Chantelle held a vivid recollection of the phone call she'd received from Daniella, and Dimitri's appearance soon after. The actress's allegations had succeeded in filling her mind with doubt and resultant anger. Anger she'd levelled at him within minutes of his arrival at her apartment.

She recalled his denial, his reassurance...and his

anger when she'd refused to accept his word as truth. One thing had led to another, and when he'd said he had to leave, she'd vowed if he walked out the door she wouldn't allow him back in.

'The food is not to your liking?'

Chantelle heard the words and registered the waiter's appearance at their table.

'I'm sure it's fine,' Dimitri offered, and brushed aside an offer to bring a fresh serving, qualifying, 'Thank you. No.'

His mother had been critically injured? He'd had to return immediately to New York?

The words reverberated inside her brain with alarming confusion. 'You should have told me,' she managed quietly, regretful she hadn't given him the chance.

'She remained in a coma for several weeks. Andreas and I took it in turns to sit with her. In the end we had to accept she had no hope of recovery.'

She was silent for several long seconds, unable to utter a word. 'I'm sorry,' she offered at last. 'I wish I'd known,' she said quietly as she attempted to come to grips with the words she'd flung at him in anger...testing his control, and breaking it.

With devastating result...for both of them.

'Andreas took a long holiday with his sister in Sydney and decided to make the city his base, handing control of the corporation to me.'

Chantelle closed her eyes, then opened them

again. Like a long-unfinished puzzle, some of the missing pieces were falling into place.

It explained much, yet left an aching void for what might have been.

To continue sharing his table, his company, was more than she could bear.

'If you don't mind, I'd like to leave.'

His gaze never left hers. 'We're far from finished.'

Emotion welled up inside, making her feel physically ill. 'For tonight, we are.' She stood to her feet and extracted a note from her evening purse.

'Don't even think about it,' Dimitri cautioned in chilling warning as he signalled the waiter for the bill.

'There's no need for you to leave,' Chantelle protested stiffly.

'Yes, there is.'

She moved ahead of him, aware he followed close behind her as she crossed the marble-tiled reception lounge to the concierge.

'I'll ring tomorrow and arrange a suitable time to spend a few hours with Samuel.'

No. 'I'm unsure what my parents have planned.' The words tumbled from her lips in quick succession, and incurred his steady gaze.

'Naturally you'll accompany him.'

Oh, God. 'I don't think—'

'A few hours, Chantelle.'

'He has a nap in the afternoon,' she offered in desperation.

'In that case, we'll organise a morning.'

The Lexus drew in ahead of Dimitri's hire car, and Chantelle was unprepared for his actions as he cupped her face and brushed her lips with his own.

It was a light, almost fleeting touch, but it wreaked havoc with her fragile emotions.

For a moment she could only look at him, her eyes wide and vulnerable until she successfully masked their expression.

Her mouth parted, then closed again, and without a further word she turned and slid in behind the wheel, engaged the gear, then she sent the vehicle down the incline to street level.

It was a scene she replayed again and again as she lay unable to sleep.

His scent, his touch evoked feelings she thought she'd dealt with.

Fat chance, she muttered inaudibly as she tossed and turned for the umpteenth time.

The question was...where did they go from here?

Where did she want to go?

A few days ago her life had been secure on a path of her choice. Now confusion reigned, and she didn't like it at all.

CHAPTER THREE

CHANTELLE stood at the kitchen sink and watched Samuel play with Jean-Paul. Her son, even at three and a half, was beginning to show a flair for kicking a ball.

'This morning it appeared you slept badly, and you've been troubled all day,' Anouk ventured gently. 'Is there something you want to tell me, *chérie*?'

Maternal instinct was acute, Chantelle admitted ruefully as she shook excess water from the salad greens she was preparing for their midday meal.

'Your date with Andreas' son last night did not go well?'

'It was OK.' Making light of it didn't fool Anouk, who teased,

'You were home early.'

Chantelle effected a faint shrug. 'We ate, talked a little.'

'You will see him again, *oui*?'

If only you knew! 'You share the same social circle as his father. The festive season usually involves a few parties. I imagine it's inevitable.'

Anouk placed a baguette into the oven to warm,

then she crossed to the refrigerator, removed the cooked chicken and began carving.

'One senses the chemistry. It is almost as if you have met before.'

There was never going to be a more appropriate moment. 'Dimitri is Samuel's father.' It was done.

To give her mother credit, she never missed a beat as she continued carving poultry. 'I wondered as much. So what are you going to do?'

Ever practical, Chantelle mused. 'You just took a quantum leap of four years.'

Her mother began loading slices of chicken onto a serving plate, and paused long enough to shoot Chantelle a telling glance. 'It was your choice to keep private Samuel's father's identity.'

'You never queried my decision. Weren't you curious?'

'Of course. What mother would not be?'

'And now, you have no questions as to the why and how of it?'

'*Chérie*, I know you well. You do not gift your body easily. For you to do so, the man has to be special, someone you deeply love. If that were not true, you would not have had his child.'

Emotion brought a lump to her throat. 'Thank you.'

'So,' Anouk reiterated with prosaic gentleness. 'What are you going to do?'

Chantelle began layering a bowl with lettuce and

sweet, succulent tomatoes. 'He wants to spend time with Samuel,' she offered slowly.

'Of course. But you are afraid, *oui*?'

'He wants to share custody.'

'And you do not want this.'

'I don't want anything to upset or confuse Samuel.'

'And you, *chérie*?' She carried the platter to the table, then turned to regard her daughter. 'What about you, hmm?'

'I feel as if my life is slipping out of control. If only Dimitri's visit hadn't coincided with mine!'

'But it has,' Anouk offered gently. 'And now you must deal with it as best you can.'

But what was *best*? And for whom? Samuel? Herself?

Sadly they were not the same. Her son would be captivated by Dimitri's presence in his life. Whereas she was beset by a host of ambivalent emotions.

Lunch was a convivial meal eaten alfresco on the terrace overlooking the pool. Samuel delighted in displaying his burgeoning vocabulary, both in French and English, and Chantelle had just settled him for his afternoon nap when she heard the distant peal of the phone.

'Dimitri,' Jean-Paul relayed as he informed the call was for her, and he gave her shoulder a light squeeze as she took the receiver.

'Is this a good time?' Dimitri's slightly accented

drawl did strange things to her composure, and she resisted the impulse to press a hand to her churning stomach.

'I guess so.'

'Such enthusiasm,' he chided with mockery, and she stifled a sigh of frustration.

'What is it you want, Dimitri?'

'If you don't have plans for tomorrow, I'd like to spend time with Samuel.'

'And if I do?'

'The following day, Chantelle, or the day after that.'

She didn't want to do this. Given a choice, she'd prefer Dimitri to fade into the woodwork for the duration of his stay. But that wasn't going to happen.

'Tomorrow morning will be fine.' Capitulation was the wisest course, given she couldn't keep putting it off.

'If you name the place and give me a time, we'll meet you there.'

'Pack swimming gear. I'll collect you at nine.' His voice was firm, and he cut the connection before she had the chance to argue.

Damn the man! Anger simmered just beneath the surface of her control for what remained of the day, disturbing her sleep, and priming her determination to say exactly what she thought of his high-handedness at the first available opportunity.

*   *   *

Chantelle woke to a day bright with the promise of brilliant sunshine, together with the heat and humidity of a subtropical summer.

Samuel's excitement was a tangible thing as she filled a backpack with every conceivable item needed for whatever occasion Dimitri had in mind.

'When are we going?' and 'Where are we going?' tumbled from her son's lips in five-minute intervals soon after she had relayed the morning's outing.

'Ah, *petit*,' Anouk protested fondly. 'Soon, *mon ange*.'

The faint *clunk* of a car door closing brought a mixture of relief and trepidation as Chantelle waited for Dimitri to ring the doorbell.

'Maman, Maman, the man is here.'

'Dimitri, sweetheart,' she corrected as Anouk moved to answer the door, only to reappear less than a minute later with Dimitri at her side.

Attired in designer jeans, a navy polo shirt and wearing joggers, he resembled the epitome of the businessman bent on leisure. The soft denim hugged his hips, emphasising the muscular length of his legs, and the polo shirt moulded his breadth of shoulder like a second skin.

Chantelle felt her stomach flip at the sight of him, and deliberately summoned a smile as she greeted him, watching as he solemnly extended his hand to her son.

'Samuel,' he offered warmly. 'Nice to see you again.'

The smile, she accorded silently, was for Samuel's sake, and she was all too aware of her own restraint. Four years ago she would have almost run to him, lit with the joyful anticipation of his touch, the feel of him as he pulled her close and ravaged her mouth with his own.

Now she simply caught Samuel's hand in her own, brushed a kiss to her mother's cheek, then she collected the backpack and slung the strap over one shoulder.

'Let me take that.' He reached for the backpack, and their fingers touched for a few seconds.

Liquid heat sped through her veins, igniting her senses, and she silently cursed her reaction.

Samuel, who'd been so excited only moments before, now fell silent, seemingly in awe of the man whose company he was going to share for the following few hours.

'We'll be back around midday, Maman,' Chantelle said as they walked out to the car.

'After an early lunch,' Dimitri added, and incurred Chantelle's swift denial.

'Samuel has a nap after lunch.'

'I'll have you home in time to settle him down.' He collected the junior safety seat and set it in place on the rear seat of his car, then he stood back as she lifted Samuel into it and secured the safety strap.

'I'll sit beside Samuel,' she declared as she straightened, only to have Dimitri indicate the front seat.

'*Chérie,*' Anouk intervened gently, 'he'll be fine.'

Maternal chastisement…or was Anouk bent on some subtle arrangement of her own?

Anouk couldn't help but be aware of her daughter's reticence, and God help him…Dimitri had to know she didn't favour spending several hours in his company.

Chantelle flashed each of them a stunning smile. She could do *gracious*…she just had to remember she was doing it for Samuel.

'Andreas suggested the water theme park at Coomera as a fun place for children,' Dimitri offered.

'There's lots of water. We got wet. Maman too,' Samuel endorsed with childish enthusiasm, and Dimitri chuckled.

'I gather he's already been there?'

'Once,' Chantelle admitted, unwilling to offer it was his favourite place.

'In that case, we're guaranteed he'll enjoy himself.'

We…there's no *we*, she wanted to deny, and almost did, except Samuel's immediate presence stopped her. Later, she promised herself, she'd correct Dimitri's assumption.

The theme park was well-patronised, given it was

the long midsummer school break and there was a host of visiting tourists to the area.

'Maman, we can go up there, *oui*? Please.'

Up there meant exchanging her jeans and top for a swimsuit. An action she normally wouldn't think about twice, if Dimitri hadn't been there.

She was acutely conscious of him, aware of his slightest touch, the warmth of his smile. Hell, he knew how to work it! Charm, he had it in spades. Four years ago she'd have believed it genuine. Now she wasn't so sure.

'Why don't I take him?'

Chantelle felt all her protective instincts rise to the fore. 'I don't think—'

'Dimitri,' Samuel sanctioned without a care in the world, and lifted his arms to be picked up, surprising her.

'Are you sure?' she queried dubiously, and gained an affirmative nod in response.

'Sure.'

'OK, champ, let's get rid of some clothes and go test the water.'

Her son's almost unconditional acceptance made her wonder if there was any truth in some deep recognition of shared genes.

Dimitri turned towards her. 'Why not join us?'

'Next time.' It would give her valuable minutes to steel herself to strip down to a swimsuit. Which was ridiculous.

Samuel was in his element as he took to the junior water slide, returning again and again as he delighted in the ride.

Chantelle almost convinced herself she was only watching her son, but it was the man catching him after each downward slide that held her attention longer than it should.

'Can we go up there?' Samuel begged as they returned to her side. 'Dimitri said I must have your permission.'

Oh, he did, did he? Well, she could hardly say *no*, when only a few days ago she'd taken Samuel *up there* herself.

It was a much larger slide with curves and covered sections, rushing water, and children under a certain age were only permitted to take the ride with the supervision of an adult.

They placed their outer clothes in lockers, then joined the queue for the more advanced ride.

When it became their turn Dimitri went in first and Chantelle followed with Samuel positioned closely between her thighs.

It was fun, and when they reached the end Dimitri rose lithely to his feet and caught Samuel, extending a hand to help Chantelle to her feet.

'Can we do it again, please?'

How easy it was to please a child. And how innocent Samuel appeared to be to the undercurrents between the two adults accompanying him.

As Chantelle looked at both child and man, the physical likeness between them was striking, and she glimpsed a vision of what the child would look like when he grew into a man.

Did Samuel possess any of her physical qualities? It was difficult to tell as the facial bone structure underwent a gradual change during the formative years. The dark hair perhaps, but then Dimitri's hair was equally dark.

This time out, Chantelle headed the downward ride, with Samuel held firmly in Dimitri's grasp, and afterwards they took a break for drinks and a snack.

There could be little doubt Samuel was having a ball, and neither his energy nor his enthusiasm lagged as Chantelle and Dimitri indulged him with several of the rides the theme park had to offer.

To his credit he didn't protest when it came time to change into dry clothes and leave. He remembered without prompting to thank Dimitri for bringing him to visit.

'I have a picnic hamper in the car,' Dimitri relayed as they made their way to the parking area. 'There's a picnic reserve at Paradise Point where we can eat.'

Casual, laid-back, it was a relaxed way to end the morning.

Except Chantelle was the antithesis of relaxed! She'd found it difficult when they'd been amongst a number of people, but isolated into an intimate group of three on the sandy foreshore at the picnic reserve only heightened her emotional tension.

Samuel ate well, and when he finished he drifted the few feet to the sand, where he became industriously immersed in collecting shells.

'Has it been such a hardship?'

She sipped the chilled mineral water as Dimitri packed what remained of the food into the cooler.

'Samuel had a great time.'

'And you?'

Chantelle looked at him. 'What do you want me to say?' He was close, much too close. 'I appreciate you're bent on turning my personal world upside-down? Thank the universe for throwing us together at the same place at the same time?' She was on a roll, and went with it. 'Thank you for forming an empathy with my son? An empathy I'll have to explain can only be rekindled at intervals we agree upon, or, failing that, as the law courts decree?'

'Why not take it one day at a time?'

'Whichever way I take it,' she declared with soft vehemence, 'the end result will be the same.'

'Will it?' He regarded her steadily, and the depth of his gaze tested the fragile tenure of her control. 'You can't perceive there might be a solution?'

'Maman.'

Suddenly Samuel was there, his hands cupped as he held a collection of shells, and Chantelle rose quickly to her feet and went to help him, infinitely relieved at his interruption.

'We will take them back for Grandmère, *oui*?'

'Indeed. She will treasure them.' She reached into her backpack and retrieved a plastic bag. 'We'll wash them when we get home.'

Within minutes she brushed the sand from his feet, slid on his joggers and cleaned his hands, aware that Dimitri replaced the cooler into the car, then followed it with the rug.

They were only five minutes from Sovereign Islands, and Samuel's eyes were drooping as Dimitri pulled into her parents' driveway.

Retreating was relatively easy as she slid from the car, collected her backpack, and moved to retrieve Samuel from his junior car seat.

'I'll take him.'

'It's OK.' Please, just let me get him and leave.

She badly needed to subside into her own space, as far away as possible from his. The morning had been a success, as far as Samuel was concerned. For her, it had dented the protective wall she'd built up around herself four years ago when survival of self had become paramount in her life.

'I'll be in touch.'

Was that a threat or a promise? She felt too disturbed to examine the ramifications of either.

'Thanks.' The gratitude was a mere facsimile, and one he recognised as her return to polite formality.

'My pleasure.'

He slid in behind the wheel, ignited the engine, and waited until she went indoors before reversing down the driveway.

CHAPTER FOUR

AN INVITATION to a mid-week cocktail party numbered the second party in five days. Which was something of a record for Chantelle, for, while she recognised the necessity for childcare during her working hours, she rarely employed a baby-sitter for anything other than an important social obligation.

Choosing what to wear didn't pose a problem, and, pre-warned by Anouk to pack evening wear, Chantelle selected black silk evening trousers, added a matching camisole and a black chiffon silk wrap threaded with gold. Stiletto heels, minimum jewellery, understated make-up, her hair swept into a smooth twist, and the overall look completed an image that met with her approval.

'We're going to another party?' Samuel queried as she brushed his hair, then straightened his shirt.

'Yes. Grandmère has many friends, and you, *mon enfant*, are her only grandchild. She wants to show you off.' She dropped a kiss on top of his head, then drew him close for a hug. 'There will be other children there, and you'll have fun, I promise,' she reassured.

'OK.'

His smile was matched by her own. 'Let's go.'

Would Dimitri be a fellow guest? She hoped not. She didn't want to cope with his disturbing presence.

Half an hour later she entered the opulent lounge in their host's luxurious home, after being greeted and introduced to the host's nanny and ensuring Samuel was comfortably settled in the downstairs playroom with six other young children.

Dimitri was unmistakable, standing on the far side of the room, not so much for his height and breadth of shoulder, the sculpted facial structure, or the expensive cut of his clothes.

It went deeper than that, combining a raw sexuality with electrifying passion; the inherent knowledge of how to pleasure a woman. A quality women recognised and many sought in a discreet bid for his attention. And there were the not-so-discreet few…of whom Daniella Fabrizi topped the list!

Damn. Why did the actress's name have to enter the equation?

Almost as if Dimitri sensed her presence he turned, and his dark, gleaming gaze locked with hers, held, as she offered a polite smile in acknowledgement of his presence before turning away.

He was something else. She cursed a vivid memory of how it felt to be in his arms, the sensations he was able to evoke in her without any effort at all. She was the instrument, he the master virtuoso, creating a sensual music that was uniquely theirs as they became lost in each other. Primitive, intensely passionate, he'd aroused emotions she hadn't known existed. And afterwards the degree of *tendresse* he displayed in the aftermath of a wildly erotic love-making always undid her.

Even now, she was intensely aware of him. The feel and touch of him, the satiny textured skin, the rough hairs on his chest arrowing down to the nest couching his manhood.

There had been no one else since him. No man of her acquaintance had aroused the slightest spark of sexual interest.

Introspection could become a dangerous pastime, and with deliberate ease Chantelle mixed and mingled with fellow guests, exerting her social skills without seeming effort as she greeted people she'd met at the party Anouk and Jean-Paul had hosted a few evenings ago.

'Let me get you another drink,' a familiar voice drawled close by, and her heart-rate went into overdrive as she turned to meet Dimitri's musing gaze.

'Not at the moment, thanks,' she said politely, aware of the faint aroma of his exclusive cologne. He was close, much too close, and she shifted slightly, gaining a much-needed inch or two of personal space.

'Samuel is downstairs?'

She was nervous, and that fascinated him. The

tiny pulse at the base of her throat throbbed at an increased beat, and he resisted the temptation to soothe it.

'Yes.'

'Relax, *pedhaki mou*,' he bade gently, and saw those beautiful eyes flash momentary anger. 'Save the indignation for when we're alone.'

The affectionate 'little one' got to her, for it brought back too many memories…of love, laughter, and exquisite sex.

'Now, there's the thing,' Chantelle responded coolly. 'I have no intention of being alone with you.'

'You don't envisage a truce?'

'What did you expect? That a rehashing of the day we parted would magically wipe the slate clean?' She kept her voice low. 'If you dare suggest the necessity is *for Samuel's sake*, I'll hit you.'

Something moved in those dark eyes, something she couldn't define, and sudden apprehension slithered the length of her spine.

'Be aware of the consequences of such an action,' Dimitri cautioned with chilling softness.

'You're all charm.'

A slow smile curved his generous mouth. 'And you're a piece of work.'

'How nice we understand each other.' She held out her glass. 'Perhaps I will have another drink.' Her smile was a mere facsimile. 'It's a spritzer.'

Chantelle waited until he turned towards the bar

before slipping from the lounge to check on Samuel. The happy laughter echoing from the playroom provided reassurance, and she watched unobserved as the children interacted together.

He looked so relaxed and content, and her heart went into meltdown. Nothing, she promised silently, and no one could be permitted to upset his secure world.

At that moment he lifted his head and saw her framed in the doorway.

'Maman!' He ran towards her, and his pleasure stirred her heartstrings. 'We are leaving?'

For a moment she sensed his disappointment, and hid a smile. He was a very sociable little boy. 'Not yet.'

'Good. I'm having fun.' He caught hold of her hand, his face a study of round-eyed excitement. 'Damian and Joshua are going to the park tomorrow to see the dolphins.'

'We will go to watch the dolphins one day, too.'

'We will? When, Maman?'

'Perhaps we could make it tomorrow,' Dimitri suggested from close behind her. 'If that suits your mother.'

He possessed the stealthy tread of a cat, for she hadn't heard a sound, and she steeled herself against his close proximity.

'Please say we can, Maman,' Samuel pleaded. 'I do so much want to see the sea lions too. Damian says they bark, and wave. And the dolphins jump out of the water.'

Chantelle didn't want to disappoint him, but the thought of spending several hours in Dimitri's company didn't appeal. 'Perhaps,' she qualified. 'But first we must check with Grandmère. We are her guests, *oui*?'

Hope, patience, resignation passed fleetingly over his features. *'Oui, Maman.'* For an instant his expression brightened. 'Grandmère and Jean-Paul can come too.' He turned towards Dimitri. 'Can't they?'

'Of course.' His smile was genuinely warm as he hunkered down to Samuel's eye level. 'But first, Maman must ensure there are no other plans for tomorrow, hmm?'

'Oui.' He looked up at his mother. 'May I go play now?'

'Enjoy, *mon petit*. I'll come collect you when we're ready to leave.'

She watched him rejoin the other children, then she turned and made her way to the stairs, uncaring whether Dimitri followed or not.

'You could have consulted me first,' Chantelle said in an angry undertone as he joined her.

'Only for you to refuse?'

His indolent drawl raised her anger level a notch. 'Look—'

'We agreed I should spend time with Samuel.'

Chantelle paused and turned to face him. 'It was more like you issued an ultimatum.'

'You want difficult, Chantelle? I can give you difficult.'

She could see the purpose evident, the dangerous inflexibility apparent. He had the wealth and the power to command top-flight lawyers to produce suitable documentation with breakneck speed.

'I want what's best for my son.'

'Then we're in total agreement.'

He was the limit, and she told him so. 'I wish—'

'I hadn't chosen to spend this Christmas with Andreas?'

'Yes! Damn you,' she vented, hating him.

He looked at her long and hard. 'Are you done?'

Her head tilted and her eyes sparked brilliant fire. 'For now.'

'Good.'

She was unprepared for the way his head lowered down to hers, and before she could move his mouth closed over hers in an evocative kiss.

His hands cupped her face as he went in deep, savoured, then he slid a hand down her spine and pulled her in close against him.

Oh, dear God. She couldn't think, didn't want to, as all her senses went every which way but loose and she began to respond.

In the recess of her mind she knew she should

resist, but it felt so good. Dear heaven, how she'd missed his touch, the feel of him.

His arousal was a potent force, and she gave a sigh in protest as he began to retreat, gentling his mouth until his lips lingered briefly before he lifted his head.

For a moment she was lost, unaware of where she was, only that she was with *him*. Then reality descended, and confusion clouded her eyes, leaving them vulnerable for a few seconds before she managed to mask their expression.

'That was unforgivable.'

Dimitri pressed a finger to her slightly swollen mouth.

'I hate you.'

'No,' he said gently. 'You don't.' He traced a finger over her lower lip. 'You hate having to admit even to yourself that what we once shared together is as strong now as it was four years ago.'

Oh, dear heaven, why did he have to be so right?

Yet she'd known the instant she set eyes on him again the emotions she'd harboured for him had never lessened.

Acknowledging it didn't mean she had to like it. And nothing, she determined, *nothing* would allow her to run a repeat. That way lay heartache and despair. She'd been there, done that, and had no intention of doing it again.

Chantelle closed her eyes for a few seconds, unaware Dimitri watched the fleeting emotions play across her expressive features, then she opened them again. 'I think we should return to the lounge.'

His mouth curved to form a generous smile. 'Before we do, I suggest you renew your lipstick.'

For a few seconds her eyes widened and she looked intensely vulnerable, then she masked her expression and reached into her evening purse and applied colour to her lips.

Without a further word she turned and ascended the stairs, aware he was following close behind her.

As soon as she reached the lounge she checked Anouk's location, then began threading her way across the room.

'Samuel is fine,' she assured. 'He's made two new friends, and heard first-hand accounts of the dolphins and sea lions at the marine park.'

'I suggested we might take him there tomorrow if you have no plans for the day,' Dimitri drawled from behind her, and she felt her stomach curl at his close proximity.

'Why not make it a family day?' she said quickly. Too quickly, for she glimpsed her mother's faint surprise.

'Darling, thank you, but no,' Anouk declined with a gentle smile, wondering why her daughter's composure appeared distinctly ruffled. 'You and Dimitri go ahead. Samuel will have a wonderful time.'

Without doubt, Chantelle admitted. But what about her?

'Jean-Paul is keen to take the cruiser out on Sunday,' Anouk ventured conversationally. 'Perhaps Dimitri and Andreas would care to join us?'

Maman…no. Don't do this!

'We thought we might spend a few hours at Couran Cove. It's a delightful resort.'

'You must let me take you all to lunch.'

Anouk waved a dismissive hand. 'Chantelle and I will assemble a picnic basket.' She offered a stunning smile. 'All that's required is your presence. I'll confer with Jean-Paul and ring Andreas with a time.'

Dammit, what was Anouk doing, for heaven's sake? Exhibiting a naturally kind heart, or playing matchmaker?

A relaxed cruise of the bay, a picnic on a tourist island had all the promise of being fraught with tension…*hers*.

Dimitri inclined his head. 'Thank you.'

Chantelle felt a desperate need to put some space between them, for he loomed too large and too close for her peace of mind. If she'd been aware of him before, *now* her body was a finely tuned instrument almost vibrating with need for his touch.

It wasn't fair…nothing about Dimitri Cristopoulis was *fair*.

He had no right to re-enter her life and try to command it…even for the duration of a family visit.

If she could, she'd take Samuel, organise the next flight to Paris and return to the place she'd called home for the past four years.

Yet such an action would amount to running away. Besides, it would upset Anouk and Jean-Paul...not to mention Samuel, who adored his grandparents. And how could she explain such a sudden change in plan to a little boy who was so looking forward to a Christmas far different from any he'd experienced in his short life?

No, she was doomed to get through the next few weeks as best she could. Dammit, she was an adult, and in charge of her own destiny. No one, especially not Dimitri, could change that.

So why did she have such a strong instinctive feeling she was slowly losing control?

'If you'll excuse me?' Dimitri inclined, wondering if she was aware he could read her expressive features.

'Yes, of course,' she said quickly, and glimpsed the faint mocking amusement apparent.

It was another hour before the guests slowly began to dissipate, and Chantelle breathed a sigh of relief when Anouk suggested they should leave.

Samuel was fading fast when she collected him from the playroom, and she lifted him high as she reached the stairs.

'Tired, *mon ange*, hmm?' she queried gently, and felt her heart turn over as his arms encircled her neck. He was such an affectionate child, and she pressed a kiss to his temple. It was something she hoped would never change.

Chantelle reached the top of the stairs and found Anouk and Jean-Paul waiting for them. Dimitri's presence sent the blood pumping a little faster through her veins, and she looked at him in silent askance as she joined them.

Dimitri met her gaze and held it. Then something moved in the depths of his eyes. This was the woman he'd loved and lost. The child she held in her arms was his own.

The bond between them was a tangible entity, and one he had no intention of losing.

'Let me take him.'

'He's fine,' Chantelle said quickly, unwilling to relinquish Samuel.

For a moment she thought Dimitri was about to argue, and she hurriedly added, 'He's almost asleep.'

It took a few minutes to thank their host, and make their way to the entrance lobby.

Dimitri walked at her side as if it was his God-given right, and she threw him a veiled glare.

'Nine-thirty tomorrow morning?' he queried as they paused in the doorway.

The marine park. In Anouk and Jean-Paul's presence, what else could she say except 'Thank you. We'll be ready'?

CHAPTER FIVE

THE Gold Coast was the home of theme parks, and it was almost *de rigueur* for holidaymakers with children to visit most, if not all of them.

At ten the parking area adjacent the marine park was well-filled, and with the sun shining brightly in a cloudless sky, the day promised heat, humidity and, if they were lucky, a fresh temperate sea breeze.

Chantelle had come well-prepared, with hats, sunscreen cream, bottled water, change of clothes for Samuel, each packed into her backpack. A portable stroller would prove useful when Samuel began to tire. Every eventuality covered, she mused as she slid sunglasses in place.

Casual wear was the order of the day, and she'd chosen a denim skirt, cotton shirt, and wore trainers on her feet.

As to Dimitri, even cargo trousers and a T-shirt did little to disguise his dynamic aura of power. Designer sunglasses and the NY-monogrammed cap added to the overall look of a corporate executive on holiday.

Chantelle had prepared in advance for the ticket box, and she extracted a high-denominational note.

'What do you think you're doing?' His indolent drawl held a degree of musing tolerance.

'I don't expect you to pay for us.'

'You want to begin an argument at this hour of the morning?'

It was impossible to tell anything from his expression, so she didn't even try. 'Please.' Independence was important to her, and she didn't want to owe anyone anything. Especially not Dimitri.

'No.'

Apart from initiating a tussle, there was little she could do but acquiesce and throw him an eloquent glare.

Once through the gates she focused on Samuel's delight as they viewed the underground marine world with sharks, stingrays and various large fish held in massive glass tanks.

There was a programme to observe, and first up was the dolphin show. Dimitri secured their seats, and Chantelle very quickly positioned Samuel between them. An action which drew an amused smile.

The accompanying commentary proved to be a show almost on its own, and Samuel clapped as each dolphin performed its trained act, laughing with sheer delight as the wonderful sea mammals dived and leapt on command.

'We can watch them again?' he queried eagerly

as the show concluded, and he made no protest as Dimitri swept him up to sit astride his shoulders.

'Of course,' Dimitri promised. 'Later.'

'Dimitri said we can, Maman,' he assured, blissfully happy at the prospect. 'Later.'

They exited the area, and chose time out for refreshments.

Man and child seemed perfectly at ease with each other, and there was a tiny part of her that envied the simplicity of a child's trust.

A small seed of doubt rose to the fore. Had she been wrong in keeping Samuel's existence from Dimitri? Yet she knew unequivocally that if he'd known, life as she'd known it for the past four years would have been vastly different.

He would have insisted on sharing custody. Something she hadn't been ready for then, any more than she was ready for it now.

Yet how could she deny her son? Nerves tightened into a painful ball in her stomach at the thought of explaining Dimitri was Samuel's biological father.

Surely he was too young to harbour any resentment against her?

'All done?'

Dimitri's voice broke into her thoughts, and she spared him a quick glance as she secured Samuel's hat and reapplied sunscreen.

'Where to next?' she managed brightly, and saw Samuel's attention was held by the distant monorail.

'Can we go on that ride? Please,' he added quickly, offering Dimitri an appealing smile.

'Don't see why not.' Dimitri held out his hand. 'Do you want a skyscraper view?'

As if he needed to ask! Riding a man's shoulders was a new experience, and, judging by Samuel's willingness, one he couldn't wait to repeat.

There was no doubt her son loved every minute of the day's outing. He was almost too excited to eat lunch, and following the sea lion show he began to visibly wilt.

'I'll carry him,' Dimitri said quietly when Chantelle suggested the stroller, and he simply lifted Samuel to rest against his chest, with his head curved into one shoulder. Within seconds the little boy's eyes drooped closed.

'He's already asleep,' she said quietly. 'Perhaps we should leave.'

'There's a shady spot over by those trees. Let's go sit down awhile.'

There were a few jetskis on the lake, together with a small powerboat towing a clown-suited man on waterskis.

Tricks, thrills and orchestrated spills that had the audience gasping, and she watched with pretended interest as her son slept peacefully against his father's chest.

Anyone observing them would immediately assume they were a close family unit. But that was far from reality.

'Is Daniella still on the scene?' It was a stark query, but one she felt impelled to ask.

Dimitri's gaze narrowed. 'We share mutual friends.'

An advantage Daniella had used without scruples in the past. 'Uh-huh. So you see each other from time to time?'

'Occasionally.'

Well-orchestrated occasions, seemingly innocent, yet deliberately planned by an actress who knew how to play the game.

'How remarkably—' she paused fractionally '—convenient.'

'Her purported relationship with me was nothing more than a figment of her imagination.'

That wasn't how Daniella figured it. 'So you said at the time.'

'Something you didn't believe then,' Dimitri discounted silkily. 'Any more than you do now.'

She shot him a look that lost much of its effect given he was unable to detect her expression beneath the shaded lenses. 'Perceptive of you.'

'We've done this already.'

So they had. If he was telling the truth, Daniella Fabrizi had a lot to answer for.

Samuel napped for a while, and woke to the

sound of the park ranger announcing the afternoon sea lion show on the speaker system.

Their attendance capped Samuel's day, and on arrival home he clung as Dimitri released him from the car seat. 'Thank you for taking me to see the dolphins, and the sea lions,' he added, then planted an impulsive kiss on his father's cheek.

Chantelle stood transfixed for a few seconds as Dimitri returned the affectionate gesture.

'I like you,' Samuel said with childish candour.

'Thank you,' Dimitri responded solemnly. 'I like you, too.'

'Will you come and see us again?'

'You can count on it.'

'We're going to see the fireworks tomorrow night.'

Chantelle's heart ached with emotion. Samuel—stop, she wanted to urge, only the word remained locked in her throat.

Fireworks and Christmas decorative-light displays formed part of the lead-up to Christmas, and Anouk had elicited information on all the activities available for children.

'You can come too,' Samuel invited earnestly, and she intercepted quickly,

'Maybe next time. Dimitri has a busy schedule.' She summoned a smile as she met his gaze. 'Thanks for giving Samuel such a lovely day.'

Dimitri let her make her escape. For now.

*   *   *

'We're going to see pretty lights,' Samuel declared as she selected his clothes. 'There will be lots of bangs.'

Chantelle held out her hand, and experienced a warm tide of affection as he wrapped his arms around her legs.

It had been another hot day, and the temperature hadn't cooled with the onset of evening.

Chantelle stepped into cotton fatigue trousers and a singlet top, slid her feet into trainers, and scooped the length of her hair into a ponytail, then she helped Samuel don shorts and a T-shirt, added sandals and a cap.

'We're having lots of fun, Maman.' He lifted his head and gave her an infectious grin. 'I love it here. And I love Grandmère and Jean-Paul.' He looked thoughtful for a few seconds. 'I like Dimitri, too.'

Oh, my. 'That's nice.' What else could she say? Least said, the better! 'Shall we go join Grandmère and Jean-Paul?'

Tonight's adventure took in a massive fireworks display at one of the Coast's major shopping complexes, timed to begin at nightfall.

A twenty-minute drive, time out for parking and gaining a position among the gathering crowds of people meant little spare time before the display began.

Jean-Paul hoisted Samuel on top of his shoulders,

whereupon Samuel emitted a blissful sigh. 'I can see everything. But Jean-Paul is not as big as Dimitri.'

Chantelle met her mother's gaze, saw the faintly raised eyebrow, and revealed quietly, 'Dimitri carried him on his shoulders while we were at the marine park.'

'Uh-huh.'

'Don't,' she swiftly cautioned, and Anouk offered a musing smile.

'*Chérie*, I'm merely doing the maths.'

'It won't do you any good.'

Anouk's smile broadened into a fulsome curve. 'We shall see.'

'Maman—'

The warning went unheeded as a brilliant series of skyrockets exploded in myriad sprays of vivid colour.

Samuel laughed and clapped his hands in delight. 'Dimitri. Dimitri's here.'

She wanted to vent her frustration, and almost did, except Dimitri moved in close and she made do with lancing him with a telling glare.

'Dimitri,' Anouk greeted warmly. 'How nice you could join us.'

With Samuel perched high on Jean-Paul's shoulders, it wouldn't have taken Dimitri long to pinpoint them among the assembled crowd.

His presence had an unsettling effect, and she hated the familiar curling sensation deep inside.

Unbidden, her pulse-rate picked up, and she felt its thudding beat at the base of her throat.

Could he see it in this dim light? She hoped not.

He made no attempt to touch her, but it was enough that he was *there*, positioned mere inches from where she stood.

Samuel was in his element, laughing and clapping with delight at each bang and subsequent burst of colour. The designs were many and varied, and lasted a while.

'Dimitri, look!' He twisted towards Dimitri and pointed to one spectacular star-burst.

Jean-Paul had a firm grip on his legs, and he appeared to have no sense of fear as he called, 'Look, Maman, isn't it magnificent?'

'Magnificent,' Chantelle agreed. His delight was catching, and Anouk turned towards her.

'He's a beautiful little boy. Such innocence, so much heart.'

'Indeed,' Dimitri drawled in agreement.

All too soon the display concluded, and the crowds began to disperse.

Samuel made a sweeping gesture with his arms. 'They're all gone.'

'But it was wonderful while it lasted,' Chantelle offered gently as Jean-Paul swung the little boy down onto his feet.

'*Oui, Maman.*'

She leant down and ruffled his hair. 'And now we must go home. Tomorrow is another big day.'

'We're going out on the boat.' He looked up at Dimitri. 'Jean-Paul's boat.'

'Yes, I know.' Dimitri picked him up and held him in the crook of one arm. 'Would you like it if I came along too?'

'Yes.'

There you go, Chantelle muttered beneath her breath. Male bonding achieved in record time. A few hours a few days apart, and her son had reached an almost instant rapport with Dimitri.

She should be grateful. She assured herself she didn't mind sharing Samuel…she just didn't want to share him with Dimitri.

Together they began wending their way towards the vast parking area, and Chantelle turned towards Dimitri as they reached the base of the steps. Anouk and Jean-Paul were walking ahead of them.

'I'll take him.'

'My car's not far from here.'

Within minutes they reached Anouk's Lexus, and Chantelle began settling Samuel into his safety seat.

'We'll take Samuel home, *chérie*,' Anouk offered. 'We can detour past a few of the houses displaying Christmas lights. It's still relatively early. Why don't you join Dimitri for a coffee?' She turned towards Dimitri. 'There's a delightful area at Main Beach filled with trendy cafés. Chantelle will give you directions.' Her gaze swung back to her daughter. 'You so rarely go out, and it's such a pleasure to baby-sit my grandson.'

'Grandmère will read me a story,' Samuel declared, oblivious to his mother's growing tension.

'I don't think—'

'Darling, you think too much,' Anouk chided. She crossed round the car and slid into the passenger seat, whilst Jean-Paul, the traitor, took his position behind the wheel.

She'd been neatly shanghaied, and with an adroitness part of her could only admire. But then, Anouk was an expert at subtle manipulation.

So where did that leave her? With Dimitri, and reliant on him for a ride home. She watched the Lexus reverse out and purr towards the marked exit before she turned towards the man at her side.

'If I thought for one minute you had a hand in this, I'd hit you!'

'Now, there's an interesting thought.'

His indolent drawl almost undid her, and she speared him a dark glare. 'You can skip the coffee.' She was on a roll. 'In fact, you can skip taking me anywhere. I'll take a cab.'

'And disappoint Anouk?' he queried mildly. 'Besides, we need an opportunity to discuss arrangements for sharing custody of Samuel.'

For a few seconds she was rendered speechless, then the impact of his words hit with cold reality.

'Coffee,' Chantelle capitulated, and earned his wry amusement.

He gestured towards a line of parked cars to his right. 'My car is over there.'

She didn't want to do this. Dear heaven, if she had her way Dimitri would disappear in a puff of smoke. But given that unlikelihood, she had to face facts.

A discussion. Well, there was no harm in conducting a discussion. It didn't mean she had to agree to anything.

'I assume you're aware how to reach Main Beach?' she queried stiffly as Dimitri eased the car through the exit and branched off to connect with the main road leading through the heart of Surfer's Paradise.

'I acquainted myself with a map.'

Chantelle settled for silence unless spoken to, and it was only when they neared the traffic-controlled intersection adjacent Main Beach that she offered directions.

Trendy cafés lined the attractive boulevard, and it irked a little when he slid the car into a recently vacated parking spot.

'Do you want to choose, or shall I?' Dimitri queried as he locked the car and joined her on the pavement.

She gave a faint shrug. 'Coffee is coffee.' It was

a popular area, with patrons filling most of the outdoor tables.

They wandered the southern end of the boulevard,
and secured the first empty table available.

The waitress was efficient, and appeared within
minutes to take their order.

'You've done an excellent job rearing Samuel.'

Chantelle looked at him carefully. 'Let's not play
games, Dimitri.'

'Just cut straight to the chase?'

The waitress returned with bottled water and two
glasses, then crossed to another table.

'It's a wasted exercise, because I doubt there's
anything you suggest that I'll agree to.'

'Because you fear the effect on Samuel.'

'Yes.' She drew in a deep breath and expelled it
slowly. She held up a hand, and began ticking off
opposing points on each finger. 'He's too young to
travel without an accompanying adult. I wouldn't
want to entrust him to the care of anyone other than
myself. I'm not in a position to take several leaves
of absence from work.' She paused beneath his intense interest, and endeavoured not to allow him to
diminish her in any way. 'You travel extensively.
When would you be able to fit Samuel into your
current lifestyle?' She lifted a hand, then let it drop
to the table. 'Oh, dammit, none of this is easy!'

The waitress delivered their coffee, and Chantelle

watched as Dimitri added sugar to his, then took an appreciative sip.

'What if I was to offer a solution?' He replaced the cup down onto its saucer and spared her an enigmatic look.

'Such as?'

'We could marry.'

Shock widened her eyes, and her face paled. 'Excuse me?'

'Samuel gains the security of a two-parent household,' he elaborated. 'If you choose to continue working, that's your prerogative.'

Chantelle viewed him steadily, unsure whether to laugh or cry. 'You perceive that as a neat package. Loose ends tied, you get to have your son full-time on a permanent basis.' Anger rose and threatened to burst the surface of her control. 'What's my part in all of this?'

She couldn't stop the words. 'Do I get to play whore in the bedroom, and social hostess as and when required?' Her voice lowered to a heartfelt huskiness. 'Thanks, but no, thanks.'

The thought of living with him, sharing his bed…oh, lord, don't even go there!

'Would it be so bad?'

'How can you ask that?'

'Samuel needs to know he's my son. How do you think he'll feel when we tell him I'm his father?'

Her eyes blazed. 'You think I haven't agonised over that. Lost sleep over it?'

'You imagine he won't ask why we can't live together?' Dimitri pursued as he leaned back in his chair, presenting an image of unruffled composure. 'What are you going to say to him?'

'The truth,' she managed shakily. 'To his level of understanding.'

'Which you expect him to accept?'

Her coffee remained untouched, and she looked at it dispassionately, aware that if she took so much as a sip she'd be sick.

'We have a good life. Samuel is a happy, well-balanced little boy. I don't want that to change.'

'It won't.'

'How can you say that?'

'Easily.'

Don't you know I can't live with you? she wanted to scream at him. Share your bed…and not wither and die a little each time knowing Samuel is your main concern and I'm little more than the baggage that accompanies him?

'Dimitri—'

'Think about it.' He drained his cup, and looked askance as she left hers untouched. 'Would you prefer a *latte*?'

'I'd prefer to go home.'

He wanted to extend his hand and pull her close, ease her fears and promise he'd take care of her.

There were other words he wanted to say, but now wasn't the time or the place.

If he could dispense with the barriers she'd erected... Patience, he cautioned. A lot could happen in two weeks, and he intended to capitalise on every opportunity.

He summoned the waitress, paid the bill, then rose to his feet.

Chantelle didn't offer so much as a word during the drive to Sovereign Islands. Instead, she gazed sightlessly at the tracery of lights reflected on the Broadwater, and she had her seat belt unbuckled as soon as Dimitri drew the car to a halt in Anouk's driveway.

She released the clasp and opened the door. 'Good night.'

'I'll see you tomorrow.'

For a moment she looked at him blankly, then she remembered Andreas and Dimitri were joining them for the day on Jean-Paul's cruiser.

She slid from the passenger seat and closed the door behind her without uttering a further word.

Indoors, she checked with Anouk that Samuel was settled in bed, then bade her mother 'good night.'

'Are you OK, *chérie*? You look pale.'

'A headache,' she invented, not wanting to begin a question-and-answer session, then immediately felt bad. Maternal love was a precious thing. 'Dimitri asked me to marry him.' She waited a beat. 'I said no.'

'Chantelle,' Anouk protested sympathetically. *'Chérie—'*

Chantelle lifted a hand. 'Please, Maman. I beg you. Not now.'

She made for the stairs, checked on Samuel, then quietly undressed and slipped into bed to lie awake until just before dawn.

CHAPTER SIX

SUNDAY provided little opportunity for Chantelle to discuss the previous evening with Anouk, as Samuel was inevitably within listening distance, and there was food to assemble for the day's outing on Jean-Paul's cruiser.

Andreas and Dimitri arrived at ten, and within half an hour Jean-Paul had eased the large cruiser away from the jetty and headed into the main waterway.

It was a beautiful day, the sun high in a clear azure sky, and Samuel became a focus as they headed for Couran Cove.

'He's a generously spontaneous child,' Andreas complimented, as Dimitri hoisted Samuel into his arms for a clearer view.

Chantelle proffered a warm smile. 'Yes, he is.'

'I am proud he is my grandson,' he said quietly.

'Thank you. I have yet to tell Samuel.'

'But you will.'

'Yes.'

Oh, lord, the telling would raise several inquisitive questions...the most obvious one being why they weren't living with his daddy...and worse, *when* would they?

There was no doubt he liked Dimitri. In fact, *liking* was rapidly becoming affection.

She should be pleased. It would make things easier.

Not. The mere thought of sharing custody, being forced to let Samuel go from her care for specified lengths of time several times a year was enough to throw her into a nervous spin.

As far as today was concerned, convention decreed she play the social game. As she had all too often during the past week.

Thankfully Anouk, Jean-Paul and Andreas were present to act as a buffer. And Samuel, who delighted them all with his enthusiasm, his non-stop chatter and numerous questions about the boat, the harbour, and when they berthed at Couran Cove there were the resort attractions to amuse him.

Dimitri was a natural in the role of father, always close by, so much a part of the inner family circle that to any onlooker they were a family.

Which, strictly speaking, they were. Yet it was a fact she neither wanted to recognise nor accept.

'He's very good with Samuel,' Anouk offered quietly when they were briefly alone.

'Yes, isn't he?'

Without doubt Dimitri had earned her mother's unqualified approval. Jean-Paul, a shrewd judge of character, appeared similarly won over. Samuel was a cinch...which left only *her*.

Was she insane to knock back the sensible solution of marriage with him? As far as the sex was concerned, it would hardly be a hardship, and his wealth would ensure she'd never have to worry about money.

But what about her own emotional heart? Could she exist in a marriage based on convenience? Live her life in Samuel's shadow solely for his benefit?

He was much too young to comprehend or understand such a sacrifice.

Besides, she had a very nice life on her own merit.

There was a well-paid job, a pleasant villa to live in, a small car, savings. She and Samuel were doing just fine.

But wouldn't it be good to have a man in your life? a wicked imp taunted silently. Someone to share the events of the day, to be taken care of, and a warm male body to curl into through the night?

What about *love*? Shouldn't that play an important part?

The imp declined to answer.

If Dimitri had an inkling of her inner struggle, he gave no sign. Although once or twice she caught his thoughtful gaze, and wondered at it. Then there were the few occasions when he stood close, and she felt the heat from his body, sensed the faint musky scent of his cologne...and silently damned her reaction.

It should have been a relaxing day. Yet acting a part and keeping a smile permanently pinned in place took its toll, and by the time they left Couran Cove for Sovereign Islands she was nursing a headache.

'Please stay for dinner.' Anouk extended the invitation to Andreas and Dimitri as they reached home. 'Just a simple meal of cold chicken, salads, with bread and fruit, a little wine.'

Maman, Chantelle protested silently. *Don't do this.*

Except she was overruled by Jean-Paul's enthusiasm and Samuel's whoops of delight.

'Only if you'll allow me to reciprocate,' Andreas agreed with a smile.

So it was done, and while the men tended to the cruiser, Chantelle bathed and settled Samuel for a short nap, then she helped Anouk in the kitchen.

'Are you going to tell me why you turned down Dimitri's marriage proposal?' Anouk deftly cut cooked chicken in portions and placed them on a large platter.

Chantelle's hands momentarily stilled in the process of washing salad greens. 'It wasn't so much a proposal as a convenient solution.'

'And a convenient solution is such a bad thing?'

'We're doing fine on our own.'

'Why are you so afraid, *chérie*?' Anouk queried gently.

Did her mother have to be so astute?

'I don't want to enter a marriage where love is one-sided or confined to mere affection.'

'But is it? The chemistry between you is apparent to anyone who cares to look.'

Chantelle began shaking excess water from the salad greens. 'Next you'll try to tell me I'm still in love with him.'

'Aren't you?'

Now, there was the thing. For a few seconds her mother's query locked the voice in her throat. 'Sexual attraction, Maman. That's all it is.' And knew she lied.

Samuel woke after an hour's nap, and joined the men on the terrace.

Chantelle set the outdoor table with plates, cutlery and napkins, added glassware, then carried out the food while Anouk cleared the kitchen.

'Sit with me,' Samuel pleaded minutes later. 'Maman here.' He patted the seat on his right. 'And Dimitri there.' The seat on his left received a pat. 'Please,' he added.

'You're the flavour of the month,' Chantelle murmured as she moved past Dimitri, and heard his faint chuckle.

He was too close.

'That bothers you?'

All she had to do was move an inch and her arm would touch his. 'Why should it?'

'Perhaps we could pursue this later?'

'I don't think so,' she responded in an undertone, only to cut the conversation as Anouk, Jean-Paul and Andreas crossed to the table.

It was a relaxed, convivial meal, although afterwards Chantelle could recall little of the conversation.

Dusk became night, and Samuel urged Dimitri to witness his prowess with a Play Station game while Chantelle and Anouk took care of the dishes.

Two male heads, Chantelle witnessed as she entered the family room to collect Samuel for bed. Both so dark, their body language so closely linked it brought a lump to her throat.

'Time for bed, *mon ange*,' she said gently, and saw him struggle with disappointment.

'Can Dimitri read me a story? Please, Maman.'

She wanted to say *no*, and almost did, except when it came to the crunch she couldn't do it. 'If it's OK with Dimitri,' she managed, aware of Dimitri's steady gaze before it shifted back to their son.

'Here's the deal. I read the story, and Maman gets to tuck you in.'

Chantelle watched Samuel lead Dimitri upstairs, and she valiantly ignored the sudden ache in the region of her heart.

They were becoming close. Too close for her peace of mind. For what would happen when it came time to say goodbye?

She allowed them twenty minutes, then she went up to Samuel's room.

Dimitri sat cross-legged on the floor close to Samuel's bed, with a picture storybook in his hand, his voice quiet as he read the words.

Samuel was trying to stay awake, but his eyelids were beginning to droop, then they flickered as he valiantly fought sleep, only to close as his breathing changed and he slept.

Dimitri rose carefully to his feet, and stood for a moment looking at the sleeping child, then he turned and preceded her from the room, pausing as she quietly closed the door behind them.

'Thank you.'

She raised slightly startled eyes to meet his.

'For today,' he said quietly. He lifted a hand and brushed gentle fingers down one cheek. 'Go take something for that headache.'

How could he know? She opened her mouth, then closed it again, and nearly died as he lowered his head down to hers and took possession of her mouth in a lingering kiss that took hold of her senses and sent them spinning out of control.

'I'll be in touch.'

There were words she wanted to say, but none came immediately to mind as they descended the stairs and joined the others in the lounge.

Within minutes Andreas signalled their intention to leave, and amid voiced thanks for a wonderful day, the two men bade Anouk, Jean-Paul and Chantelle 'good night.'

Another day, another theme park.

Chantelle struggled with her conscience as Dimitri eased the car into an empty space in the large parking area adjacent MovieWorld.

In truth, each and every theme park was on her list of places to visit with Samuel. So why should it make any difference that Dimitri accompanied them?

Except it did…in spades. His presence heightened her stress levels, and pitched her to tread a fine emotional edge that played havoc with her senses.

She only had to look at his mouth to be forcibly reminded of just how it felt possessing her own…and her own eager response.

This was a man with whom she'd shared every intimacy…the heat, the passion, the primeval, mesmeric hunger for each other…ecstasy at its zenith.

The memory kept her awake too many nights, and when she slept he frequently haunted her dreams, causing her to wake in a tangle of bedcovers, her skin damp with sensual heat…only to discover she was alone, empty and aching.

On the occasions she told herself she was dealing with it…there was Samuel, Dimitri in miniature, as a vivid permanent reminder of what had been.

'Are we really going to see how they make movies?'

Samuel's voice penetrated her wayward thoughts, and she caught hold of his hand as they joined the queue at the ticket line.

'It's more like a movie show with live acts and stunts,' she corrected, reaching for her purse. An action which incurred a dark glance from the man at her side. Worse, Dimitri covered her hand and firmly returned it to her side.

Chantelle's bid for independence both amused and irritated him. 'We've already done this.'

Samuel's pleasure increased as the day progressed, and he was delighted with the various action shows, fascinated by the stunt actors, and through the eyes of a child…the apparent realism.

It was proving to be a holiday he'd never forget, and although she'd planned it this way, she hadn't envisaged Dimitri having any part in it.

A chill shivered over the surface of her skin. Had Dimitri already sought legal counsel? Was a team of lawyers preparing custody papers ready to serve on her? Or was he hoping to persuade her marriage to him was a more satisfactory option?

Doubts swirled inside her head. Was she being selfish denying Samuel a family life? Could she marry Dimitri and be content with a *convenient* marriage? Would it be enough? Sacrifice her life for that of her son?

Dimitri had made it sound so simple, so *feasible*. So, independently, had Anouk.

Did *she* have it so wrong?

Maybe Dimitri could view the arrangement with favour…hell, why wouldn't he? A wife in his home, his *bed*…not to mention full-time custody of his son and heir.

'Dimitri.'

The feminine voice was incredibly familiar, and one Chantelle would never forget.

'Darling, what on earth are you doing *here*?'

Daniella Fabrizi. Tall, incredibly svelte, her dark auburn hair loose in a flowing mass of curls, and her make-up a work of art. Attired in a cream linen suit whose skirt hemline rested several inches above her knee, and whose jacket was slashed to a low V and revealed an enviable cleavage.

The question had to be what Daniella was doing here.

Following Dimitri? Or was the actress unaware of his plans? Chance was a fine thing, but Chantelle knew Daniella left nothing to chance. So it had to be a calculated trip from her native New York.

'Daniella.'

Dimitri's voice was an indolent drawl, and it was impossible to detect much from his expression.

'I flew in yesterday with Victor LaFarge,' the actress revealed. 'He's thinking of shooting a movie here and wanted to check out the location, the studios.'

And you just decided to tag along? Actresses didn't usually check out locations and studios…did they?

'We must get together, darling.' A slight pout of those beautifully moulded lips was a contrived gesture. 'I rang and left a message with Andreas.'

Dimitri didn't confirm or deny he'd received it, and Daniella's gaze shifted to Chantelle.

'Why, you're here, too. I thought you'd moved abroad.'

'Daniella,' she acknowledged with as much politeness as she could muster.

The actress's gaze shifted to Samuel. 'What a cute child. Your nephew?'

'Samuel is my son,' she said quietly, and saw Daniella's gaze narrow, followed by the moment comprehension dawned.

'Well, now,' the actress began with silken vehemence as she swung back to Chantelle. 'Aren't you just the cleverest little thing?'

She wanted to pick Samuel up and move away, and she almost did, except only cowards ran.

'I didn't realise this visit represented doubleduty,' Daniella commented, shooting Dimitri a stunning smile. 'It won't, of course, create an obstacle.'

What in hell was the actress talking about? Samuel's existence wouldn't cause an obstacle to *what*? Daniella's plan to cohabit with Dimitri? Maybe even marry him? An act that would catapult Daniella into the position of part-time stepmother?

Not in this lifetime, Chantelle vowed silently. She deliberately checked her watch, then turned towards Dimitri. 'Samuel and I will be at the Batman show. It's due to begin soon.' Somehow she managed a warm smile, although it failed to reach her eyes. 'Do stay and chat with Daniella.'

'I would hate to keep Dimitri from an obligation.'

She was a first-class witch. But what else was new?

'Oh, *please*,' Chantelle assured. 'Dimitri is free to do whatever he wants.' With that she took Samuel's hand and began leading him away.

Not that she got very far before Dimitri joined her.

'You had no need to run away.'

She spared him a dark look. 'Correction. I was removing myself from the line of fire.'

'Would you believe I gave her no inkling of my visit to the Coast?'

'Doubtless your secretary organised your flight.' What point subtlety? 'Daniella is a very resourceful woman.' She couldn't help herself. 'And very good at ego-stroking. You must be flattered.'

Dimitri wanted to shake her, then kiss her senseless. If Samuel hadn't been present, he'd have tossed convention to one side and opted for the latter.

Instead, he did neither.

'I don't possess an ego,' he drawled with musing humour. 'Nor do I covet flattery.' He spared her a sideways glance. 'Unless you want to offer yours?'

'Are you kidding?'

'Maman,' a small voice intercepted, 'are you angry with Dimitri?'

You have no idea, she accorded silently. *Anger* doesn't begin to cover it.

'Look,' she encouraged him, indicating the scene ahead. 'Batman.' As a distraction, it worked wonderfully well, and she didn't even protest when Dimitri took Samuel from her and hoisted him onto his shoulders.

For the remainder of the afternoon she kept up a civil front...for Samuel's benefit.

It was after four when they exited the gates and made their way to Dimitri's car. Samuel was fading fast, and she knew he'd fall asleep within minutes of the car being in motion.

Chantelle didn't offer any conversation during the drive to Sovereign Islands, and she unlatched the door as soon as Dimitri brought the car to a halt in Anouk's driveway.

'I'll take Samuel,' she said quickly. 'He might wake.'

'Will that be a disaster?'

'Of course not.' She looked askance as he crossed round to her side. 'Dimitri—'

'Chantelle?' he gently mocked.

'Don't be facetious,' she flung beneath her breath, and incurred a dark glance. She refused to be reduced to an undignified struggle, so she simply stood aside and let him unclip the restraints holding Samuel secure in the safety seat.

Which meant Dimitri got to carry Samuel indoors.

'Oh, poor *petit*,' Anouk murmured as she saw her grandson asleep in Dimitri's arms. 'Take him straight upstairs. Even if he only naps for a little while, it will be better than the short time he has already had.'

'I'll take him,' Chantelle said swiftly, and sent up a silent prayer to the deity Dimitri would hand Samuel over. She didn't want to share this indomitable man's presence in the confines of Samuel's bedroom, for Dimitri's height and breadth would swamp the room.

However, the deity wasn't listening, and she merely received a musing look as Dimitri moved past her and headed towards the stairs.

'Maman,' she protested, only to have Anouk direct her a telling glance.

'*Chérie*, you are very tense. Has it not been an enjoyable day?'

What could she say? Nothing, at least not right now. 'I'd better go check.'

Samuel rested silently on the bed, and Chantelle carefully tucked a cellular cotton blanket over him.

She turned and encountered Dimitri's dark gaze, and for one electrifying minute she was unable to move.

Then his mouth widened into a slow smile, and the spell was broken as he stood aside for her to exit the room ahead of him.

Chantelle stepped quickly from the room, and all but ran down the stairs, supremely conscious that Dimitri followed close behind her.

'How is he?' Anouk queried. 'He didn't stir?'

'He's asleep, Maman.'

'Good.' Anouk turned towards Dimitri. 'Will you join us in a drink?'

'Thank you, but no. Another time, perhaps?'

Was he anxious to leave so he could call Daniella? She told herself she didn't care…and knew she lied.

CHAPTER SEVEN

CHANTELLE opted for a quiet day at home with Samuel instead of accompanying Anouk and Jean-Paul to a nearby shopping complex. Especially as they'd visited the day before so Samuel could see Santa with all the other children.

Parking was at a premium, the crowds many, and she didn't want Samuel becoming over-tired.

'Shall we bake a cake for Grandmère?'

'A surprise.' Samuel's eyes lit up at the thought. 'Chocolate, Maman.'

'Chocolate it is.'

She set to work, and had just popped the cake into the oven when the phone rang.

It was Anouk, sounding agitated, which was unusual. Her mother never became agitated.

'*Chérie*, I'm at the hospital. Jean-Paul tripped and fell. The stupidest thing. He was avoiding a boy riding a skateboard at speed in the car park.' She paused fractionally. 'We are waiting on X-rays. It's possible he has fractured his collarbone.'

'Are you OK?' Chantelle queried at once. 'Do you want me to come sit with you?'

'No, I'm fine. But I don't know what time we'll be home.'

Late afternoon, with Jean-Paul in obvious pain and wearing a protective sling.

He was required to rest, and the next few days were spent quietly at home. The news of his accident spread, and Dimitri called in for a visit, spent time with Samuel, and was about to leave when Anouk opened the drawer of an escritoire and retrieved two embossed tickets.

'Jean-Paul and I were to attend a charity ball to-morrow evening.' She handed them to Dimitri. 'Please, take these. You and Chantelle can attend in our place.' She turned towards her daughter. 'I'll mind Samuel. Six-thirty for seven. Black tie. It's to aid the Leukaemia Foundation.'

What if I don't want to go? Chantelle almost que-ried, only to be outnumbered before she had a chance to decline.

'Please,' Jean-Paul acceded. 'It's a good table, and a fund-raiser for a worthy cause. Anouk is on the committee.'

Thirty-six hours later Chantelle stood in the large lounge adjacent the hotel ballroom and glanced with interest at fellow guests assembled there.

Men attired in dark evening suits, the women in designer gowns and jewellery, real and faux.

The evening's affair was indeed an *event*. Capacity attendance, she surmised as she sipped champagne and orange juice.

Dimitri was something else in a superbly tailored dinner suit, white shirt and black tie. He had the look, the stature that set him apart from other men. Add an aura of power, and the result was devastating.

He drew women's attention like bees sensing a honey pot. Feminine interest, blatant and discreet, but apparent none the less. Four years ago she would have smiled and silently voiced 'you can look, but I get to take him home'. Then she had known how the evening would end, with a loving that lasted through the night.

Now they'd spend the evening together as social equals, pretend they were enjoying themselves, then he'd deliver her to Anouk's door, and they'd occupy separate beds in different houses.

Did he lie awake at night aching, as she ached for him? The long, sweet loving, the passion? So intense, like twin souls transcending reality and merging into one.

Standing close to him like this, she was aware of him to an alarming degree. The musky aroma of his cologne mingling with the clean smell of freshly laundered clothes acted like an aphrodisiac, heightening her senses, and accelerating her heartbeat.

It was crazy, but she had an urge to slip her hand into his, feel the warmth and strength apparent, and have his fingers thread through her own. To have

his eyes warm with sensual heat in silent promise…
for her, only for her.

Oh, dear God…*get a grip*.

Conversation. Chantelle reached for it like a
drowning person reaching for a life-raft.

'When do you return to New York?'

She was nervous, Dimitri observed, idly watching
the throbbing pulse at the base of her throat.

'New Year.' He placed the palm of his hand between her shoulder blades and moved it gently in
silent reassurance. An action that earned him a startled glance as his hand slipped to rest at her waist.
'The second of January to be precise.'

A week before she was due to return to Paris with
Samuel.

'I'm surprised you were able to structure such a
long break.'

'My life isn't entirely given over to business.'

The faintly accented drawl brought a tinge of colour to her cheeks. 'I didn't imagine it was.'

'No?'

There was something going on here she didn't
know about. An elusive, almost mesmeric interac-
tion she could only guess at.

Dammit, what game was he playing?

'Dimitri!'

Chantelle steeled herself to present a polite façade
as she turned towards Daniella and Victor LaFarge.

The likelihood of this being a chance encounter was remote.

'You should have told me you'd be here tonight.'

The actress did provocative reproach well. The faint pout, the slight tilt of her head...and a sultry gaze that exhibited blatant lust.

Overkill, definitely. But what man wouldn't react?

'Where are you seated?'

If Daniella suggested they occupy the same table, she'd *scream*. Then common sense prevailed; seating arrangements had been organised in advance.

Chantelle noticed the three sets of double doors were now open, and guests were beginning to vacate the lounge.

'Shall we go in?' Dimitri inclined.

Was it deliberate, or merely a courtesy? Chantelle wondered as he urged her towards the ballroom entrance.

His hand remained at her waist, and she could have sworn his fingers effected a soothing squeeze.

What was he doing, for heaven's sake?

Efficient organisation ensured the guests were directed to their reserved seating, and Chantelle sank gracefully into a chair at a table close to the catwalk.

'Ah, there you are.'

She could only look on with startled dismay as Daniella collected two place-names, replaced them with hers and Victor's, then quickly transferred the place-names to the table she and Victor had been assigned.

'That's better.' The actress promptly took the chair next to Dimitri.

It was? Chantelle couldn't imagine anything worse. Whatever happened to good manners? Had Daniella no shame?

Apparently not.

'Darling,' Daniella purred with feline sensuality as she placed a hand on Dimitri's arm. 'You didn't return my calls.'

With deliberate care he removed her hand. 'No.'

Oh, my. He was rejecting her advances? In public?

'It was very impolite of you, *caro*.' The pout was back, and although a smile was in evidence, her eyes were green ice.

'You think so?'

Victor seemed fascinated with their exchange, and Chantelle reached for her water glass. She needed something stronger, but the wine waiter had yet to appear at their table.

'Victor and I'll be on the Coast for another few days, then we fly down to Sydney to check out the studios there.'

'Indeed?'

Mercifully the wine waiter provided a welcome distraction…one that extended several minutes as

Dimitri effected a round of introductions to the four guests sharing their table.

The MC announced the purpose of the evening, noted the charity, and introduced the chairwoman, who gave a splendid speech on the Leukaemia Foundation's goals and achievements. After which a popular singer came on and produced a stirring rendition of a familiar ballad.

Chantelle was supremely conscious of Daniella's attempts to gain Dimitri's attention. And his apparent disinclination to play *polite*.

The starter was served, and she almost died when he forked a small shrimp from his plate and offered it to her.

What was this? He was feeding her? It had been something they did whenever they'd dined together in the past. So why *now*? Nothing had changed... had it?

She wasn't so sure of anything any more, especially not *him*.

There was a break between the starter and the main, during which time the MC showed slides of children with leukaemia and encouraged the guests to dig deep with donations and the purchase of raffle tickets.

Chantelle made a contribution, and barely contained her surprise at the high denominational bills Dimitri added to the basket being passed around their table.

'Victor, take care of it,' Daniella commanded languidly.

The waiters began serving the main course, placing alternate plates of fish and chicken…the usual practice at such events.

'Oh, please, take that away and bring me a salad,' the actress said with disdain.

Daniella Fabrizi excelled at playing the diva. Four years ago the actress had been a new kid on the block, but fame and fortune had obviously wrought changes…none of which Chantelle considered an improvement. But then, she had every reason to be biased!

'I imagine you hired a baby-sitter for…Sam, isn't it?' The actress directed the query to Chantelle.

'Samuel,' she corrected. 'My mother is looking after him.'

'How convenient for you.' Daniella's voice dripped barbed cynicism beneath the superficial smile.

'Yes,' she agreed, and watched the actress transfer her attention to Dimitri.

'We really must get together for dinner.' Her hand rested on his thigh, and her eyes glittered with suppressed anger as he calmly removed it. 'The four of us, of course,' she added quickly.

'I don't think so.'

Chantelle consciously held her breath for a few

seconds, aware all conversation at their table had come to a sudden halt.

'Darling, why ever not?' Daniella pursued with a tinkling laugh. 'We've been intimate friends for a long time.'

Dimitri rested his cutlery. 'We were never intimate. Your deliberately orchestrated interference caused unutterable grief and denied me the pleasure of sharing Chantelle's pregnancy and the first three and a half years of my son's life.'

'Oh, really, how can you say that when we—?'

'Shared one date five years ago.'

The silence was electric. The muted music, the guests' chatter…it all faded into the background.

'Since then you've contrived to elicit invitations to the same functions I attend,' Dimitri continued with dangerous silkiness. 'Almost everywhere I turn, be it Athens, London or Rome…you manage to be there.'

'Don't be ridiculous.'

She was good, Chantelle complimented silently. She did injured indignation to perfection.

'It amounts to stalking, Daniella.'

'How can you say that?'

'Easily.' He waited a beat. 'If you won't desist, I'll have no option but to take out a restraining order against you.'

'I don't understand how you can be so cruel.'

Pathos was evident, and seemed incredibly genuine as the actress recoiled from what she perceived to be an unjustified attack.

'I travel extensively on location. My visit here has been at Victor's invitation.'

Victor remained silent. Integrity, or a desire to distance himself? Probably the latter.

'Your inclusion at tonight's function?' Dimitri persisted silkily.

'Publicity. It's an essential part of an actor's career.'

'I have it on authority the venue was fully booked.'

'So? Someone must have cancelled.'

'And the several messages you left on Andreas' answering machine?'

'Why shouldn't I look up an old friend?'

'We're merely social acquaintances, Daniella. Accept it and move on.'

The waiter appeared at their table and placed a delectable salad in front of the actress, who took one look, and demeaned him with attitude. 'Is this the best you can do?'

The anger simmering beneath Daniella's control threatened to erupt into an explosive scene.

The waiter apologised and requested the actress's specific requirements.

'The food is appalling. Don't bother.'

Temperament was one thing, but nothing excused bad manners.

Chantelle picked at the food on her plate, rearranging the artistic vegetable compilation, forked a morsel of fish, then reached for her wineglass.

Dimitri calmly collected his cutlery and finished the contents on his plate.

Doubtless he was accustomed to shooting people down in flames. Maybe he did it in business on a daily basis. However, she needed a temporary escape from the tense atmosphere.

With deliberate movements, she pushed her plate aside, folded her napkin, then she excused herself.

It seemed feasible to freshen up, given the main event...a fashion show...was due to begin when guests had finished the main course.

How long could she remain absent? Five minutes, ten? It didn't take long to reapply lipstick and powder her nose, but she waited ten minutes before entering the vestibule.

Only to come face-to-face with Daniella, whose transformation was something to behold.

'Don't let that little performance fool you,' the actress vented in barely controlled fury. 'Dimitri is mine, he always has been.'

Chantelle drew in a calming breath, hating the scene she knew was about to unfold. 'I don't believe you,' she said steadily, and took a backward step as Daniella moved close.

'Are you calling me a liar?'

Oh, hell. She didn't want a cat-fight, but she was

damned if she'd remain quiescent. 'Did it never occur that you're delusional? Or that you possess an unhealthy obsession for a man who wants nothing to do with you?'

'*Bitch.*' Daniella's hands clenched and unclenched with rage. 'Just because you bore him a son—'

Chantelle held up a hand. 'Stop it right there,' she warned, and made to walk away, except she wasn't quick enough as Daniella's palm connected painfully with her cheek.

'Don't mess with me. I can have you taken out—' she clicked a finger and thumb together with expressive emphasis '—like that.'

'You think Dimitri wouldn't put two and two together?' Chantelle challenged, and felt the first stirring of fear as Daniella's eyes darkened to emerald.

'I can make him want me. I know tricks—'

She'd had enough. Without a further word she pushed past the actress and walked to the lift, which mercifully opened as soon as she pressed the call-button.

At Reception she had the concierge summon a cab, which appeared within seconds, and she slid into the rear passenger seat, gave the driver Anouk's address, then focused on the passing traffic, the nightscape, in an effort to dispel Daniella's vengeful image.

It didn't work, nothing worked, and she alighted

from the cab feeling as if she'd run an emotional marathon.

Anouk met her at the door, her features creased with concern.

'What is it, *amie*? Dimitri has called, not once but twice. *Merde,*' she breathed. 'What is that mark on your face?'

'Maman—don't ask.'

'But of course I will ask!' The sudden peal of the phone provided a momentary distraction. 'That will be Dimitri again.'

'I don't want to speak with him. I don't want to see him.'

'*Alors*—I must answer that.' She did, and Chantelle gathered little from her mother's end of the conversation other than she confirmed Chantelle was home.

'He is on his way here now,' Anouk revealed as she cut the connection.

'Maman, if you let him in the door, I swear I'll take the next flight out of here.' Stupid, angry tears threatened to spill, and she brushed at them in a futile gesture. 'I'm going upstairs to bed. We'll talk in the morning.' She caught the concern on her mother's features, and relented a little. 'Promise.' Then she crossed to the stairs and went to her room.

With care she removed her make-up, then slipped out of her clothes. There was a tense moment as she glimpsed the beam of reflected car-lights in the driveway, and she swiftly turned the safety lock in position.

Dimitri might get past Anouk, but she was damned if she'd face him tonight.

Within minutes there was a light tap on her bedroom door. 'Chantelle. Dimitri insists on speaking with you.'

She took a deep, calming breath. 'Whatever he has to say can wait until morning.'

It was a while before she saw car-lights switch on and his car reverse down the driveway. Then, and only then did she unlock the door and check on Samuel before retreating to her room to lie in bed staring at the shadowed ceiling.

CHAPTER EIGHT

CHANTELLE slept badly, and woke to find Samuel tugging at her arm. With automatic movements she reached forward and gave him an affectionate hug.

'Maman, wake up. Dimitri is here, and Grandmère is waiting to take me to the beach with Jean-Paul.'

What on earth was the time?

Eight, she determined with a silent groan. 'I need to shower and dress, *mon ange*. Go downstairs and wait for me. Fifteen minutes, OK?'

'OK,' he said happily. 'I've had breakfast, and Grandmère is packing a picnic.'

Ten minutes later she donned jeans and a singlet top, slid her feet into sandals, then she caught her hair into a ponytail. Make-up? Forget it.

Subterfuge was alive and well, she perceived as she entered the dining room. Dimitri stood with Samuel hoisted in his arms as they both surveyed Jean-Paul's cruiser moored at the jetty stretching out from the water's edge.

Jean-Paul, his arm in a sling, looked distinctly bemused, and Anouk was slotting bottled water and juice into the portable cooler.

Dimitri turned as he sensed her presence, and gave the appearance of being totally relaxed...until she met his gaze, and she glimpsed something she didn't care to define.

'Maman is here,' Samuel said at once, and looked at his grandmother. 'Can we go now, Grandmère?'

'Of course.' Anouk ran a quick check. 'Sunscreen, hat, insect repellent, change of clothes, swimsuit, towels...yes, that's everything.'

'Grandmère is going to show me how to catch fish.'

She is? Well, now, that has to be a first.

'We're going to eat it for dinner,' Samuel informed as Dimitri released him to stand on the floor. *'Au revoir, Dimitri. Maman.'*

'The coffee is hot,' Anouk declared. 'And there are croissants warming in the oven.'

'I'll help you with the cooler.' Dimitri crossed to where it stood and followed Anouk, Jean-Paul and Samuel out to the car.

Chantelle poured fresh juice, drank it, then filled a cup with coffee, choosing to take it black and sweet. Her nerves were in shreds, and the thought of food repelled her.

Minutes later she heard the car start, and she steeled herself for Dimitri's return. Even so, his reappearance in the kitchen surprised her and she almost spilled her coffee as he entered the kitchen.

For a moment he simply looked at her, and she met his searching gaze with fearless regard.

Soft denim jeans and a polo shirt did little to minimise his impact on her senses, and, unless she had it wrong, it didn't appear he'd slept any better than she had.

'Would you care to tell me why you walked out last night?'

His voice was silk-smooth and sent shivers scudding across the surface of her skin. 'I gather Daniella wasn't forthcoming?'

He thrust a hand into each pocket of his jeans. 'She denied speaking to you. At first.' The memory of his confrontation with Daniella still had the power to anger him, and he clenched his fists in silent frustration.

'I can take care of myself.'

He moved to stand within touching distance, then he lifted a hand and cupped her cheek. 'You have the beginnings of a bruise.' He brushed a thumb-pad gently over her cheekbone.

Beneath his touch she felt strangely helpless. 'Dimitri…'

He cupped her face and tilted it so she had to look at him. 'From the moment I met you, there has been only *you*. In the past four years no one—nothing—has come close to what we shared together.'

He lowered his head and brushed his lips to her

cheek, then trailed a path to the edge of her mouth. 'I want you in my life.'

'You can't always have what you want.'

His mouth covered hers in a kiss so incredibly sweet it made her want to cry. 'Yes,' he said softly, 'I can.'

'Because of Samuel.'

He was silent for a few seconds, and she tried to wrench away from him, only to be held fast where she stood.

'That requires a *yes* and *no* qualification. Yes, because I want to be part of my son's life. And no, because *you* are more important to me than anything or anyone else. Without you, I merely exist.'

Love…what about *love*?

'You want me to spell it out?'

His gaze held hers, and she couldn't look away.

'I fell in love with you within days of when we first met. It never changed, even after we went our separate ways.'

Daniella had contrived to poison what they shared then, and now, with manipulative effect. Except this time it hadn't worked.

'I won't allow it to happen again.'

Dared she believe him? She wanted to, desperately.

He pulled her close, one hand holding fast her head while the other slid down to cup her bottom.

Then his mouth closed over hers, and she became lost in the taste and feel of him.

It was magical, mesmeric…a passionate intoxication of all her senses.

When he lifted his head she could only look at him, and her bones began to melt at the raw desire apparent.

'This is one level on which we communicate,' Dimitri said in a husky groan, as he slid his hands beneath her singlet top.

Her skin was like satin, so smooth and silky, and delicately scented. He wanted to taste every inch of her in a long, slow loving that would drive them both wild, bury himself inside her and watch her spiral out of control, then join her in the ride.

'I need you. Dear heaven, you can't begin to believe how much.'

'I don't think—'

His mouth possessed hers, and any thought of resistance was lost as her hunger matched his.

She couldn't get enough of him as instinct ruled, and she made no protest when he swept her into his arms and made for the stairs.

He entered her bedroom, and she retained little recollection of dispensing with her clothes, his. There was only *now*, the heat and the passion in a fast and furious lovemaking that tore the breath from her body and left them slick with sensual sweat.

Dear heaven. She felt as if she'd been consumed

by an emotional storm so intense she *burned* from it.

All her senses were on high alert, and she could feel every inch of her body…inside and out.

Dimitri cupped her chin and gently turned her head towards him. 'I love you.'

The warmth of his smile melted her bones and she offered a tremulous smile.

'Marry me, Chantelle.' He dropped a kiss at the edge of her shoulder. 'I want to share your life.' He nibbled a path across her collarbone, then slipped low to nuzzle at her breast. 'And have you share mine.'

He trailed his lips to her navel, dipped the tip of his tongue and teased the hollow there before moving to one hip and kissing a path to her knee.

He knew where to touch, the location of each sensual pulse-beat, and he explored them all with such excruciating slowness she was almost begging when he sought to gift her the most intimate kiss of all.

She cried with the pleasure of it, and reached for him, exulting in his quickened heartbeat, the thudding of his pulse, and he entered her to indulge in a long, slow loving that left them both sated and sensually replete.

'You haven't said yes,' Dimitri ventured as he drew her in close against him and pillowed her head into the curve of his shoulder.

'Not fair. You have me at a disadvantage.'

'*Agape mou,*' he murmured against her temple, 'I plan to keep you at a disadvantage on a permanent basis.'

She lifted a hand and teased her fingers through the swirling hairs on his chest. 'You do realise it's the middle of the day?'

'And that makes a difference, because?'

'We should get up.' She made a slight effort to move, and thought better of it.

The warmth of his smile reached down and touched her soul. 'Soon, hmm?'

'Anouk and Jean-Paul—'

'Won't return until after four.'

'A conspiracy, huh?'

'Good management,' he corrected.

Chantelle lay quietly, exulting in the languid warmth of a woman who had been thoroughly loved. This was where she wanted to be, with this man, for the rest of her life.

'Yes,' she said simply.

Dimitri stilled. 'Is that *yes*, it was good management, or have you agreed to marry me?'

A light laugh bubbled from her lips. 'Both. Besides, we've just had unprotected sex. Twice. The last time we did that, I fell pregnant. I think I should make an honest man of you.'

He tunnelled his fingers through her hair and settled his mouth over hers in a long, evocative kiss that almost made her weep.

'Soon. Very soon,' he promised. 'We'll organise a licence and get married before we leave for Paris.'

'Whoa, not so fast,' Chantelle protested. *'Paris?'*

'You need to give notice and pack everything you want to transfer to New York.'

'We? You're coming with us?'

'Pedhaki mou,' he assured with musing indulgence, 'I don't intend letting you out of my sight.'

It was an hour before they rose and shared a shower, then, dressed, they went down to the kitchen and raided the refrigerator for a late lunch, choosing to eat out on the terrace overlooking the sea.

Chantelle sat quietly as she sipped chilled white wine, and became lost in reflective thought.

If she hadn't returned home for Christmas; if Dimitri hadn't chosen this particular festive season to visit his father... They might never have met again, never had the chance to experience the joy, the passion of two people so perfectly in tune with each other.

'I love you,' she said gently, turning towards him.

'Cristos.' The word emerged with heartfelt warmth. 'Now you tell me.' He rose from the chair and pulled her to her feet.

'What are you doing?'

'Taking you inside.' He threaded his fingers through her own. 'I don't want to shock the neighbours.'

CHAPTER NINE

'MAMAN, we are home. Grandmère helped me catch a fish.'

There was a moment's silence as the child absorbed the scene in front of him. Slowly he turned towards his grandmother. 'Grandmère, why is Dimitri kissing Maman?'

'They are standing beneath the mistletoe, *mon ange*, are they not? It is a Christmas tradition, *oui*, for adults to kiss beneath the mistletoe.'

'Only adults?'

Dimitri lifted his head and turned towards his son.

Then he swept wide an arm as he beckoned Samuel to join them.

Samuel ran, and was lifted high into his father's arms. He wriggled a little, pressed a kiss to his mother's cheek, then impulsively gifted another to the man who held him.

'This is nice.'

'Nice enough for you to share Maman with me?'

Samuel looked thoughtful. 'Are you going to be my daddy?'

Chantelle held her breath.

'Would you like that?' Dimitri queried solemnly.

123

'*Oui*. Maman doesn't know how to catch fish, and she won't let me have a proper bicycle. But I'm getting big, and I won't fall off.'

Anouk smiled and caught Jean-Paul's hand. 'In this case, three isn't a crowd, but five definitely is. Let's go look at the garden for a while.'

Christmas was the season for family, with love, laughter, gifts and giving.

For Chantelle it held special meaning, for from this moment on she'd always connect the festive season with being reunited with the love of her life.

Three weeks ago she would never have imagined in her wildest dreams she'd be planning her own wedding. Or that she would reveal to her son his real father's identity.

Miracles had been worked to ensure the marriage could take place amongst family the day before their departure for France.

Returning home for Christmas had brought more than she could have ever dreamed of, and she lifted her face to meet Dimitri's warm gaze as Jean-Paul handed out gifts assembled beneath the Christmas tree.

The brief touch of his mouth on hers was a vivid reminder of what they would soon share together.

'Dimitri is kissing Maman again,' Samuel announced, and encountered his father's broad smile followed by his teasing drawl.

'You'd better get used to it.'

Samuel grinned and shrugged his shoulders. He didn't mind. His mother was happy, Dimitri was cool, and, by the number of brightly packaged gifts beneath the tree, Santa had rewarded him well.

What more could anyone want?

A PRINCE
FOR CHRISTMAS
Rebecca Winters

CHAPTER ONE

"ERIC? Will you forgive me for calling you this late?"

"Maren?"

Thirty-year-old Eric Thorvaldsen, fifth in line to the Frijian crown, a fact that pleased him no end because he was almost a hundred percent certain he'd never have to rule, jackknifed into a sitting position on the bed. The black Lab Thor lying at his feet lifted his head before putting it down again.

A quick glance at his watch told him it was four in the morning. "Have you made me an uncle?" This would be his sister's first child.

"Not quite yet, brother dear. I had contractions and Stein took me to the hospital, but they finally stopped. Our baby's going to be born prematurely no matter what. But the doctor is hoping I can last one more week, so he has ordered me to bed."

"Four more days and it's Christmas!"

"Wouldn't it be something if my little baby were to have a birthday on the most wonderful day of the year?"

If that were the case, Eric already felt sorry for the baby who would be his nephew. He'd be cheated out of his own special birthday, one he shouldn't have to share with a holiday, but Eric kept that thought to himself.

"It'll be wonderful anytime."

"I know. I can't wait. Anyway, because I've been put on bed rest, I have a favor to ask of you. Please don't say no before you hear what it is. This is really important!"

Everything was important to his compassionate sister who championed a dozen causes in the name of the homeless, the sick and aged, orphans, abused animals.... The list went on and on.

"I would have asked Knute or mom, but he's out of the country attending that economic meeting in Hamburg and won't be back for a few more days. Mother went with him to do some shopping. That leaves you."

Since their father's death from a fatal heart attack last year, their older brother Knute was now king. By Maren mentioning his name, it meant this favor had something official about it. "Official" was a word Eric shied away from—whenever it was possible.

"Eric? I can tell you're cringing."

He chuckled. "Am I that bad?"

"You're worse! Seriously, this is so important I'll have to risk the baby coming early and take care of it myself if you can't."

He blinked. "Well—you've put me in a position where I can hardly refuse now, can I," he drawled.

"I love you."

"I love you too."

They were like twins, only a year apart with her being the elder. They were their parents' second family.

Knute was seven years older. Thank heaven he didn't know any better than to do his duty. With two sons who were being raised to succeed him if anything happened, followed by Maren and her soon-to-be-born-son who'd be third and fourth in line to the throne, Eric had been left free to pursue his work as an oceanographer.

"Do I have to come to the palace?" Thorsvik was only a half hour away from where he lived.

"No. You can stay right there in Brobak."

"That's a plus."

When he wasn't working in the city or attending oceanographic seminars around the world, he preferred to spend what little free time he had at his home in the little village south of the capitol. On a steep slope far away from other people, he could look down on the Oslo fjord and feel rejuvenated.

"I'll ask someone from the palace to bring your ceremonial suit to you in the morning."

Eric's brows met in a frown. He hadn't had to look official since a family photograph had been taken at the time Knute became king.

"This is something I have to do tomorrow?"

"Yes, but let me explain. A year ago the Chocolate Barn in the market square decided to expand their Christmas exports to include a hot chocolate mix.

"Instead of putting the traditional gnome on the packaging, they ran a contest to find the right little Frijian girl to display on the labeling around the can. They're hoping she'll become a recognizable icon throughout the world.

"A child in America, of Frijian descent won the contest. Her prize was a trip to Frijia before the Holidays with her family and—"

"And the highlight would be a special audience with Princess Maren, at the Chocolate Barn, where she'll be given a year's worth of chocolate treats to take home," Eric broke in.

"Something like that," she murmured. "They asked me to do this a year ago, and I agreed. She'll be there at two o'clock to meet you."

"Have you ever turned anyone down for anything?"

"I try not to if it's for a worthy cause. The Chocolate Barn is going to donate part of the proceeds of this new product to my animal rescue charity."

"Surely the owners and the girl's family will understand when they find out you're about to have a baby?"

"Of course they will. But we're talking about a little girl here. A darling little five- or six-year-old who still believes in fairy princesses and castles and magic. No doubt she's been waiting and waiting for tomorrow to come."

He let out an exasperated sound between a laugh and a groan. "I'm hardly going to fill the bill, Maren."

"You're the genuine royal article, and you look like Prince Charming when you're dressed as if you're ready to attend a coronation. Her child's heart will fall in love with you on the spot. She'll forget all about wanting to meet me.

"The palace photographer will be there to take a picture of the two of you for a souvenir to be sent to her, then you can go enjoy your Holiday."

"That's good. I'm through with work until January and planned to fly to Kvitfjell tomorrow with Bea for a day of skiing before Christmas."

"I'm glad. A certain source has told me she's in love with you."

"The press will say anything, Maren. We've had some good times together, but don't read too much into it."

"I've seen pictures of the two of you in the paper. She's beautiful and I hear she's very smart. You couldn't go wrong with a woman like her."

"You're right."

"Maybe when you get back, you'll bring her to the palace to meet all of us?"

"I don't know about that."

"Eric—" she cried in exasperation.

"If I'm in love with her by then, I'll introduce you."

His sister moaned in defeat.

"I don't want to make a mistake, Maren."

For several years now the *paparazzi* had labeled him Europe's biggest playboy. It was a lie they continued to perpetuate in order to sell papers, but he refused to let it bother him.

There was a pause before she said, "I wouldn't want you to do that. Make a mistake I mean."

Eric could always count on his sister's love.

Unlike Knute and Maren who'd married spouses of royal lineage in case either of them or their children had to rule, Eric could marry a woman of his own choosing, even if she was a commoner. That was the agreement he'd worked out with his father before he'd passed away.

Oddly enough, being allowed to find his beloved in the same way any nonroyal could, had made Eric reluctant to jump into marriage. He preferred to get it right the first time and not end up divorced.

The other day his best friend Olav, who'd recently married, reminded him that marriage was for an awfully long time so he'd better be sure before he took the fatal step.

For once Eric hadn't been able to tell if his oldest childhood buddy was teasing or not. Since that comment, Eric had the distinct impression Olav's marriage was already in trouble.

It put the fear in Eric.

"Don't worry about tomorrow. I'll do my best to represent you. What you need to do is take care of yourself and that baby."

"Thank you, Eric. You're the greatest."

No he wasn't. Knute would have agreed to fill in for her without hesitation. Anything for the good of Frijia. Their brother was a noble soul. Eric admired and loved him.

In an attempt to assuage his guilt over his distaste for duty Eric said, "I'll let you know how the day went before I leave on my ski trip."

"I'd appreciate it. Promise me you won't break a leg so the rest of the Holidays are ruined for you."

"I'm hardly going to do that."

"Even an expert skier like you can have an accident, Eric. Just be careful. You know how mother is looking forward to all of us being together on this particular Christmas."

Eric was very much aware their mother was still grieving and needed her family around. Knute had been inspired to take her to Germany with him. Hopefully she hadn't had time to brood. Thank goodness their sister would soon be giving her another grandson to dote on.

"Don't worry. I'll only be gone a couple of days. Make sure you do as the doctor tells you, Maren. Goodnight."

"Hold still for a minute, sweetheart."

A couple of bobby pins to secure the embroidered red cap in Sonia's mass of shiny brown curls did the trick.

"There." Kristin, born Kristin Remmen, gave her niece a kiss. She'd looked after her since the death of her beloved sister. "Now you're ready."

"Do you think the Princess is here yet, Aunty Kristin?" Sonia shifted from one leg to the other in excited anticipation of what was about to happen.

Kristin eyed her five-and-a-half-year-old niece whose sightless brown eyes shone like stars. She'd been so good, but the thought of meeting Princess Maren of the Frijian royal family had been all she could think about for the last month. It couldn't come soon enough for Kristin.

"I don't know. We're supposed to wait in here until the owners send for us."

The Severeids had given them the use of the employee's lounge at the rear of the world famous Chocolate Barn to do any last minute preparations.

She and Sonia had gotten ready at the small, quaint hotel a block away from the barn. For the occasion Kristin had bought a cherry red wool coat-dress with gold buttons that ran from hem to neck.

The tailored look played down her curvaceous five foot five figure.

The appearance of Princess Maren meant one inevitable throng of photographers and television journalists. So, Kristin wanted to look her best and had swept back her honey blond hair in a French twist to reveal tiny gold earrings in the shape of jeweled Christmas ball ornaments.

The whole promotion had been tied in with Christmas and was to be the top human interest story for the evening news not only in Europe but all over the world.

"If your great-great-grandmother were alive to see you in the same clothes she brought over from Frijia for her little girl, she'd be so proud."

According to Kristin's family history, Anton Remmen, who'd worked on the family farm on the Varland Fjord, came to America in 1900 with his wife and their son and daughter Sonja, after whom little Sonia was named.

The red vest and black skirt reflected that region of the country they originated from, with the famous Varland lace on the white linen blouse and apron. In red stockings and black burnad shoes with silver buckles, Sonia looked the epitome of a traditional Frijian child.

Now Sonia's picture adorned the label on the cans and packets of hot chocolate manufactured at the Chocolate Barn in Brobak.

Blessed with an engaging wide smile and dimples, many older people who remembered the famous Olympic ice skating champion Sonja Henie, remarked how much Sonia looked like her.

Kristin could see a superficial resemblance. Certainly there was a vivaciousness about her niece that captivated people.

The fact that she was so photogenic and adorable in her grandmother Sonja's authentic outfit had prompted Mr. and Mrs. Severeid to pick Sonia's picture from the hundreds that had been sent in from Frijia, Europe and America for the contest.

"Do you think Grandpa Elling will see me on TV?"

"He wouldn't miss it for the world."

Kristin lowered her head. She felt a pang in her heart at the thought of her grieving father who'd been too sick with a bad flu bug to come on their three day trip to Brobak and the surrounding towns in Frijia.

If Sonia's parents were still alive, they would have brought her here instead of Kristin. They would have been able to see everything and feel the thrill of being back in the beautiful country of their ancestors.

"Ms. Remmen?" At the sound of Mrs. Severeid's voice, Kristin turned around. "Could I speak to you for a minute?" she asked in Frijian, a language

Kristin spoke fluently and taught for the American-Frijian Cultural Exchange Institute in Chicago.

"Is the Princess here now?" Sonia said excitedly.

"Just a minute, sweetheart, and I'll find out. Sit on this chair."

Kristin left her squirming niece long enough to go to the door. "Yes?"

"There's been a change in plans," the older woman whispered. "We've just been told by someone from the royal palace that Princess Maren's first child is due any day now and she's been put on bed rest. Therefore her brother Prince Eric has come in her place.

"This is terribly exciting because he rarely makes public appearances. We're very honored by his visit. I thought you should know about it to prepare your niece. I'll signal you when it's time to walk to the front of the store with her."

"Thank you," Kristin murmured, but her heart had dropped to her feet. Her anxious gaze darted to her niece who'd been counting on meeting the Princess ever since she'd heard she'd won the contest.

In truth, it was the only reason Kristin had brought her to Frijia. The precarious situation had to be handled with extreme delicacy.

She walked back and knelt down next to Sonia. "Sweetheart? Guess what I've just found out?"

"What?" Sonia asked breathlessly, almost falling off the chair she was so excited.

"Princess Maren is ready to have a baby."

"A baby—" Sonia's eyes widened. "You mean right here?"

"No, sweetheart. She'll have it at the hospital, but for the moment she's home in bed."

"Is she sick?"

"No. But the doctor wants her to rest until the baby comes."

"Are we going to the palace to see her then?"

Kristin hugged her, praying for some inspiration. "I'm afraid not, but she has sent someone else to meet you."

Sonia's lower lip started to tremble. Not a good sign.

"I don't want to meet anybody else!"

"Not even her brother?"

"He's not a princess—" she blurted in a tear-filled voice that could probably be heard beyond the confines of the back room.

Kristin moaned inwardly. "I know, sweetheart, but her brother is a prince and a very special person. His name is Prince Eric. He's as famous as his sister."

Except that infamous was probably more like it.

Over the years Kristin had seen pictures of the handsome royal family on television and in magazines, as well as in the Cultural Exchange's own newspaper. It was in one of their editions that the Chocolate Barn's contest had been advertised with the promise of the winner being able to meet Princess Maren.

Her brother, Prince Eric, was even better looking than his elder brother who was now king. The eligible playboy prince appeared more often in the news than the rest of his family. He'd been linked with the great beauties of Europe, and was reputed to have broken many hearts.

"But I want to meet the Princess!" Sonia cried loud enough for everyone in the entire store to hear her.

"I know you do, but this can't be helped. Remember how Grandpa Elling couldn't come with us because he's been sick? Well it's the same thing with the Princess."

"But she's not sick. She just has to rest," Sonia reasoned in her child's mind before she broke down sobbing and clung to Kristin. "Please can't we call the Princess on the phone?" she begged, totally out of control.

"If you tell her how much I want to meet her, she'll let me come. I *know* she will."

Tears streamed down her blotchy cheeks, panicking Kristin who hadn't seen her niece like this since she'd awakened in the hospital to learn that her parents had gone to heaven.

"I p-promise not to make any n-noise or do a-anything wrong, Aunty Kristin. I'll be s-so good. T-tell her I'll be g-good."

Sonia's hysteria stemmed from a lot more than disappointment that she wouldn't be meeting a real live princess. She was still too fragile after losing her mother and father.

Kristin was frantic because a member of the royal family along with television crews and photographers were waiting in the store for the appearance of the lucky little girl who'd won the Chocolate Barn's contest.

This was turning into a nightmare!

"Maybe I can help," said a low compelling male voice in English with only the slightest trace of accent.

CHAPTER TWO

KRISTIN turned her head in the direction of the door. The second her light blue eyes caught sight of the Prince, resplendent in ceremonial dress, she let out a surprised gasp and stood up.

His coloring was similar to Sonia's, in that he had dark brown hair and eyes. Tall and powerfully built like his brother and father, he stood six feet two or three, and possessed an aristocratic bearing.

Dressed in dark blue with the wide royal red band crossing his broad chest from shoulder to hip, Kristin's niece would be awestruck if she could see him.

While Kristin studied him, she discovered that he was studying her just as thoroughly.

His gaze wandered over her face and figure with unmistakable male interest. She swallowed hard before averting her eyes.

In the next instant he moved toward them and hunkered down next to Sonia who was sobbing harder than ever and refused to be comforted.

"I understand you're called Sonia," he began. "So you're the girl who came all the way from America to meet my sister."

His words produced another paroxysm of tears.

Kristin noticed the play of hard muscle beneath his suit jacket. She could tell he was striving to come up with a different approach to an impossible situation.

"My name is Eric. Do you think you could stop crying long enough to talk to me for a minute?"

She rubbed her knuckles against her wet eyes. "I—I don't want to talk to a-anybody 'cept the P-princess."

"I know exactly how you feel. When I was a little boy and very upset about something, I always ran to my sister to talk to her because she's my best friend and the kindest person I know. Do you have a younger brother?"

"No." Sonia hiccuped. "My m-mommy and daddy died before they could g-give me one."

Kristin felt the Prince digest those words. She had the grace to feel sorry for the royal bachelor playboy who she figured had never been forced to deal with a crisis quite like this before.

"My sister asked me to come in her place because she couldn't. I know you wanted to meet a real princess, but I *am* her brother." He wiped some of the moisture off her cheeks. "Will a prince do for today?"

No woman young or old could be immune to that humble yet compelling male entreaty, not even

Sonia, who finally lifted her tear-ravaged face to him.

"D-do you h-have your c-crown on?" she asked in a tremulous voice.

The Prince's intelligent gaze swerved to Kristin's in distinct puzzlement. At this point she realized everything had fallen apart before Mrs. Severeid had found the time to tell him about Sonia's condition.

"My niece is blind," Kristin tapped him on the shoulder and silently mouthed the words.

Their eyes held for endless moments while he absorbed the tragic revelation. As he continued to stare at Kristin, his expression underwent a dramatic transformation. Lines of incredulity darkened his features, making him appear older.

His dark brown eyes looked pained before they settled on Sonia once more. Strong masculine hands reached out to grasp her niece's little fingers in his.

"I didn't have time to put it on," he said in a solemn tone.

"H-how come?" Sonia wanted to know. Small tremors shook her body, but miracle of miracles, her hysterics were subsiding.

"Because it's in another town."

"Where?"

"At a cathedral in Midgard with some other family crowns."

"How come? If I had a crown, I'd put it in my room on the dresser."

Kristin's eyes closed tightly. The "how comes?" had started, and now there'd be no end to them.

"My crown's too heavy to wear all the time, so I keep it locked up in the church where it will be safe."

"Does it hurt your head?"

She sounded so concerned about that, the Prince flashed Kristin an intimate smile in spite of his shock that Sonia couldn't see. Already he'd discovered her niece possessed a potent charm of her own. It was unbelievable to Kristin that her ex-fiancé Bruce hadn't been affected by it.

Encouraged by the progress the Prince was making, Kristin couldn't help but smile back.

"I get a headache when I have to wear it for a long time," he said, still looking at Kristin as if he couldn't tear his eyes away.

"Does the Princess's c-crown hurt her too?"

His gaze eventually swerved back to Sonia. "No. It's smaller and lighter."

"Is her crown at that church?"

"No. I think she keeps it with her."

"Do you live at the p-palace with the Princess?" Sonia asked before she hiccuped again.

"Not since I became a man."

"When did that h-happen?"

Out of the mouths of babes.

Kristin struggled not to laugh at Sonia's innocent question.

This time the Prince sent Kristin a slightly wicked smile before he concentrated on Sonia and murmured, "I'm not sure. When I turned twenty-three I decided to get my own place."

"My Aunty Kristin's twenty-three. How old are you?"

"I turned thirty on my last birthday."

"My daddy was thirty when he died. Do you live in your own palace?"

"No. I live in an old sea captain's house."

"I thought you were a prince!"

His low laugh excited Kristin. "I am, but I love the sea. My house sits high on a hill where I can look down and watch all the boats."

Sonia shivered. "I don't like the water."

He frowned. "Why?"

"Cos I was on a sailboat with my mommy and daddy when they drowned. Now I live with my Aunty Kristin."

At that news, the Prince subjected Kristin to another intense yet solemn appraisal before he said, "You're a lucky little girl to have her."

"That's what Grandpa Elling says. Don't you miss the Princess?"

"Yes," he whispered, "but she has a husband and pretty soon she's going to have a baby boy. They need their own place."

"Do you live all alone?" Her voice trembled.

"No. I have a dog."

Her expression brightened. "Is he big?"

"Yes."

"What's his name?"

"Thor."

"That means thunder!"

The Prince chuckled softly, but Kristin felt it resonate deep inside of her. "That's right."

"Is he mean?"

"He's as sweet as my sister."

"We couldn't keep a dog at our apartment."

"That's too bad. Every little girl should have one. How would you like to meet mine?"

What? Kristin's heart thudded.

"Could I?" Sonia cried in delight.

When the Prince turned to Kristin, she shook her head. "Please—that's not necessary," she whispered, but by then the Prince had plucked Sonia from the chair and held her in his strong arms.

"I tell you what. Let's go out in front of the shop so the photographer can take our picture with the Severeids. Then we'll walk across the square to Santa's post office. After that we'll visit Thor."

Sonia threw her arms around his neck and gave him a kiss on the cheek. She'd never done that with Bruce in the whole time Kristin had known him.

The Prince reciprocated with a spontaneous hug that looked so genuine to Kristin, he could have been Sonia's daddy loving her.

"Hold on to my hand and don't let go," he said after putting her down.

"I won't. Come on, Aunty Kristin."

The Princess had been forgotten for the moment, but Kristin feared a new problem had arisen, one that might be much more difficult to fix by the time this experience was over.

"I'm right behind you, sweetheart."

Kristin had a hard time crediting that any of this was happening. The moment was surreal.

With Sonia in her native dress and the handsome Prince looking as if he'd just stepped from the pages of a fairy tale. Kristin had to admit that the two of them entranced the eye.

Everyone, including the security guards, must have thought so too judging by the hush that fell over the crowd of locals and television people. They'd congregated around the Chocolate Barn's sixteen foot high chocolate Santa waiting for the Prince to join the owners.

"Your Highness," Mrs. Severeid spoke up, "we are honored that a member of the royal family could be here today to meet the winner of our contest, Sonia Anderssen from Chicago, Illinois, in the United States.

"She's a true daughter of Frijia and we are proud for her picture to appear on every can and packet of hot chocolate, the Chocolate Barn's newest product to the world.

"Out of the fifteen hundred children's photographs sent in by Frijians from all over the globe for our contest, Sonia's picture captured our attention and our hearts."

Fifteen hundred? Kristin had no idea the competition had been so fierce.

Mrs. Severeid bent down to put the microphone in front of Sonia. "Will you tell everyone about the dress with the Varland lace you have on, Sonia?"

"My great-grandma wore this when she came to America from Frijia a long time ago with her mommy and daddy."

"You look lovely in it. Can you tell the people watching how it happened that your photograph was sent in?"

Uh-oh. Sonia was a precocious child. Kristin held her breath, half afraid of what was going to come out next.

"Grandpa Elling sent it because he loves me."

"Did you know he'd entered you in our contest?"

Sonia shook her head. "No. Not till Aunty Kristin told me I was going to meet the Princess. But she has to rest cos she's going to have a baby boy any minute."

No, Sonia—

"So she asked her brother to come. They're best friends. He couldn't wear his crown cos it's in a church and gives him a headache, but he's going to let me meet his dog who lives at the Captain's

House. Thor's not mean. Prince Eric says he's as sweet as the Princess.''

Stop—

The press was going to seize on all those private juicy tidbits, especially the fact that the Princess was expecting a son, another royal heir to the throne. Kristin was sure the gender of the princess's unborn child wasn't supposed to be common knowledge yet!

While Kristin hid her face in her hands, excitement and laughter rippled through the mesmerized onlookers as video cameras rolled and flashes popped by the dozens.

When she peeked through her fingers, she saw that the Prince had gathered Sonia in his arms once more. To Kristin's shock, he was smiling at her with his eyes as well as his mouth. If he was upset, it didn't show.

"As you can see, it was my lucky day Princess Maren asked me to represent her on this delightful occasion. I'm sure the whole world is as charmed by Sonia as I am.

"I think it only fitting that everyone meets the woman who made it possible for Sonia to be here.'' His gaze sought Kristin's in the crowd. "If you'd come up here, please—''

With a royal summons like that Kristin had no choice but to join them, yet her legs felt like rubber.

She prayed she wouldn't embarrass herself by stumbling on her way up to the mike.

"Sonia?" the Prince said. "Will you introduce your aunt?"

"She's my Aunty Kristin and I love her cos she takes care of me and brought me to Frijia. I love Grandpa Elling too."

The Prince's eyes leveled on Kristin in such a personal way it made it impossible for her to look away, let alone breathe. His gaze traveled over her features and seemed to rest on her mouth.

"This is a great day for Frijian-American relations. Don't you agree?" he asked in a deep, drawling tone.

Kristin nodded like a tongue-tied school girl before getting control of herself. "This experience is something Sonia will treasure all her life. I speak for my father, Elling Remmen, when I say thank you to the Severeids and Your Highness for this once-in-a lifetime opportunity."

More flashes went off, then Kristin turned to shake the owners' hands.

With a happy smile, Mr. Severeid took over the mike. "For the next year we'll be sending Sonia a chocolate treat from our store every month so she won't forget us.

"In her honor, we've had a mold made of Sonia and will now present her with a chocolate figure of herself she can hang on her Christmas tree at home in Chicago.''

That was a surprise the Severeids hadn't said anything about until now. It warmed Kristin's heart. She knew her father would be overjoyed to see his darling granddaughter honored this way. She was his pride and joy.

Everyone clapped and cheered as the owner handed Sonia the five inch high chocolate ornament covered in a transparent wrapper with the blue, red and gold ribbon made expressly for the Chocolate Barn.

Sonia clutched it in her hand.

''Say thank you,'' Kristin whispered to her niece.

''Thank you everybody. Can I eat it after Christmas?''

''You can do whatever you want.'' The older man knew about Sonia's blindness. By now his compassionate eyes had filled to the brim with tears.

''I'll put your ornament in my purse for safekeeping,'' Kristin whispered to her niece.

When that was accomplished she started to take Sonia from the Prince, but he held her closer to him as if to say he wasn't about to relinquish her yet.

''Shall we go to Santa's post office now?''

CHAPTER THREE

ONE of the salespeople helped Sonia on with her coat before the Prince carried her to the entrance. Surrounded by security men, they made their way out of the Chocolate Barn to be confronted by a vast throng that had gathered because word had spread the Prince was in the marketplace.

Kristin walked alongside them, trying to hear the running dialogue between him and Sonia. It was difficult because her niece was in his arms and their faces were close together.

With her adrenaline working overtime, Kristin didn't feel the cold even though the temperature which, according to the post office's exterior thermometer, indicated it was only a few degrees above zero.

A traffic sign bordered in red with a rotund figure packing a big bag stood in front of a darling three-tiered wooden Christmas house with balconies and a peaked roof.

Kristin had already been told by the tour guide who'd brought them to Brobak that this shop had been designated by the Frijian Foreign Ministry as the official post office for Santa Claus.

The inside looked like storyland, and was filled with doll houses and toys and baskets of handmade *nisses,* the Frijian Santa Claus. While Kristin suffered to think Sonia couldn't see anything, the Prince was busy describing everything in sight to her niece, making it come alive for her.

Every once in a while his penetrating gaze flicked to Kristin, sending her a private message that said he was loving this.

So was Kristin.

So was her niece!

Sonia's brown eyes shone while she listened in rapt attention to his vibrant male voice as he pointed out items to her in his inimitable way. In the process he'd seduced Kristin as well as the mesmerized child in his arms.

This was a side of Prince Eric the *paparazzi* had never shown to the world, a remarkable nurturing side the tabloids had failed to capture. He was turning this day into a magical experience for Sonia. Kristin loved him for it, but she wished her heart wouldn't race so fast whenever he looked at her.

He moved to the counter where he could help Sonia make her wish list to send to Santa.

''What is it you want more than anything in the world?''

At this point Sonia had discovered the epaulets on his shoulders and was fingering them. ''A Seeing Eye dog. *They're* not mean.''

Kristin bit her lip. She hadn't known anything about Sonia's secret desire. Someone at the hospital must have talked to her about it out of Kristin's hearing.

"You're right. A wonderful dog like that will be your best friend for life," he said in a husky voice. "I'll write that down for you."

An employee behind the counter rushed to hand him paper and a pen.

"Do you think Santa will bring me one? My teacher says they're spensif."

It sounded as if kindergarten was the place Sonia had heard about a Seeing Eye dog.

"Why don't you let Santa's elves worry about that?" he said with another kiss to her forehead. "Here you are." He handed her the envelope with the letter inside. "Go ahead and drop it in the mailbox."

Sonia squeezed her eyelids shut, then let it fall.

"Now it's on the way to the North Pole," he told her.

She let out a happy squeal. "You have to make a wish too."

"I plan on making several." He wrote something on another sheet of paper and put it in an envelope. "Do you want to mail this one too?"

"Yes."

"All right. Let it go."

When that was accomplished he said, "Why don't we pick out a present for you."

No, Kristin cried inwardly, shaking her head. This was all too much. The Prince only smiled benignly at Kristin, then moved toward a display of toys to delight any child's heart.

"Do you like mice?"

"I love fat ones like in Cinderella."

"So do I." He chuckled. "Right now I'm looking at a collection of the cutest stuffed mice you ever saw. There's a baker, a candle maker, a chimney sweep, a nurse and a grandma with knitting needles."

"Can I have the grandma, please? Grandma Astrid died last year. I want to give it to Grandpa Elling so he'll feel better."

Again the Prince turned to Kristin, visibly touched by Sonia's sweetness. Then she heard him say something in Frijian to the saleslady, but it was too low and fast for her to make out words.

The woman put the mouse in a box with the same kind of striped ribbon on Sonia's ornament and handed it to her with a smile.

"Are you ready to come to my house and meet Thor?"

For a reward, Sonia kissed his cheek again. "Yes, please."

The black limo with the royal insignia and one-way glass climbed the narrow road above the town, giving Kristin a breathtaking view of the scene below. At ten after four in the afternoon, the sun had already been to bed for an hour.

Lights flickered on the water from Niflheim fortress which guarded the entrance to the fjord. Beyond it was Glatheshim Island.

She kept her gaze focused out the window so she wouldn't be tempted to stare at the Prince. He sat across from her with Sonia on his lap. She chattered nonstop the way she used to do before the accident.

Prince Eric was a captive audience who never seemed to tire of Sonia's questions and answered each one with patience and occasional bursts of laughter. He appeared to really be enjoying himself. The difference between Bruce's behavior with Sonia and the Prince's was like night and day.

As far as Kristin was concerned, he'd gone far beyond anyone's expectations by agreeing to appear at the Chocolate Barn in Princess Maren's place.

But even if Sonia was blind, Kristin couldn't understand why he was lavishing all this extra interest and concern on her niece. He'd done what his sister had asked of him. No one could have imagined him doing anything more.

In real life you didn't meet a royal and end up going home with him the same day, yet that's what was happening.

The second he'd asked Sonia if she would like to

meet his dog, the matter had been taken out of Kristin's hands.

It frightened her to watch her niece respond to the Prince the way she'd done with her own father who'd been a fun loving man. What made the situation even more more curious was the fact that both men had been given the same first name of Eric.

Since the boating accident two months ago, Sonia had turned into a somber child not even her own grandfather had been able to make smile very often.

When he'd become ill and couldn't fly over with them, he'd insisted that Kristin bring Sonia to Frijia. He thought the trip and the opportunity of meeting the Princess might help restore his granddaughter's spirits to some semblance of her former bright, happy self in spite of her blindness.

Kristin's father must have been inspired. He wouldn't recognize the happy, giggling child listening to a funny story the Prince was telling her about three naughty *nisses*.

Though it thrilled Kristin to see this change in her niece, she felt a growing alarm for the moment when the Prince returned them to the hotel in town and Sonia had to say goodbye to him. Kristin actually shuddered at the thought.

"Are you all right?" he asked sotto voce.

She jerked her head away from the window to look at him, unaware he'd been watching her.

"Of course," she lied.

How could she possibly be all right? She was riding in a car with Prince Eric of Frijia. This kind of thing just didn't happen!

Not only was he the most attractive man she'd ever met in her life, he was wonderfully down to earth and normal. Sonia already adored him. Everything was perfect! Her niece wasn't the only one who didn't want any of it to end.

But for everyone's sake it *had* to, as soon as possible.

"We're so excited we feel like we're in the middle of a fantastic dream, don't we, Sonia?"

That's what it was. A fantastic dream. That was all it could be. Which was why this whole experience couldn't be allowed to go on any longer than it took to meet the dog.

To Kristin's shock her niece's face fell. She wrapped her arms around his neck. "We're not in a dream, are we?"

His eyes narrowed on Kristin as he hugged the little girl clinging to him. "No, *elskling*. This is very real."

The look in his eye, the deep intonation in his voice when he'd called her little darling in Frijian, shook Kristin to the core of her being. She glanced out the window once more, afraid to meet his gaze again for fear he'd divine her unwitting attraction to him.

"How come your Aunty Kristin didn't bring her boyfriend to Frijia with you?"

A gasp escaped Kristin's throat. He didn't know if she had a boyfriend or not. He'd thrown out the question to see how Sonia would answer it, and she didn't disappoint him.

"They had a fight when he found out I was going to live with her. Grandpa Elling said Bruce was jealous—"

"That's enough," Kristin broke in hot-faced and horrified for the Prince to have heard something that was no one's business.

Before the trip her fiancé, who'd said he couldn't get the time off from work, had asked her why she would bother to take Sonia to Frijia when she couldn't see anything.

Absolutely shocked by his question, Kristin realized she didn't know this man who'd put a ring on her finger two weeks before tragedy had struck their family.

When he admitted that he was reticent to take Sonia on after they got married, she gave him back the engagement ring and told him goodbye.

But that knowledge had never been meant for other ears!

Unfortunately Prince Eric's reputation preceded him. He was an expert's expert at eliciting information he wanted to know when it came to women. Especially from a little girl he'd already enamored.

What child wouldn't be flattered by that kind of attention?

Kristin didn't delude herself into thinking the Prince was interested in *her*. He was only making conversation with Sonia to pass the time.

"Do *you* have a girlfriend?"

Oh, Sonia—

The guileless question had put the shoe squarely on the other foot. Kristin held her breath while she waited for his answer.

"I've had several."

"How come you didn't get married yet?"

"My mother asks me that all the time."

"Don't you want to?"

"Well for one thing, Thor has to love the woman I pick."

"Doesn't he love *any* of your girlfriends?"

"Not yet, but I know he's going to love you. You're just his size and you give better hugs than anybody."

Her whole face glowed. "I do?"

"Yes. How about another one right now."

Kristin averted her eyes against the display of affection the two exhibited toward each other.

It was one thing for him to be kind and solicitous to her in front of the camera. But more than ever Kristin couldn't fathom what prompted his loving behavior toward Sonia now that they were in the limo. In truth, she couldn't understand why he'd done something as unheard of as to invite them to his home.

As soon as she could speak to him alone for a minute, she would tell him he'd done too much for Sonia already. Any more time spent with him and it would be too hard on her when they had to leave for Chicago in the morning.

He didn't realize what a breakthrough this was for Sonia to come out of her despondency. But it was only temporary. After meeting the Prince, she would fall back into a more severe depression once it was time to leave him and this enchanted day behind.

Kristin was already dreading the moment. She had the strongest feeling Sonia would dissolve into the kind of hysterics that would require a sedative to calm her down.

"We're coming to my house. It's a big rectangle made of wood and stone. The corners of the roof tip up. Right now there's a layer of snow everywhere. In summer the garden is full of wildflowers of every color. Behind the house are the woods. Thor loves to run through them."

The limo passed beyond a guarded gate and continued following the winding road lined with trees and dense shrubbery. Suddenly she glimpsed his house nestled in the scenery. Kristin had never seen anything like it before.

Such a solid structure seemed to be a part of the

landscape itself, totally reminiscent of Frijia's Viking heritage. Only a person of royalty could afford to live on top of a fjord in a home of such superb workmanship.

Sonia could have no idea...

As Kristin climbed out of the limo and followed the Prince into his house, she had the impression she'd just entered a storybook.

CHAPTER FOUR

A BEAUTIFUL black Labrador preceded the Prince's housekeeper into the foyer.

He rushed up to the Prince and rubbed his head against his trousers with a moan of joy.

"Thor? I want you to meet someone very special." He put Sonia down. "Lift your paw and give her a handshake."

The well behaved dog obeyed without question. The Prince guided Sonia's hand. She grabbed hold of the dog's paw and shook it. Her bright brown eyes shone before she laughed and threw her arms around the dog's neck.

"I love you, Thor!" she cried. The patient dog stood there with his tail wagging and let her do whatever she wanted, then gave her a lick that made her giggle.

The Prince sought Kristin's gaze. "My dog is bilingual. Frijian-American relations couldn't be doing better could they?"

"Yes," she whispered. Things were going too well. Kristin was terrified.

"Let's remove your coat, *elskling*."

After unzipping her parka, the Prince handed it to

the housekeeper. "Eva? I'd like you to meet Sonia Anderssen and her aunt, Ms. Remmen. This is the young lady who won the Chocolate Barn's contest. They've come all the way from Chicago, Illinois."

"I'm delighted to meet you," the older woman said, shaking Kristin's hand. Her eyes flicked to Sonia. "I can see why you won. You look adorable."

Before Kristin could prompt her niece to respond, Sonia said, "Thank you. It's nice to meet you." She lifted her hand, but it wasn't high enough.

The housekeeper frowned in bewilderment until the Prince whispered something in her ear. Immediately the older woman's eyes teared up. She found Sonia's hand and shook it, then hugged her as if she couldn't help herself.

"I bet you're cold and hungry. What would you like to eat?"

"Could I have hot chocolate and a sandwich, please?"

"I'll fix it right now."

"We'll be in the living room," the Prince murmured.

After the housekeeper told him in Frijian about an urgent call from a woman named Bea, she disappeared with Sonia's coat.

Kristin had the distinct feeling it was one of the Prince's girlfriends anxious to get in touch with him. No doubt in doing this favor for Princess Maren, he'd had to put his own plans on hold. Why on earth had he brought Kristin and Sonia to his house?

By now he'd turned his attention back to her niece. "Hold on to Thor's collar, and he'll take you on a tour of the house. Just tell him which rooms you want to see."

Sonia let out a squeal of delight. "Thor—let's go to the dining room first!"

The dog made another low moan, then slowly, carefully, started walking through double doors leading to the left side of the house. With that marvelous animal intuition, he sensed Sonia needed his help and paced himself accordingly.

Kristin's eyes blurred at the touching sight.

The Prince's held a tenderness that stunned Kristin. "Now that we're alone, I'd like to know what your friends call you," came his deep male voice.

She cleared her throat. "Kristin."

"My name is Eric. I'd like you to use it."

Avoiding his eyes she said, "I'm afraid we won't be here long enough for that, Your Highness."

"None of my friends refer to me that way. My sister would have asked you to call her Maren if she'd been able to meet Sonia today."

Finally she lifted a troubled blue gaze to his. "Did she ask you to do all this?"

"All what?"

"I—I'm quite sure that everything you did for

Sonia after we left the Chocolate Barn went beyond the call of duty," she stammered.

His dark brown gaze pierced through to her insides. "To quote my sister, *'We're talking about a little girl here. A darling little five- or six-year-old who still believes in fairy princesses and castles and magic. No doubt she's been waiting and waiting for tomorrow to come.'*"

Kristin bit her lip. "With understanding like that, she's going to make a wonderful mother."

"I couldn't agree more. Maren's known for her heart of gold. Far be it for me to let her down."

"You've done your part so well, Sonia's not behaving like the same child I brought to Frijia." Her voice shook. "She's happy and laughing again. No one else has been able to bring her out of her shell. It's wonderful to see.

"But if you thought you saw and heard an unhappy little girl in the back room of the Chocolate Barn because the Princess wasn't coming, just wait until she has to say goodbye to *you* in a little while."

He studied her through narrowed lids. "Who said anything about goodbyes?"

She took a fortifying breath. "Sonia and I are flying back to Chicago in the morning. I have to make certain she gets a good night's sleep first. Any more time spent with you and she won't want to leave."

"Let's not worry about that right now." There

was an underlying note of authority in his voice he probably wasn't aware of. "I want to hear more about the accident that took her sight. If her condition is operable, I know a specialist who would be happy to examine her and operate. If it's a matter of finances—"

"It's not." Kristin shook her head. "That's very kind and generous of you, but Sonia has hysterical blindness."

He pondered her comment for a long moment. "You mean she *could* see if her mind would allow it?"

"Yes. The psychiatrist on her case believes she's feeling guilty about something to do with her parents' death. She can't forgive herself, so her subconscious won't allow her to see. It's a form of self-inflicted punishment."

Lines marred his attractive features. "She's only a child. How could she feel guilt like that at such a tender age?"

"I don't know," Kristin cried softly.

"Does she remember how the accident happened?"

"If she does, she won't talk about it. That's why the psychiatrist believes guilt over something has prevented her from opening up."

"When did it happen?"

Kristin's eyes closed for a moment. "Two months ago."

"So recently," he murmured sounding far away before he put a hand on her arm. "You're trembling. Let's go in by the fire and warm you up."

The contact sent a fire all its own coursing through her veins. He didn't relinquish his hold until he'd guided her through the double doors on the right side of the hallway. They walked to one of the couches placed next to the living room's enormous hearth.

The heat from the flames of burning pungent pine seeped into her system, warming her from the inside out.

She could well picture a descendent of a fierce Norseman residing in this essentially male room, yet only a prince could live in such magnificent surroundings with inlaid wood flooring and a handcarved wood ceiling that dated back hundreds of years.

The intricate handcarved furniture gleamed in the firelight. The seafaring appointments of the room gave it the unique flavor of Frijia's past. She imagined the Prince had looked through the telescope near the windows many times to see the stars as well as ships entering the fjord.

"Here we are."

Kristin looked toward the doorway in time to see Sonia and Thor, followed by Eva who carried a tray. She set it down on the coffee table in front of the fire.

"Thank you," the Prince murmured to his housekeeper. He called to the dog who walked over to his feet and lay down. "What do you think of my house, Sonia?" This he asked after he'd picked her up and seated her next to him on the couch facing Kristin.

"It's a lot bigger than Grandpa Elling's. How come you don't have carpets?"

"Because these are wood floors with special designs," Kristin said before he could. "You'd never want to cover them up. Now it's time to eat these delicious looking ham sandwiches the housekeeper has made for us."

The Prince fixed Sonia a plate and handed it to her. Kristin poured the hot chocolate into Christmas mugs.

"Here's your drink. It's the perfect temperature so it won't burn your tongue. There's the cutest little *nisse* on your cup looking out of a barn door." She placed it in Sonia's fingers. "When you're through, there are some Christmas cookies too."

"Yum."

The room was silent while they began to eat. It appeared everyone had an appetite, especially the Prince who finished off a whole sandwich in no time at all.

"If you two will excuse me, I'll be right back. Thor," the Prince said after getting to his feet, "stay with Sonia."

"Where are you going?"

"It's not polite to ask," Kristin reminded her.

"I'm sorry."

"That's all right. I have an important phone call to make."

"Hurry then," Sonia urged him.

Before Kristin put her head down in embarrassment, she saw the smile that broke out on the Prince's arresting features. "I'll be back by the time you've started on the cookies."

"Can Thor have one?"

"Why don't you give him part of a sandwich instead? He loves ham."

"Okay."

"First you need to eat the rest of your food," Kristin admonished her niece when she saw that she was ready to give up her own half.

"I hope he comes back soon," Sonia said between bites after he'd disappeared.

"I do too."

For your sake as well as mine, we have to leave and get out of Frijia as fast as possible.

"Maren? How are you holding up?"

"I'm fine now that you've called. I've been waiting to hear from you and thought you must have left for Kvitfjell already."

"No. I'm still at my house with Sonia."

"I thought you were going skiing with Bea!"

Bea... He'd forgotten all about her.

"That came out wrong. Sonia's the little girl who won the Chocolate Barn's contest."

There was a long silence. "You took that child *home* with you?" she finally cried in shock.

Eric realized he'd done something totally unprecedented. "Yes."

"What happened? Did she become difficult when she found out I couldn't be there?"

"At first, but then she settled down and was perfect. You'll see it all on the six o'clock news. Maren—I need a favor from you."

"Of course," she said in a quieter tone. "Anything—"

"I'd like Sonia and Kristin to meet you. If we leave here now, we could be at the palace within forty-five minutes."

"Kristin?"

"She's the little girl's aunt. I don't have time for more explanations. We'll watch the telecast together. Make sure you're wearing your crown when we get there."

"But Eric—" she blurted. "What about your trip with Bea?"

"It's been canceled." At least it would be as soon as he got off the phone with his sister. "I'll see you shortly."

He hung up and rang Bea. While he waited for her to answer, he found Sonia's parka laid over a chair.

"Eric? When I didn't hear from you, I was beginning to worry something was wrong."

"I'm sorry. The favor I had to do for Maren has turned out to be more complicated than I thought. I'm afraid we won't be able to go to Kvitfjell."

"If you mean this evening, I suspected as much. We can go in the morning."

"I think we'll have to put it off."

"But Eric—"

"I'm sorry, Bea. The last thing I want to do is disappoint you, but a situation has arisen I have to see through. It might take me more than a few days to deal with it. By then Maren's baby will probably come. The family will want me around."

"Will we at least be able to see each other Christmas Eve?"

He could hear the edge in her voice, but something had happened to him today. Something he couldn't explain. All he knew was that he didn't want Sonia or her aunt to disappear from his life. Not yet...

"Maybe."

"Is this your way of saying goodbye to me?"

I don't honestly know.

He took a deep breath. "Bea—this is about a little blind girl with a deep psychological problem."

"Blind?"

"Yes. I'll tell you about it later. If you watch the

evening news, you'll see her. I promise I'll call you.''

He heard her hesitancy before she said, ''I'll be waiting.''

After ringing off, he hurried to his bedroom to change into informal clothes, then he strode swiftly to the front of the house with Sonia's parka.

Once back in the living room his breath caught to see the way the firelight outlined Kristin's exquisite profile. His gaze fell lower to the shape of her lovely body clothed in the stunning red wool dress. Her hair gleamed like spun gold.

She turned at his approach and stood up. Those light blue eyes held a shimmer more bedazzling than any crown jewels.

Whether young or old, the Remmen women were incredibly attractive. It was the reason Sonia had been chosen to represent the Chocolate Barn's latest export.

What kind of fool was the man Kristin was involved with? Eric couldn't fathom it.

''It looks like you two have finished eating. Now we can leave.''

Sonia had been rubbing Thor's ears. When she heard Eric's voice she lifted her head, startled. ''Where are we going?''

Purposely ignoring Kristin, he sat down next to Sonia and helped her on with her parka. ''To see the Princess.''

"At the palace?" she cried out in ecstasy.

"Yes. She's waiting for us."

"Can Thor come too?"

"I don't see why not."

"That's very kind of Your Highness, but we have to return to the hotel," Kristin protested just as he'd expected her to.

Sonia immediately started to cry that she wanted to see the Princess. Eric gave her a hug. "Wait here, Sonia."

He stood up to meet her aunt's anxious gaze. "Could I speak to you in the foyer please?" he whispered the words.

Though he sensed she wanted to refuse him, her good manners prevailed. She followed him out to the hallway.

"Before you say anything," he began, "I thought that arranging a meeting with my sister would satisfy Sonia so she'll be easier to manage for the trip back to the States."

That was the best excuse he could come up with for the moment. He hoped she would buy it because there was no way he was ready to let her and Sonia go.

Her classic features looked pained. "It isn't that I don't appreciate all you've done, Your High—"

"Eric," he cut in on her.

"E—Eric," she stammered. Her fingers looked white as they clutched her handbag in what looked like a death grip. "But it wouldn't be right to impose on your sister, not as this stage in her pregnancy."

He stared into her anxious eyes. "Kristin," he addressed her by her first name. Whether she liked it or not, it felt good to get on a more personal basis with her. "Maren wants to meet Sonia.

"When she called me earlier to ask me to stand in for her, she said that if I couldn't do it, she would go against doctor's orders to keep that appointment with Sonia.

"Even if it meant she went into early labor, that's how important it was to her. She can't wait to be introduced to your niece."

Kristin's breathing seemed to be more shallow all of a sudden. "How long do you think it will take?"

No woman of his acquaintance had ever run the other way from him before. Anything but. This was a new experience for him.

He didn't know if Sonia's welfare was the sole reason Kristin was so reticent to spend more time with him, but he was determined to find out, even if he had to lean on his title to press his advantage.

"If we leave now, I can have you back at your hotel by eight o'clock. Sonia had a dream to meet the Princess. I'm not willing to take that away from her. Neither is my sister. So I guess the decision is up to you whether we leave for the palace or the hotel."

CHAPTER FIVE

"Please can we go see the Princess? I promise to be good."

Kristin twisted her blond head around to discover Sonia standing in the doorway, clinging to Thor's collar.

The pleading expression in her eyes defeated Kristin who was struggling to get on top of an impossible situation.

"Do you promise that after you've met her, there won't be any more tears when you have to go back to the hotel?"

Sonia nodded.

Her niece meant it right now, but Kristin knew that when the moment came to say goodbye to Eric, the hysterics would start up again much worse than before.

"All right," her voice shook. "I tell you what. I'll stay behind at the hotel and start packing while you go with the Prince." She'd made the suggestion for her own self-preservation.

"But I don't want to go without *you!*" Sonia cried out in absolute panic.

The dark frown that broke out on Eric's face was

equally disconcerting. Thor's low moan seemed to second their feelings.

"If we don't leave now, we'll miss watching the telecast with the Princess," Eric persisted. At this point, he held Sonia in his arms.

"She's waiting for us, Aunty Kristin."

Kristin's mouth had gone dry. "Does your sister know I'm coming too?"

Maybe it was a trick of light but Eric's eyes looked more black than brown. She'd angered him when it was the last thing she'd wanted to do.

"Of course."

She expelled a deep sigh. "Then we'd better go so we don't keep her up any longer than necessary. I don't want to be the reason she goes into premature labor."

With a satisfied smile, Eric ushered them out the front door to the waiting limo. Thor climbed in last and lay down next to the Prince who held Sonia on his lap. They sat across from Kristin who stared blindly through the glass.

The drive to Thorsvik only took a half hour.

Eric gave her niece his complete attention and acted as a tour guide at the same time, rendering fascinating facts only someone in the royal family would be privy to.

Sonia was in heaven.

Kristin's heart ached for her sister's child because this adventure would be over in a few hours, never to be repeated. They would return to Chicago, a world far removed from the Prince and Thor. Sonia's heart would be broken.

The only thing Kristin could see that might help mend it would be to buy a pet for Sonia. A Seeing Eye dog would be the answer for her in the future. But that required time and money.

For the moment she needed a devoted dog like Thor on whom she could lavish her affection and receive love in return. Just watching her interact with Eric's dog had convinced Kristin it would be a wonderful idea.

The manager of the apartment where she lived didn't allow pets either. When Kristin had given the ring back to Bruce, she'd decided it would be best if she and Sonia moved in with her father until Sonia started school at the blind center the next fall. It would give Kristin time to find an apartment that was friendly to children and animals.

She knew her dad was lonely without her mom, and still grieving for the loss of his elder daughter. He would love it if Kristin and Sonia lived with him for a while, dog and all.

While her mind was busy planning for the future, she hadn't realized they'd already reached the heart of the city. The huge, wide yellow and white three-story palace built in the mid 1800s sat on a hill at the end of Thorsvik's main thoroughfare.

Its lighting against a dark velvet sky brought out

the unique architecture, making it look as fantastic as the day itself had been.

Drawn by a compulsion stronger than her will, she found herself studying the wonderful man who was telling her niece about his childhood. Worlds apart from Sonia who'd been born to parents who could only afford a small apartment, he'd been the offspring of royalty. This magnificent palace was his earthly home.

Yet inside the limo, dressed in charcoal trousers and a light gray cable knit pullover, she could pretend he was simply a man whose heart had been touched by a little girl's inability to see. He was a brother who'd taken time out of his busy life to help his sister and had gone the extra mile to make a difference in Sonia's life.

If Kristin were to give the press a headline, it would state that despite Eric's reputation as a playboy, he was a prince of a man, title or no title.

"We've arrived, Sonia. We're going to enter the palace through a side entrance. There's a staircase that leads to my sister's apartment on the second floor. Are you ready?"

"Yes." She looked excited enough to burst. What child wouldn't be overjoyed that she was about to meet a real princess?

Eric captured Kristin's gaze, reading her mind. Her heart turned over before she looked away.

"Do you want me to carry you, or would you like to walk?"

Sonia flung her arms around his neck. "Will you carry me please?"

He laughed gently. "I was hoping you'd say that. Come on, Thor." The three of them got out of the limo first.

There were several security people in another limo behind them. One of them helped Kristin from the back seat and up the steps into the palace where staff stood in attendance.

Once inside the doors, the interior was more sumptuous than Kristin had imagined. But even if her niece could see everything, Kristin had an idea she wouldn't be looking at anything or anyone except the man who was treating her like she was a fairy princess.

A third of the way down the gilded corridor of the second floor and the Prince opened one of the double doors. He was greeted by a dark blond man Kristin recognized from pictures as Stein Johansen, the husband of Princess Maren.

After introductions were made, they proceeded to a small drawing room which had been personalized with the conveniences of modern living.

Kristin spotted the lovely brunette Princess in a maternity nightgown half lying on a couch in front of a television set with a quilt thrown over her.

The resemblance to Eric was uncanny.

To Kristin's surprise, his sister was wearing her tiara. That meant Eric had told her to put it on for Sonia's sake.

Kristin's feelings for him were growing stronger by the second.

He waited for her to catch up with him. With Sonia in one arm, he placed his other hand at the back of Kristin's waist and urged her forward.

The gesture was far too personal. His touch sent a lick of flame through her sensitized body, but she didn't dare try to break away from him, not in front of his family.

"Maren? I'd like you to meet Sonia Anderssen, the new poster girl for the Chocolate Barn, and her aunt, Kristin Remmen."

The two women shook hands while they eyed each other for a brief moment. No doubt the Princess was wondering what on earth was going on.

"How do you do, Your Highness. This is a great privilege. Please forgive us for disturbing you."

"I'm thrilled you did. It's wonderful to meet you, Kristin. Please call me Maren."

"Thank you."

The Princess was as down to earth and gracious as her brother.

She switched her attention to Sonia. "Come here, darling." She held out her arms. Eric lowered Sonia to the Oriental rug covering the conversation area of the room, then removed her parka.

"Sonia had an accident two months ago and can't see."

The Princess underwent a transformation not unlike her brother's when he'd first found out Sonia was blind.

She sat up and reached for Sonia's hands, drawing her close to her. Tears spilled down her flushed cheeks. "I'm so happy to meet you, Sonia," she said in a husky voice. "Will you forgive me for not being there today?"

"Yes. Eric said you had to rest cos you're having a baby boy."

"That's right. Do you want to feel him?"

"Can I?" Sonia's eyes lit up in wonder.

"Here." She put Sonia's hand on her protruding belly and moved it around. "Maybe he'll kick for you."

Sonia jumped when a little foot jabbed at her hand. "That's the baby prince inside?" she squealed incredulously.

"Yes, darling," Maren murmured.

"What's his name?"

"We haven't decided yet."

"I think you should call him Eric. That was my daddy's name."

At the unexpected bit of information, Eric darted Kristin a searching glance. It was one more reason why Sonia had felt an affinity to the Prince, Kristin was certain of it.

"Does he have a crown?"

The Princess let out a laugh. Sonia had a charm that infected everyone. "Not yet, but I'm wearing mine. Would you like to try it on?"

"Could I?"

"Let's take off your cap first," Eric said. As if he did it every day, he proceeded to undo the bobby pins so he could remove it. Kristin put everything in her purse.

"There," he said, smiling down at Sonia. "Are you ready to be crowned?"

Sonia giggled. "Yes!"

He lifted the tiara from his sister's hair and placed it on Sonia's head. She felt it for a moment, then turned to Kristin with a smile that took up her whole face.

"How do I look, Aunty Kristin?"

"Just like a princess. I wish I had a picture to show your grandpa."

"No problem," Maren's husband interjected before several flashes went off in succession.

Eric got down on his haunches beside her. "Does it hurt?" he teased.

"No," she said in frustration, "but it keeps slipping."

His laughter was so infectious and male, it sent a shiver of delight through Kristin's nervous system.

Just then another flash went off.

Kristin caught the jeweled tiara before it reached

Sonia's nose. "That's because this was made for the Princess. I think it's time to give it back. Don't you?"

"Yes."

Kristin handed it to Eric who'd leveled his gaze on Kristin and refused to look away.

"Thank you," she mouthed the words.

He put the crown on a nearby table before whispering in her ear, "The pleasure's all mine."

The feel of his warm breath made her insides quiver.

"I hope the news hasn't started yet—"

The sound of a rather breathless female voice caused Kristin to tear her eyes from his. Another surprise awaited her to see Sofia, the brunette wife of Eric's elder brother, enter the room with her two boys.

They ran over to Eric and practically jumped on him and Thor. Obviously he was a favorite with them.

"Easy, boys," he said in English. "We have guests. Sofia, may I introduce Kristin Remmen and Sonia Anderssen from Chicago, Illinois, in the United States."

Everyone shook hands.

"Jan and Knute? Meet Sonia. You can try out your English on her."

"How do you do," they both said.

"Hi!" Sonia answered back. She turned in Eric's

direction. "Who are they?" she asked in a loud whisper that made everyone chuckle.

"My nephews, my brother's boys. Jan is six and Knute is eight."

Kristin could hear Sonia's mind working. "Their daddy's the king?"

"Yes."

"Do they have to bow in front of him?"

Eric laughed hard. "No."

"You speak Frijian?" Knute asked in stilted English.

"I know some words. *Broe, vann, kjott* and *potet.*"

At her response everyone chuckled again.

Sonia's lower lip trembled. She turned to Eric. "Why are they laughing?"

He swept her up in his arms. "Because you're so smart and pronounced the words for bread, water, meat and potatoes perfectly. Not many visitors from America can do that. With those four words, you'll never starve while you're in Frijia, *elskling.*"

Out of the corner of her eye Kristin saw the way both women stared at Eric as if they couldn't believe his behavior.

"Here's the news," Stein interjected. "Why don't we all sit down and watch."

"You can sit on my lap and I'll tell you everything that's going on," Eric said to Sonia. They sat down on the nearest seat. Then his dark brown gaze swung to Kristin. He patted the place next to him.

Her cheeks felt hot, yet once again she had no choice but to join him. When their thighs brushed against each other, she started to tremble and couldn't stop.

The boys sat on the floor in front of the television set while their mother found a chair next to Stein's.

Sure enough the top story of the night was the visit of Prince Eric to the Chocolate Barn where he met Sonia.

His nephews whooped it up to see their uncle in front of the giant chocolate *nisse*. The footage didn't stop there. It followed them through the square to the post office shop.

The boys asked their mother if they could visit both shops the next day like Sonia. She told them they'd talk about it later.

Then the camera zoomed in on Kristin and Eric as he was helping her into the limo.

Judging by the way they were looking at each other at that particular moment, the viewer could be forgiven for thinking they were in love. In truth they were responding to something Sonia had just said about giving Santa Claus a dog for a Christmas present.

Evidently the journalist had the same impression as Kristin because he ended the segment by saying, ''Sources tell us the Prince whisked Sonia and her beautiful aunt Kristin to his home as part of their fairy-tale visit to Frijia. Was this too in the name of duty? Or could it be that Europe's most eligible Prince is finally playing for keeps?''

CHAPTER SIX

"WHAT did the man mean about playing for keeps?" Knute asked his uncle.

By this time someone had turned off the television. A crimson-faced Kristin leaped to her feet ready to leave.

"I'll tell you what," Eric answered in kind without missing a beat. "Why don't you and Jan take Sonia to your playroom."

No!

"I asked the staff to put some presents in there for all of you. Just remember that she lost her sight two months ago, so Thor will lead her around."

Jan looked wounded. "She's…blind?"

"That's right."

The shocking news subdued the boys who stared hard at Kristin's niece.

"Sonia? Hold on to Thor." He'd switched to English. "He knows where there's a surprise waiting for you. The boys will go with you."

She jumped in place. "What kind?"

Eric grinned. "You'll have to wait and find out." He placed Sonia's hand on the dog's collar.

Kristin stifled a moan. She'd hoped they'd be able

to say their goodbyes and slip out of the palace, but no such luck.

"Here, Thor!" Knute prompted the dog, behaving like the adult. Kristin watched the four of them start for the entrance. The boys showed great deference to Sonia who jabbered in English all the way to the double doors. Who knew how much the young princes understood?

"I'll go with them and supervise," Sofia volunteered before leaving the room.

Suddenly Kristin felt a strong masculine hand on her arm. "Come with me," Eric murmured before ushering her out. "I'll show you the apartment where I grew up."

Once they were in the corridor, Kristin pulled back in panic, forcing him to let go of her. "I—I'd rather wait outside for Sonia in the limo."

"If that's your wish."

Surprised at his easy capitulation, she walked slightly ahead of him before she realized she was displaying terrible manners. At the bottom of the staircase she turned to him out of breath.

"Forgive me. I haven't even said goodbye to your family or thanked the Princess."

"Don't worry about it," he murmured. "I'll explain that I wanted to be alone with you and that's why we didn't return."

While her heart slammed against her ribs so hard it hurt, he told one of the security men hovering close by to bring Sonia and Thor to the car when they were ready. Then he escorted Kristin through the outer doors to the waiting limo.

Once they were settled across from each other in the warm interior, he leaned toward her. "Do you have a job you must get back to before Christmas?"

Why did he want to know that? "No. I'm off until January Third."

"What a coincidence. So am I. What kind of work do you do?"

"I'm involved with the AFCE in Chicago."

His dark eyes fired with genuine interest. "That's a program my brother is interested in. What's your precise job?"

"I train elementary teachers from your country for an exchange teacher program."

"Have *you* been on the exchange program?"

"Not yet."

"Why?"

"My mother was ill for a long time before she passed away last year. I never felt I could leave my father alone." She kneaded her hands, wondering how to steer the conversation away from her. "What kind of work do you do?"

He sat back in the seat, eyeing her with an enigmatic expression. "You mean you actually believe I do something to justify my existence besides stand around looking official?"

"I have no idea what you do," she came back

quietly, "but I know your life couldn't possibly be the continual party the press would have the world believe."

"How do you know that?"

He was beginning to sound like Sonia.

"Because I see how close you are to your family. The rapport with your nephews tells a lot about you. Your sister would never have asked for your help today if she didn't trust you implicitly. You've been wonderful to Sonia... Thank you," she said in a husky voice.

"You don't need to thank me. I wouldn't have missed this experience. Sonia's a remarkable child. When she cries, it's never over her blindness. She's a joy to be around."

"I love her desperately."

"I can see why. After being cooped up on a submarine for the last month, you could have no idea how much I've enjoyed today."

A submarine? "Are you in the military?"

"After my naval training, I became an oceanographer. More recently I've headed a project that is studying the fjords.

"With the use of satellite remote sensing, we're able to do better underwater mapping. Hopefully it will aid us in the process of undersea exploration and drilling to discover new resources for our country that won't harm the environment."

"Now I'm the one who's impressed," she whispered. ''With responsibilities like that, it's a miracle you have any time for a personal life.''

''I make time for family, but it's true I spend most of it working or attending international oceanographic conferences. Unfortunately the *paparazzi* never miss the opportunity to photograph me with some woman.

''Usually it's a total stranger walking along the sidewalk next to me, or a woman from a seminar who happens to be seated at my table for dinner.''

Kristin believed him.

''That isn't to say there haven't been a few women in my past.''

She moistened her lips nervously. ''You mean like Bea?''

His lips twitched. ''When Eva informed me Bea had called, I didn't realize you understood Frijian to that extent. She's a woman I've been seeing for a short while. If my sister hadn't asked me to fill in for her, Bea and I would be in Kvitfjell for a day of skiing before Christmas.''

''Where is that?''

''Near Lillehammer in Norway.''

''I see.'' Naturally he was involved with someone. What went on in his personal life shouldn't matter one way or the other. But it did...

Cross with herself, Kristin struggled to maintain a nonchalance about their whole conversation.

''I think you're a great brother to put off personal

plans in order to accommodate your sister's wishes. However there's always tomorrow.''

"You're right,'' he said on a satisfied note that hurt Kristin because she would love to be the woman who spent the whole day with him, and all the days after that. "I'm looking forward to it.''

She didn't want to hear any more about the latest woman to capture his interest. "Eric—would you mind bringing Sonia out to the car? You know how children forget everything when they're playing.

"No doubt my niece is having the time of her life, but I do need to get her back to the hotel. We have to leave for the airport at seven in the morning.''

"Of course.'' He used the limo phone and rang someone inside the palace to fetch Sonia. When he'd finished and had hung up he said, "She'll be with us in a moment.''

Kristin avoided his eyes. "Thank you.''

He didn't try to engage her in further conversation. She didn't know whether to be happy or sad about it.

Before long she saw the palace doors open. Thor raced down the steps and climbed into the limo to curl up next to Eric.

Stein followed carrying a chattering Sonia in his arms. The two boys walked on either side of them, followed by someone on the palace staff holding a large shopping bag which was put in the trunk.

There was a flurry of conversation from all the children as Stein handed Sonia over to Kristin. While the boys asked Eric in Frijian if Sonia could stay overnight, she begged Kristin in English for permission to sleep over.

"We haven't finished playing fort yet, Aunty Kristin. We were having a big war and everything!"

"Please, Ms. Remmen," Knute begged politely. Apparently the children had gotten along well.

"I wish she could stay, Knute. I'm sorry," Switching back to English she said to Sonia, "Remember what you promised? You told me you wouldn't cry if I let you visit the Princess."

Sonia's lower lip quivered on cue. "I'm not crying," she said, but she was close to it. So was Kristin who hadn't spent nearly enough time with Eric.

"Boys? I'm sorry to bring your fun to an end, but we're leaving for America in the morning. Sonia needs her sleep," Kristin said in Frijian.

And your Uncle Eric has a date to go skiing.

"Thank you for being so good to her. You've made it possible for her to take home another wonderful memory. Please thank your mother for watching her. Goodbye."

"Goodbye," they muttered. Two glum faces were the last things Kristin saw before she and Stein said goodbye to each other and he shut the limo door.

"Can I sit on your lap, Eric?" Sonia asked in a tear-filled voice.

"What do you think?" He plucked her from Kristin's arms and hugged her.

"Where's Thor?" she cried.

The dog inched his way closer to lay his head on her lap. He was bilingual all right.

A lump lodged in Kristin's throat.

More than anything in the world she wanted to join that threesome for the return trip to Brobak. Secretly she ached to feel Eric's arm around her.

Determined to get her mind on something else, she gazed out of the window at the moon which would be setting in a few hours. It was so strange to have daylight for about five hours and then go to bed before the moon did.

By the time they reached the hotel a half hour later, Sonia had fallen asleep against Eric's shoulder.

"I'll carry her to your room," he mouthed the words to Kristin. "Come, Thor."

The dog made a low moan before obeying his master.

Because it was the Prince, special arrangements had been made for them to slip in through a back entrance. With the aid of a couple of security men to clear the way, they rode the elevator to the third floor and entered Kristin's hotel room without being observed.

As he started to lay Sonia down on one of the double beds, her eyelids opened. "Daddy?"

His concerned dark gaze met Kristin's for a fraction of a moment. "No, Sonia, it's Eric."

"Will you stay with me?"

"I'll be right here until you fall asleep again."

"Why don't we get ready for bed first, sweetheart?"

"Okay. We'll be right back. Don't leave me."

"I promise I won't move."

Eric handed Sonia to Kristin. She hurried her niece into the bathroom to help her undress and brush her teeth. Then she led her into the other room.

Kristin noticed one of the men had brought up the shopping bag from the trunk of the limo and had placed it on the dresser before disappearing.

"Eric?" Sonia called out. "Will you help me say my prayers?"

"I was just going to suggest it."

Sonia knelt down by the side of the bed where he was sitting. "You go first."

Kristin stood there mesmerized.

With his hands clasped, he bowed his head. "Dear God—" he began. "We thank you for this wonderful day. Please help Sonia to tell me and Thor about the accident because we love her and we're all best friends who don't keep secrets from each other. Amen."

With those words Kristin knew what she'd suspected in her heart since the moment he'd quieted Sonia's tears in the back room of the Chocolate Barn. *She'd fallen in love with him.*

At the realization, she sank down on the end of the bed because her legs would no longer support her.

Sonia forgot about her own prayers. She climbed in bed and let Eric pull the covers over her.

"Where's Thor?"

"Right here."

"Can he sleep with me?"

"Of course." He gave a command to the dog who got up on the bed and found a comfortable spot with his head on Sonia's stomach. She patted him.

"Daddy told me to stay down in the boat, but I got scared cos of the big waves. I started to run to him. He-he screamed at me to go back down. Then I fell in the l-lake. Mommy t-tried to get me. So did Daddy. But they c-couldn't r-reach me. I was a bad g-girl cos I didn't listen to him. Now they're in h-heaven."

The last came out in a strangled sob.

Eric had his arms around her before Kristin could join them from the other side of the bed. "You weren't a bad girl, *elskling.* You could never be bad. It was an accident! You were frightened.

"If Jan and Knute had been on that sailboat with

you, they'd have been frightened too and would have tried to run to their daddy.''

"Are you sure?"

"I'm positive." He cradled the back of her head. "Your daddy was only trying to protect you. That's a daddy's job. But the wind was too strong for you to make it to his arms. He would never blame his little daughter for an accident.

"Right now your parents can see you from heaven and they think you're the bravest girl in the whole world. They want you to be happy with Kristin, don't they, Thor."

The dog barked as if he'd understood every word.

Sonia lifted her tear-stained face. "Y-you promise they're not m-mad at me?"

"I promise."

"Eric is a Prince, Sonia," Kristin broke in. *A prince among men.* "When he makes a promise, you can believe it. Now go to sleep, sweetheart, and dream about all the wonderful things we did today."

Sonia's eyelids fluttered closed and she lay back against the pillow with a deep sigh. Under a minute she was sound asleep.

Without conscious thought Kristin leaned over Sonia to grasp Eric's arm. She lifted wet eyes to his. "You've just accomplished something miraculous—" she whispered shakily.

He moved closer and pressed a warm kiss to her lips. "Let's hope it's the start of one. I'll be by for you in the morning to drive you to the airport. Goodnight, Kristin.''

Almost as if he couldn't help himself, he cupped her face between his hands. This time he kissed her mouth deeply and hungrily before disappearing out the door.

He left Kristin so shaken with longings he'd brought to life, she had to cling to the end table so she wouldn't fall down.

CHAPTER SEVEN

WHEN the phone rang, it felt like the middle of the night because it was still dark outside. Kristin groped for the receiver wondering if it was her father, but it turned out to be the wake-up call from reception downstairs.

Eric would be here soon to drive them to the airport. He'd been all she could think about last night. The thought of him produced such excitement within her, she felt actual physical pain to her heart with every beat.

"Come on, Sonia. It's time to get dressed and eat breakfast downstairs before our trip home."

She turned on the light and looked over at her niece. But Sonia wasn't in her bed and there was no sign of Thor. Her pajamas lay on top of the covers.

"Sonia? Are you already up, sweetheart?" She slid out of bed and ran across the room to the bathroom.

It was empty.

Kristin's body broke out in a cold sweat. When she searched in the drawers, she discovered one of Sonia's jeans and top was missing. So was her parka which Kristin had hung in the nook near the door to the room. Her walking boots were gone. Everything!

Was it possible her niece had decided to go on a walk with Thor? There was just one problem with that scenario. The hotel wasn't familiar territory to Eric's dog.

Maybe Eric had come by the room early to take her and Thor for a walk. Would he do that without informing Kristin of his intentions first?

Or had some lunatic seen Sonia on television and decided to kidnap her? Even hold her to extort a ransom from the Prince himself?

Terror seized Kristin's heart.

She raced across the room and phoned reception to inform them that her little niece was missing. The concierge sounded horrified by the news. He said he would alert the police and send the hotel staff on a hunt for her and Thor.

Kristin threw on a pair of wool pants, a sweater and coat. After lacing up her walking boots, she hurried out of the room to look for Sonia. Maybe she was trapped in the elevator and couldn't get out.

Frantic with fear, she ran down the hall and rang for it to come. When it stopped on her floor the door opened, but all she discovered was a young couple on their way to breakfast.

When she asked if they'd seen Sonia, they said no but offered to help in the search. It was agreed they would start with the staircase to see if by any chance Sonia was playing there with Thor.

The second the elevator arrived at the main floor, Kristin flew out the doors and proceeded to collide with a rock-solid male body.

"Eric—" she gasped.

He clutched her to him. "What's wrong?"

"Sonia and Thor are missing. When I woke up, they were gone—" she cried out in agony. "The concierge has notified the police, but I thought, I prayed, they were with you."

He held her tighter. "No. I've just arrived. We'll find her. I swear to you we'll find her." His voice shook with barely restrained emotion.

She leaned her head back so she could look into his eyes. "Do you promise?"

His dark brown gaze pierced through to her soul. "Yes. I'm a prince. When I make a promise, you can believe it. Those were your words to Sonia last night. Remember?"

Kristin fought not to break down. "I do."

"Wherever she is, Thor will protect her with his life." He reached for his cell phone and made several calls. At this point the concierge rushed over to them.

"We have staff and security searching every floor, every room, Your Highness. So far we haven't found her." The bad news brought a moan to

Kristin's lips. As Eric slid his arm around her shoulders and pulled her against him, the police arrived.

Eric rapped out orders to the lieutenant to search every lane and street in Brobak, starting with Badeparken, which he explained to Kristin was the fjord-side park where he'd often walked Thor.

"Come on." He grasped her hand. "We'll search the Bathavna area."

Kristin knew that was Brobak's boat harbor. She hurried with him through the hotel to the rear entrance and climbed into the limo. By now the whole area swarmed with security and police. Eric gave his driver instructions and they drove off.

She clung to his hand. "The sun won't be up for several more hours. Anything could happen to her if someone hurt Thor and she's wandering around alone."

"Shh." Eric leaned over and silenced her with his lips. "We'll find her."

"Oh, Eric—she's so precious. If I lost her, I don't know what I'd do."

"We're not going to lose her. She has so much faith in Thor, she probably told him to take her for a walk."

"But he can't open doors."

"He's smart enough to lead her to one so she can open it herself. Those two have uncanny radar. It's a gift we lose by the time we're adults."

"We need it now," she half sobbed the words.

"What I don't understand is how she knew where to find all her clothes? She didn't see me hang up her parka. She had no idea where I put everything."

Eric hadn't wanted to alarm Kristin, but he'd asked himself those same questions the second she'd collided with him in the foyer and had told him Sonia and Thor were missing.

His instructions to his own security men had been to treat this as a kidnapping which would put the whole town on the highest alert. He phoned Eva and told her the police would be scouring the grounds and the road leading up from the town for any sign of Sonia and Thor.

For the next two hours he and Kristin walked every square inch of the harbor area and marketplace, exhausting all possible areas where she might have gone with his dog.

Kristin kept calling out to her niece in the darkness until she didn't have a voice left. It ripped Eric's gut apart to witness her pain. In truth, he'd never experienced this kind of agony before either.

Little Sonia had stolen her way into his heart. The thought of anything happening to her terrified him, but he had to remain strong for Kristin. He'd made a promise to her, one he'd keep or die trying in the attempt.

He'd already received phone calls from his sister and his brother who'd just heard the news from one

of his bodyguards. Knute and their mother were on
their way back from Germany to help in the search.

Kristin vacillated whether to let her father know
what was going on. But in the end she used the
phone in the limo to call him and tell him Sonia and
Thor were missing. Eric thought it was wise to alert
him just in case she was found too late to make the
flight home.

His admiration for Kristin escalated when she remained calm while reassuring her father everything
possible was being done to locate Sonia. ''The
Prince himself is helping me look for her, Dad, so
don't worry. We're going to find her. Say a prayer
for us.''

Eric crushed her against his side, his emotions
raw.

Kristin finally hung up the phone. ''Dad's amazing. He says he knows we'll find her. Oh, Eric—
where do you think Sonia could be?''

His mind had been replaying various conversa-
tions with her. ''She was so fixated on my crown,
maybe—''

''Maybe in her child's mind she met someone and
asked them to drive her to Midgard—'' Kristin
blurted. ''It's worth looking into.''

''I agree.'' He got on the phone to security and
told them to follow up on that lead. Then another
idea came to him and he called Sofia at the palace.

''Have you found her?'' Knute's wife cried.

"Not yet."

"She's an engaging child, Eric. Last night I really fell in love with her."

"Sonia has that effect on everyone. Do me a favor and put both boys on different extensions. I need to talk to them."

After a few seconds, "I'm here, Uncle Eric." It was Knute's voice.

"So am I," Jan piped up.

Eric pushed the monitor button which acted like a microphone so Kristin could hear everything.

"Listen, boys. This is vitally important. As you know, we can't find Sonia or Thor. While you were playing with her last night, did she talk about something she wanted to see or do before she left Frijia? Think really hard before you answer."

Kristin clung to his arm while they both waited for a response.

"We asked her if she wanted to play fort. She said she wanted to be the cowboys and we could be the Indians," Jan explained.

"Let me explain," Knute cut in. "We told her it was a Frijian fort and we were fighting the enemy."

"Yeah," Jan inserted. "She didn't know we have forts too."

"I was talking, Jan," Knute said. "I told her we needed to sink a big ship so we could escape with our country's gold, she got really excited and said she didn't want to be the enemy, but she wanted to be a Frijian too.''

Eric's eyes closed for a minute. "So what else did she say?"

"She said she wished she could see that fort. I told her it was a museum now. She asked if people could visit it."

"We told her yes," Jan finished the rest.

"Eric—" Kristin clasped his arm tighter without being aware of it. "Maybe that's where she went."

He hated to take away any hope from her, but Kristin didn't realize Sonia would have to ride the ferry to reach it. Though there'd been a breakthrough last night about her guilt over the accident, that didn't mean she'd ever be able to set foot on a boat again.

"Can you think of anything else?"

"No," they both said at the same time.

"Thank you, boys. Will you put your mother back on?"

"Eric?" Sofia said. "I don't recall any other conversation either."

"Thank you, Sofia. It's been a great help. We'll keep in close touch."

"Tell Ms. Remmen we're all thinking of her and Sonia."

"I will."

One of the security men knocked on the door of

the limo which was still parked at the harbor. He'd brought them coffee and rolls.

Eric thanked him, then urged Kristin to eat with him. "We have to keep up our strength."

While he phoned the head of security to cover the car ferries and all of the area around Niflheim fortress on the off chance Sonia might have asked someone to take her there, he watched in relief as Kristin ate a roll and drank her coffee.

Only good news would do something about her pallor. Yet she was one of those women with a classic beauty that needed no artifice.

Yesterday she'd caught her hair back. This morning the honey-blond silk tumbled about her shoulders in attractive disarray. Minus any lipstick, her light blue eyes sodden with pain, she looked almost ethereal in the semidarkness of the interior. He wanted to take that pain away.

"Better?" he asked when they'd both finished the last of their coffee.

"Much. Thank you."

"Are you ready for another trek around the village?"

"Yes."

"We'll stick to the smaller lanes where cars can't go. Sonia may have fallen asleep somewhere and Thor's keeping her warm."

Anything was better than sitting here waiting for the phone to ring. He didn't want to entertain the possibility Sonia had been kidnapped. But the longer time passed without word of her, his fear foul play was involved grew greater.

In the next half hour the sun had come up, but their search proved fruitless. They'd just reached the parked limo when Eric answered another call on his cell phone.

"Did they find her?" Kristin cried.

He clicked off. "No. We're going back to the hotel. The police want you to help them choose some of Sonia's belongings from the room. They're going to make a door-to-door search with bloodhounds, hoping to pick up her trail."

"Dear God—to think it's come to this—"

Eric crushed her in his arms and held her for the short trip to the hotel. "We'll find her, Kristin. You have to believe that." He rained kisses in her hair.

"I do. It's just that Sonia might have been gone a long time. It's always night to her. Who knows when she left the room."

The limo pulled up to the back entrance which had been cordoned off to everyone except the police. Eric grabbed Kristin's hand and they rushed toward the door of the hotel.

"Aunty Kristin!" a familiar little voice cried out.

CHAPTER EIGHT

KRISTIN and Eric both spun around in time to see Thor and Sonia climb out the back of a medium-size van parked next to the building. It had the hotel's logo painted on the side.

The dog rushed to greet Eric joyously. Sonia was right behind him and ran into Kristin's arms.

"Thor and I have been waiting and waiting for you."

"Sonia!"

Kristin swung her niece around and around, laughing and crying at the same time. "I've never been so happy to see anyone in all my life." Her gaze flew to Eric's. His handsome face radiated joy and relief as great as hers.

"To think she's been here all the time," he whispered against her ear before biting the lobe gently. Then he gave his attention to Sonia.

"Where did you go, *elskling?*"

"I wanted to see that lady before we went to the airport."

"What lady?"

"The one that rows mommies cross the water cos they're going to have a baby!"

Eric burst into laughter and pulled her into his arms. "You mean Jacobine, the harbor mistress. It's the statue on Hovedgata we passed just minutes ago," he explained to Kristin.

Dazed, she stared at him, then Sonia. "But how did you even know about it?"

"That tour lady told us."

"You're a very intelligent girl to remember something like that," Eric exclaimed before giving her a kiss on the cheek. "Why didn't you tell your aunt you were leaving the room with Thor?"

"You were asleep, and Thor needed a drink. We went outside and I fed him some snow. Then we went to see the statue. We weren't gone very long."

"Sweetheart—didn't you know I would worry if I woke up and couldn't find you?"

"Yes, but we came back fast and then I couldn't open the door. So we got in that car and I locked it so nobody could get in."

She pointed to the van. "It was cold in there, but Thor got on the floor with me and kept me warm."

Eric murmured, "The police must have assumed that if they couldn't open the doors to the van, she couldn't either, so they didn't make a thorough search of it."

Kristin nodded. "Sonia? When you could hear people talking out here, why didn't you ask one of them to let you in the hotel?"

"Cos they were policemen. I was afraid they'd get mad at me."

"How did you know they were policemen?" When Kristin thought about it, she couldn't understand how Sonia even knew the van was there to climb into.

Eric slid his other arm around Kristin's shoulders and pulled her close to him and Sonia. "You can see again, can't you, *elskling?*"

Sonia's sparkling brown eyes smiled into Eric's like a full-sighted person's. "Yes."

With that revelation, Kristin reeled. *"You can honestly see?"*

Her niece nodded, causing her disheveled brown curls to dance.

"When did it happen?"

"When I woke up. Thor was panting cos he was thirsty. I saw his big black head."

Eric roared with laughter. "Did you know the whole town has been looking for you?"

"It has?"

"You're more famous than my brother."

"You mean Jan and Knute's daddy?"

"That's right."

Sonia turned toward Kristin with a trembling lower lip. "The boys didn't want me to leave. I wish we didn't have to go home today."

"You can't go home today," the man kneading Kristin's shoulder declared with a triumphant ring.

"Your plane already took off. How would you and your aunt like to spend Christmas at my house?"

"Oh—" Sonia made a sound of utter bliss. "Can we, Aunty Kristin? Please?"

Two pairs of pleading brown eyes gazed soulfully at Kristin. Three if she counted Thor's.

"Please?" Eric whispered. "It's one of the wishes I put on my list for Christmas."

Whether he'd made that up or not, right now the blessing of sight had returned to Sonia because of Eric's inspiration, making it impossible for Kristin to think beyond this moment.

She lifted tremulous eyes to him. "We'd love to spend today with you, but we'll have to leave first thing in the morning."

"How come?" Sonia cried mournfully.

Kristin reached for her niece, but she grabbed Eric around the neck and wouldn't let go. "Because your grandpa's still too sick to fly here. We wouldn't want him to be all alone on Christmas, would we?"

Sonia's expression sobered. "No. He would cry."

"That's right. So we'll have to fly home tomorrow. But we've got today to enjoy ourselves."

One more day…

Sonia patted Eric's cheeks. "Can we go see your crown?"

A chuckle escaped his lips. "I don't see why not. While I stay here to talk to the police, why don't you and your aunt go to your room and call your grandpa to tell him you're safe. Then we'll leave.''

"Okay. Come with me, Thor.''

As the dog trailed after her, Eric brushed his mouth against Kristin's lips. "Hurry.''

With her heart pounding out of control, Kristin rushed inside the hotel after Sonia. Since the moment she'd discovered Sonia was missing, Kristin had let her guard down with Eric. They'd both been emotionally upset which accounted for their familiarity with each other.

But though she didn't doubt his attraction to her was genuine, that's all it was. *An attraction that couldn't possibly go anywhere.*

Eric had girlfriends, but Kristin couldn't consider herself one of those.

If her father hadn't sent in Sonia's picture for that contest—and if Princess Maren hadn't been put on bed rest—Kristin would never have met Prince Eric.

This whole chance experience had been a complete fluke from start to finish.

One day when he decided to marry, the woman he chose would have to be from a family of royal lineage like Sofia's or Stein's.

For that reason, Kristin was doubly thankful she could use her father's illness as an excuse to fly home in the morning. She needed to meet that deadline before she did something really stupid like believe that maybe Eric had fallen in love with her too and didn't want her to leave.

There'd be time enough when she returned to Chicago to wonder how she was going to exist for the rest of her life without him. She didn't even want to think about Sonia's reaction.

"This church sure is big!"

"It's very old and beautiful," Kristin said in a quieter voice, hoping Sonia would lower hers.

Her niece walked between them holding their hands, still overly excited from flying on Eric's small private jet where they'd eaten a fabulous brunch on board.

But the whole time they were touring the medieval cathedral in Midgard, Kristin was aware that if Eric hadn't granted his sister a favor yesterday, he would have flown Bea in that same jet to Kvitfjell today for some skiing and very probably a night of loving.

"This is the room where they keep the crowns, *elskling*."

Kristin marveled to think they could view them in private behind the glass partition. Her eyes widened like Sonia's when she saw the various crowns. They were fabulous.

"Which is yours, Eric?"

"Why don't you guess?"

Sonia walked back and forth. "This one." She

pointed to a tall jeweled masterpiece with gold bands and white stones leaping out against red velvet. On top was an amethyst cross.

He grinned: "How did you know?"

"Cos it looks the heaviest."

"Like I told you earlier today, you're a very intelligent young lady."

His comment made her giggle. "Put it on."

Kristin sensed his hesitation. "Since we're locked in this room, I will for you, but don't tell anyone."

"I won't."

"It will have to be our secret. Promise?"

"I promise," she said solemnly.

He reached for it and lifted it on to his head. "How do I look?"

Sonia sucked in her breath. "Like a king!"

He *did* look like a king. One day it was possible he *would* be king. Kristin still couldn't credit any of this was happening. Yet she couldn't doubt that his love for Sonia was real, not now...

"It was made for the coronation of one of my ancestors, King Carl, almost 200 years ago."

"What's a coronation?"

Eric flashed Kristin a private smile before he said, "When a king is crowned king."

"Are you going to be king someday?"

"I hope not."

A wealth of emotion went into that comment, giving Kristin more insight into Eric's remarkable character.

"I'm glad you're just a prince."

"How come?" he teased her with one of her own questions before putting the crown back in its spot.

"Cos Jan and Knute said their daddy doesn't play with them very much."

"A lot of conversation went on in that playroom," he muttered, but Kristin heard him. "My brother has the worries of the whole country on his mind, Sonia. When he heard you were missing, he came home from his trip to help me look for you."

She blinked. "Does he know you found me?"

"I'm sure he's been told by now."

"Aunty Kristin?" Her big brown eyes looked up at her. "Can I thank the King?"

"Yes, sweetheart. In fact, we have a lot of people to thank. When we get back to Chicago, we'll send letters to everyone."

Suddenly her niece ran to Eric and threw her arms around his legs. "I love you. I wish you could be my new daddy."

No.

Kristin averted her eyes. "Let's just be grateful Prince Eric is your good friend." She'd mentioned his title deliberately. "Now we'd better leave so we can go see the Viking ships in the museum. Come on."

She grabbed hold of Sonia's hand. When they

reached the door, Kristin knocked for the guard to let them out of the room.

The conversation had touched on treacherous ground. She'd been afraid this would happen before the day was over. Kristin needed to have a private chat with her niece before Eric caught up to them. The best place for that would be the rest room she'd seen at the rear of the church.

Once inside where they could have privacy, she knelt down in front of Sonia. "Sweetheart—I know how much you love Eric, but he can't ever be your daddy."

One tear trickled down her flushed cheek. "How come?"

Kristin shook her head in pained exasperation. "Because he was born into a family where he has to marry a woman who's also from a royal family so their children will be royal."

"How come?"

"It's a law that was made hundreds of years ago by the first king."

"Are Jan and Knute royal?"

"Yes, because their mommy was a princess."

"Will the boys have to marry princesses someday?"

"Yes."

Her precious little face fell. "Oh."

Sonia, Sonia. "Just think how lucky you are that Eric is your special friend."

Instead of becoming hysterical as Kristin feared, Sonia finally said, "Can we go now?"

"Yes."

As she stood up, Sonia ran out the bathroom door. Kristin rushed after her, but not before her niece reached Eric who stood at the main doors of the entrance to the cathedral waiting for them.

The sight of him so tall and devastatingly appealing in his black coat and boots took Kristin's breath away.

By the time she caught up to her niece, he'd swept Sonia into his arms. "What's the big hurry, *elskling?*"

"Can I play with Jan and Knute after we look at the ships?"

"They're planning on it."

"Sonia—we've already been to the palace," Kristin reminded her. "We can't go there again."

He shot Kristin an enigmatic glance. "It's already been decided Knute and Sofia will bring the boys to my house. My brother's anxious to meet both of you."

Sonia's head jerked around. A smile illuminated her face. "We're going to meet the King! Now I can thank him."

CHAPTER NINE

"ERIC? While mother's talking to Sofia and Kristin, come here for a minute," Knute whispered.

He left the women and children who were playing in the living room with the dog, and followed his brother into his library.

Knute shut the door, then leaned against it to study Eric. "Kristin told me about your prayer and the miracle that followed. How does it feel?"

Eric's eyes smarted. "I'm still in shock."

"Do you know what Sonia asked me after she thanked me for flying home to help in the search?"

"I can't imagine, but knowing her as I do, it was something completely original."

"You could say that." His brows lifted. "She said, and I quote, 'Could you make a law to turn me into a princess so I can be Eric's little girl, cos I *love* him?'"

His brother had done a perfect imitation of her.

The revelation didn't come as a surprise. Sonia had already asked Eric to be her daddy when they were in Midgard earlier in the day. But hearing this from Knute touched him in the deepest recesses of his soul.

He cleared his throat. "What did you say back?"

"I told her I'd have to think hard about it. She asked me how long it took me to think hard about things." Eric started to chuckle. "I said it might take six months."

Knute's answer brought Eric up short. "Six months?"

"Well…after considering everything, I wanted to be sure there was enough time for you to win her Aunty Kristin around before you proposed an official alliance of the three of you."

A long silence ensued before he said, "I've got competition, Knute. There's a man in her life."

His brother shrugged his shoulders. "I didn't see a ring on her finger."

"You know that doesn't necessarily mean anything. Sonia let it slip the guy doesn't want to raise Kristin's niece. It means they've been talking marriage."

"Nevertheless, their problem sounds serious. Now's your chance, if you know what I mean."

"It's all I've been able to think about."

Knute clapped a hand on his shoulder. "I always figured when you met the right woman, you'd know it instantly."

Eric nodded. "I haven't been the same since I heard Sonia sobbing her heart out in the back of the Chocolate Barn because Maren couldn't come.

"When I walked to the rear of the store and

Kristin looked up at me with those gorgeous blue eyes, helpless in the face of Sonia's disappointment, I felt something zap my insides from my heart to my stomach.

"Finding out Sonia was blind only intensified my feelings for both of them." His eyes closed tightly for a moment.

"They're heartbreakers all right. Sonia has an artless charm about her that draws you in. The boys are crazy about her. I can see why. Do you know she asked me to play with them more because they miss me *very, very* much?"

Eric smiled again. "That sounds like my *elskling*. Anyone who meets her is drawn to her." He stared at his elder brother. "She's not the only one wanting a favor from the King."

Knute's mouth quirked in amusement. "Is that right?"

"There's something I'd like you to arrange, but we'll talk about it after I've put Kristin and Sonia on the plane in the morning."

"Come to the palace as soon as they've gone."

"I thought you had a meeting scheduled."

"It's been canceled. I've decided to take Sonia's advice and spend every moment of the holiday with my family. After hearing about the death of her parents, it has made me reassess my priorities."

"I know what you mean," Eric murmured, anxious to get back to the other room. First, however, he had a certain phone call to make to Bea.

CHAPTER TEN

WITH Sonia in his arms, Eric walked Kristin through the empty body of the 747 to the front of the plane. No other passengers had been allowed to board yet.

"We didn't fly over first class!" Kristin cried softly.

His dark brown eyes searched hers. "Maybe not, but you're returning home that way."

Sonia was already in tears and clung harder to his neck. "I wish we didn't have to go." Kristin echoed her niece's sentiments. It was killing her to think she'd never seen Eric again. "Will you come and see us?" her niece begged.

Kristin groaned. The flight home was going to be a nightmare.

"There's nothing I'd like better, *elskling*."

By the time he'd lowered her into a window seat, Sonia was verging on hysterics. Kristin turned to her niece. "Remember what I told you? Eric has important work to do for his country on a submarine."

"Can't you tell the s-submarine to come to America?"

"No, sweetheart, he can't!" Kristin answered for him.

Eric wiped the tears from her flushed cheeks. "I'll phone you tomorrow and find out what Santa brought you for Christmas."

Kristin lurched in her seat.

"We'll be at G-Grandpa's. Do you know his number?"

"Yes."

"Does T—Thor know I've gone?"

"I haven't told him yet."

"Eric has to leave now so the other passengers can board the plane. Say goodbye, sweetheart." Kristin tried to act as matter-of-factly as possible, determined to hide her own pain from him.

"Bye, Eric." The words came out like a croaking sound before Sonia crawled into Kristin's lap and broke down sobbing against her neck.

Kristin looked up at Eric dry-eyed. "You'd better go, Your Highness," she mouthed the words. "Thank you for everything."

His expression sobered. She sensed he wanted to say something else, then thought the better of it.

There was a sharp intake of breath before he strode out of the first-class compartment taking her heart with him.

"Dad? I'm going to run over to the apartment and get a few things I need, then I'll be back."

"Take your time, honey." He was still examining

the grandma mouse Sonia had chosen for him with Eric's approval.

"Do you want to come with me, Sonia?"

"No. Eric's going to call me."

Maybe. Maybe not.

It was already five in the afternoon. She knew he wouldn't have kept Sonia waiting without a good reason.

"All right. I'll hurry."

She left her niece in front of the Christmas tree playing with her new fort consisting of Frijian submarines and cruisers on the floor.

Surrounding her were all the rest of the toys Eric had brought to the plane without Kristin's knowledge, including the full set of mice from Santa's post office shop.

When she and Sonia had deboarded in Chicago to go through customs, an airport official had met them and ushered them out to a limousine filled with bags of beautifully wrapped packages.

Eric's generosity extended to signed photographs taken at the Chocolate Barn, a wool scarf for Kristin's father and an exquisite light blue silk scarf for herself.

"To match your eyes," the inserted note had said. The message made her breath catch.

She hadn't given Eric anything for Christmas, but she would rectify the matter when she and Sonia sent thank-you letters to everyone.

No sooner had she driven herself to the house where she rented the basement apartment from an elderly woman, than her cell phone rang again. She checked the caller ID. It was Bruce.

She wanted nothing to do with him, but this was his twentieth attempt to reach her in the last six hours. After walking down the steps at the side of the house, she let herself in the door and answered it.

"Hello?"

"Kristin? It's Bruce."

Once upon a time the sound of his voice excited her, but no more. A telemarketer's unwanted intrusion would have been more welcome.

"I know."

"I'm pulling in the driveway behind your car and would like to come in for a minute. I've changed my mind about Sonia. Please don't say no, honey. This is far too important to our future."

If he'd said those words when she'd tried to give him back the ring, she might have listened.

But everything had changed in the last week. A certain prince had appeared on the scene, showing her what a real man was all about. No other male would ever be able to measure up to Eric. Not in a lifetime…

"You can have five minutes. Then I have to get back to dad and Sonia."

She'd barely hung up and turned on lights when he entered the apartment and reached for her.

"I've missed you, honey. Forgive me for being such a fool about Sonia? We'll work it out."

Work it out?

"This last week without you has been pure hell. I'm putting my ring back on your finger where it belongs."

He sounded like he meant everything he said, but she wasn't moved by his apology or his emotions.

"No, Bruce."

She pulled away from his arms, aware that he was at least four inches shorter than Eric and didn't have his powerful build. If she noticed those things, it was because it no longer felt right to be with Bruce. *He* didn't feel right to her.

"What do you mean, no?" She heard the hurt in his voice. His dark blond looks were very attractive, yet whatever she'd once felt for him was gone.

Kristin let out a sigh. "You're a wonderful person, Bruce, but I meant it when I said it was over between us. Please hear me out—" she asked when he started to protest.

"I'm grateful for your honesty about Sonia. It's an enormous responsibility to raise a child, especially when it's not yours. I loved Sonia before she was even born, so it was natural for me to want to be her mother now that she's alone. She'll always need me and dad.

"And though I appreciate the fact that you've had a chance to think about it and want to try to be a father to Sonia, I know it won't work.

"You deserve to marry a woman who's unencumbered so the two of you can enjoy married life for a while before you start your own family. I know that one day you'll make a terrific father.

"The truth is, even though Sonia's vision has been restored, her daddy is a difficult act to follow." In fact there's only one man I know who could make the sun light up her universe again.

"What?" Bruce muttered incredulously. "Her sight's come back?"

"Yes. The doctor said it might, *if* she ever got over her feelings of guilt."

His face lost color. "When did it happen?"

"She woke up one morning on the trip and could see Thor's head lying near her pillow."

He frowned. "Thor?"

"Prince Eric's dog."

Her ex-fiancé studied her for a full minute. "I watched the TV coverage on you. Evidently the playboy prince had to take his sister's place for the duty appearance with Sonia. There's a rumor he's interested in you. Is it true?" he demanded.

His color had returned. Now his cheeks looked ruddy.

"No. What he did was behave like Prince

Charming and make Sonia's trip to Frijia one of enchantment. Now the enchantment is over.''

Bruce grasped her upper arms. ''What does he mean to you, Kristin?''

''What *could* he mean to me?'' she answered in a level voice.

A haunted look entered his eyes. ''I don't know, but there's something different about you. He got to you, didn't he?'' Bruce whispered in shock.

Yes.

''What he did was win Sonia's confidence to the point that she told him about the accident. When he found out she blamed herself for it, he convinced her it wasn't her fault. Obviously she believed him because the next day she could see.''

Tears filled Kristin's eyes. ''It was a miracle. I love him for what he did.''

''You love him for more than that. I can hear it in your voice. Did he kiss you?'' He shook her gently.

Kristin wasn't about to lie to him. ''Yes.''

His breathing grew shallow. ''Did you kiss him back?''

Remembering that hungry kiss she'd returned with equal fervor at his house on the first night, she averted her eyes. ''Yes.''

A sound of grief escaped Bruce's lips. ''If I'd taken the time off to go Frijia with you, none of this would have happened.''

You're wrong, Bruce.

When the Prince walked to the back room of the Chocolate Barn and their eyes had met, she'd felt herself falling helplessly through space. It was the defining moment of her life, but would have to remain her secret.

"Because things worked out the way they did, Sonia has her sight back. We can all be thankf—"

There was a knock on the door, cutting off the rest of her words.

"It's probably Mrs. Coretti. Just a minute."

Kristin walked over to the door and opened it expecting to see her landlady. When she discovered who was standing in the stairwell, she almost fainted.

"Merry Christmas, Kristin."

CHAPTER ELEVEN

"ERIC—" she cried, holding on to the door so she wouldn't collapse.

Jeans and a black wool pullover couldn't disguise his princely bearing. His intense gaze played over her face and figure relentlessly.

"Your father told me I'd find you here."

"You've seen dad?" Her voice squeaked the question.

His smile reached clear down into her soul. "Him, and my little *elskling*."

"Aren't you going to introduce us?" sounded a cold voice directly behind her.

Good heavens—she'd forgotten all about Bruce, let alone her manners.

"Of course. Please—come in."

Eric crossed the threshold, bringing the freezing air off Lake Michigan inside with him. The temperature outside wasn't that different from Frijia's. She shut the door.

"Bruce Hancock, please meet His Royal Highness, Prince Eric."

The two men shook hands.

"I saw you on television with Sonia and Kristin.

She tells me you're the one responsible for her niece being able to see again.''

Eric took his time responding. ''Before Sonia went to sleep, she asked me to say my prayers first. Heaven did the rest.''

Kristin could hardly breathe. She had the grace to feel sorry for Bruce whose Adam's apple bobbed several times.

The Prince turned to her. ''If I'm interrupting something important, I'll come back at a better time.''

''No—'' she cried, revealing the state of her chaotic emotions. ''Bruce was just leaving.'' She opened the door so he'd be forced to go.

He eyed both of them for a moment. The regret in his eyes saddened her for his sake, but she was glad this was the end of a relationship doomed for failure. Better now than after they'd said their vows.

When he disappeared up the outside stairs, she closed the door and turned to Eric.

''I—I can't believe you flew here on Christmas.'' Her voice throbbed with too much emotion.

''This is a special day for me. Maren had a Christmas baby. He looks like Stein.''

''How wonderful! Did you tell Sonia?''

There was a gleam in his eye. ''I even let her know they've decided to name him Eric.''

"That must have thrilled you."

He nodded. "Of course mother's ecstatic and totally preoccupied with her newest grandchild. Knute took his family skiing after they opened presents. Everyone had a place to go and something to do. It gave me the excuse I was looking for to come after you."

Come after her?

She felt her heart skitter all over the place.

"From what I learned from Sonia in the limo that night, you and Bruce must have been planning marriage."

"We were, but I broke our engagement before leaving for Frijia."

He studied her with a grave expression. "Now that she has recovered her sight, is it possible you two will be getting back together again?"

"No," she replied without hesitation.

"You're sure?"

"Very. Not every man can embrace another man's child. Bruce came over here tonight to tell me he's willing to work at it. But that's not enough. From the beginning Sonia has sensed he hasn't been able to accept her.

"I told him he should look for a woman who doesn't have a child. I'm afraid I come with a niece who needs me and my father desperately."

"I met Professor Remmen. He's a terrific person. You didn't tell me he's a mathematician."

"Actually he's the chairman of the department at the university."

"That's an honor for a man who's obviously brilliant."

"Sonia takes after him."

"So I gather. However, she resembles her grandmother. He showed me pictures of her and your sister, Marthe. Beauty runs in the Remmen family."

"Thank you."

"You are beautiful, you know."

Kristin didn't want him to say things like that. It would only deepen the pain when he left again. She rubbed her arms.

"Why did you really come here, Eric?"

He stood there with his legs slightly apart. "I found that I missed you and Sonia, so I decided to get on a plane."

Her eyes widened. "That's the reason?"

"The only one. Have you missed me?"

"W—what kind of a question is that?"

"Why are you so flustered? Sonia acted happy to see me. How about you? Do you wish I hadn't come?"

"The truth?" she cried in anguish.

"Of course."

"It would have been better if you hadn't."

After a pause, "At least that's honest. My apologies for intru—"

"No—" she broke in on him. "You don't understand—"

"Then help me."

"Sonia wasn't the only one you enchanted, but we're home now, and the fantasy has to stop."

"I enchanted you?"

"You know you did," her voice trembled. "But it would be pointless to spend any more time with you because—because there's no future in it."

"What if there were?"

A gasp escaped her lips. "Now you're sounding like Sonia, but I can't afford to dream impossible dreams. You'd better go."

He remained where he was. "Kristin—long before my father passed away, we had an understanding that when I felt the time was right, I could marry any woman of my own choosing."

The blood pounded in her ears. "Any?"

"Yes. Now I'm going to ask that question again. Have you missed me as much as I've missed you over the last forty-eight hours?"

"Till I've wanted to die."

"That's all I needed to hear." On a groan, he pulled her into his arms. Their mouths and bodies met in a frenzy of need. Before she knew how it had happened, they were on the couch and Kristin found herself clinging to him.

"I can't believe I'm holding you in my arms," she whispered against lips that roamed her flushed face and neck with increasing urgency. "You've changed my whole life, Eric."

"That's how I felt when I walked in the back room of the Chocolate Barn and saw this beautiful blond woman in red, kneeling next to a little girl who was crying her heart out. Mine melted on the spot when you looked at me with those incredible blue eyes.

"I'd marry you tonight if I could have my own way, but you've just come out of an engagement and need time. Would you and Sonia be willing to move to Frijia for a few months so we could really get to know each other?

"Knute is making arrangements for you to be an exchange teacher in Brobak at an elementary school where Sonia could attend. There's a house for rent close by. We'd be able to spend every possible moment together.

"I need you and Sonia in my life, darling. I'm a better person for being with you. If you can't see yourself leaving the States right now because of your father, then I'll come here because my life will never be the same witho—"

"We'll come!" Kristin declared against his lips. "Maybe it's too soon to say I love you, but I have to say it. I love you. It's an all-consuming love I feel in my heart." She clutched him tighter. "Oh darling—what if dad hadn't entered Sonia in that contest?"

"Don't think about the what-ifs. There are too many of them. Right now all I want to do is kiss us both senseless. Do I have your permission?"

Kristin threw her arms around his neck and drew him down to her, leaving him in no doubt that his wish was her desire.

Three months later...

"I now pronounce you, Prince Eric, and you, Kristin Remmen, man and wife. In the name of the Father, the Son and the Holy Ghost. Amen."

To Kristin's shock, the priest suddenly produced a small golden tiara. He motioned for Sonia to come to the altar. She left her grandpa's side to approach the priest who set it amongst her shiny brown curls. It was a perfect fit.

"From this day forth, King Knute has declared you'll be known as Princess Sonia."

Kristin had an idea Eric had asked his brother if he would make a law so Sonia could be a princess.

Their gazes locked. He was too wonderful. Kristin loved him too much and tried to tell him with her eyes before he gave her a kiss unlike any other.

It was the possessive kiss of a husband. One full of passion and the promise of the wedding night to come.

Sonia's giggle of pure joy finally caused him to

relinquish Kristin's mouth. He grasped their daughter's hand. She looked like an adorable angel in a white tulle gown that floated when she walked.

"Daddy?" she whispered loud enough for all the guests assembled in the palace chapel to hear. "Am I a real princess now?"

Eric, resplendent once more in his ceremonial suit, smiled down at her. "Yes, you are."

"Can I keep my crown on my dresser?"

"If you'd like."

"Does it mean I can marry a prince someday?"

Quiet laughter whispered through the congregation.

"If you want to, but it won't be for a long, long time."

"How come?"

Oh no.

Kristin moaned loud enough to capture her new husband's attention. He was loving this, but the altar of the chapel was hardly the place for a running conversation with Sonia.

"Because I want to enjoy my daughter for a lot of years first."

She looked up at both of them. "Mommy? Will you and Daddy give me a little brother?"

Kristin's face went crimson. "Sonia—"

Eric chuckled before flashing her a wolfish glance. "We'll do our best, won't we, Your

Highness? Now...shall we go meet our guests, *els-kling?*"

"Yes. The boys and Thor have been waiting and waiting for me."

THE MILLIONAIRE'S
CHRISTMAS WISH

Lucy Gordon

PROLOGUE

IT WAS the most glorious Christmas tree in the world: eight feet high, brilliant with baubles, tinsel and flickering lights, with a dazzling star shining from the top.

Around the base brightly coloured parcels, decorated with shiny bows, crowded together, spilling lavishly over the floor.

The whole thing presented a picture of generous abundance. It was a family tree, meant to stand in a home, surrounded by happy children eagerly tearing the wrapping from the parcels, revealing longed for gifts.

Instead, it stood in the corner of Alex Mead's huge office. The presents were fake. Any child removing the pretty wrapping paper would have found only empty boxes.

But no child would do so. The whole confection had been designed and carried out by Alex's secretary, Katherine, and as far as he was concerned she had wasted her time.

She entered now with some letters in one hand and a newspaper in the other, and he noticed that she couldn't resist glancing proudly at the tree as she passed.

'Sentimentalist,' he said, giving her the brilliant grin that won him goodwill at every first meeting. Often the goodwill was short-lived. It didn't take long for rivals and associates to discover the predator who lived beneath the charm.

'Well, it looks nice,' she said defensively. 'Honestly, Alex, don't you have any Christmas spirit?'

'Sure I do. Look at your bonus.'

'I have and it was a lovely surprise.'

'You earned it, Kath. You did almost as much as I did to build this firm up.'

He was a generous man where money was concerned. Not only her bonus but that of several other vital employees had been more than expected. Alex knew how to keep good staff working difficult hours.

'Some of them want to come in and thank you,' she said now.

'Tell them there's no need. Say you said it for them, and I said all the right things—Happy Christmas, have a nice time—you'll know how to make it sound good.'

'Why do you have to try to sound like Scrooge?'

'Because I *am* Scrooge,' he said cheerfully.

'Liar,' she said, with the privilege of long friendship. 'Scrooge would never have let his employees go a day early, the way you're doing. Most firms keep everyone there until noon, Christmas Eve.'

'Yes, and what's the result? Nobody does any

work on Christmas Eve morning. Half of them are hung over and they're all watching the clock. It's a waste of everyone's time.'

She laid the newspaper, open at the financial page, on his desk. 'Did you see this?'

It was the best Christmas gift an entrepreneur could have had. There was a page of laudatory text about Mead Consolidated and its meteoric rise, its impact on the market, its brilliant prospects.

Backing this up was an eye-catching photograph of Alex, his grin at its most engaging, telling the world that here was a man of charisma and confidence who could steer his way skilfully through waters infested by sharks. You would have to look very closely to see that he was one of them.

The picture was cut off halfway down his chest, so it didn't show the long-limbed body that was just a little underweight. He was thin because he forgot to eat, relying on nervous energy for nourishment, just as he relied on nervous force to make an impact.

It was Alex's proud boast that he had no nerves. The truth, as Kath knew, was that he lived on them It was one of the reasons why he looked older than his thirty-seven years, why his smile was so swift and unpredictable, and why his temper was beginning to be the same.

When she'd come to work for him his dark eyes had sparkled with ambition and confidence and his complexion had had a healthy glow. The glow was gone now, and there were too often shadows under his eyes. But he was still a handsome man, only partly through his looks. The rest was a mysterious talisman, an inner light for which there were no words.

She had been on business trips with him and seen the female heads turn, the eyes sparkle with interest. To his credit he had never collected, although whether that was out of love for his wife or because he couldn't spare the time from business, Kath had never quite decided.

'"Here's the one to watch,"' she read from the newspaper. '"By this time next year Mead Consolidated will threaten to dominate the market." Well, you might try to look pleased. It's so brilliant you might have written it yourself.'

He laughed. 'How do you know I didn't?'

'Now you mention it, you probably did. You're conceited enough for anything.'

'So conceited that if *I'd* written it I wouldn't have stopped at "threatened" to dominate. That's not good enough for me. I have to be at the top, and I'm going to get there.'

'Alex, you only started eleven years ago, practically working from a garden shed. Give yourself time.'

'I don't need time. I need Craddock's contract, the biggest that's ever come my way.'

'Well, you've got it.'

'Not until he's signed it. Dammit, why did he have to get this tomfool idea about going to the Caribbean?'

George Craddock, the man whose signature he was determined to get by hook or by crook, had been all set to sign when he'd been struck by the notion of a gathering on the tiny Caribbean island that he owned. He'd called Alex about it that very afternoon.

'And a big contract signing party to end it,' Alex groaned now. 'It's a pointless exercise because the deal's already set up.'

'So why the party?' Kath asked.

'Because he's old, foolish and lonely and has nobody to spend Christmas with him. So I have to forget my plans and catch a plane tonight.'

'Weren't you supposed to be seeing your family over Christmas?'

'Part of it. I was going to arrive tomorrow and stay until the next day. Now I'll have to call Corinne and explain that I've been called away. I just hope I can make her understand.'

Tact prevented Kath from saying, *Sure, she understands so well that she's divorcing you.*

'You should have told Craddock to get stuffed,' she told him robustly now.

'No way! You know how hard I've fought for this contract, and I'm not going to see it slip through my fingers now.'

Seeing disapproval on her face he said, defensively, 'Kath, there'll be other Christmases.'

'I'm not so sure. Children grow up so fast, and suddenly there aren't other Christmases.'

'Now you're being sentimental,' he said gruffly.

That silenced her. 'Sentimental' was Alex's strongest term of disapproval.

'I'm sorry,' he said. 'I'm not in the best of moods. Go home, Kath. Have a nice Christmas.'

'And be in early on the first day,' she said in a reciting tone.

'I never need to tell you that.'

When she'd gone he sat down tiredly and stared at the phone. What he had to do could not be put off any longer. If you had to break a promise it was best to do it quickly and cleanly.

He hoped there wouldn't be any trouble with Corinne. She was used to the demands of his job, and the fact that it often took him away from his family. The only time she'd ever fought him about it was at Christmas.

And it would have to be Christmas now, wouldn't it? he thought, exasperated. Just when he'd wanted to put a good face on things and show that he wasn't a neglectful father, as she'd accused him!

He'd planned to join her and the children tomorrow, just for one day, because that was all he could spare. But he would have arrived, overflowing with presents, and they would have been impressed whether they liked it or not. They would have *had* to be. He would have seen to that.

So the sooner he called, the better. Dial the number, say, I'm afraid there's been a change of plan—

He reached for the phone.

CHAPTER ONE

'MUM, it's the best Christmas tree we've ever had. A tree fit for Santa.'

Bobby was nine, old enough to have his own ideas about Santa, kind enough not to disillusion his adults.

'It's beautiful, isn't it, darling?' Corinne agreed, regarding her son tenderly.

The tree was five feet high and covered in tinsel and baubles which had been fixed in place by eager, inexpert hands. Perhaps the star on top was a little wonky, but nobody cared about that.

'Do you think Dad will like it?' Bobby wanted to know.

'I'm sure he will.'

'You will tell him I did it, won't you? Well, Mitzi helped a bit, but she's only a little kid so she couldn't do much.'

'She's six years old,' Jimmy said, from where he was standing behind Corinne. 'It's not that long since you were six.'

'It was ages ago,' Bobby said indignantly.

Jimmy grinned. He was a cheerful young man with a round face that smiled easily, the kind of man who seemed to have been designed by nature for the express purpose of being an uncle.

He was in the army, on two weeks' leave, and had gladly accepted Corinne's invitation to spend Christmas. They were only third cousins, but, with no other family, they had always clung to their kinship.

'You thought you were a big man at six,' he reminded Bobby.

'I was,' the child said at once. 'And I'm an even bigger one now. Put 'em up.'

He lifted his fists, boxer-style, and Jimmy obligingly responded with the same stance. For a moment they danced around each other, Jimmy leaning down to get within the child's range.

Suddenly he yelled, 'Help! He got me, he got me,' and collapsed on the floor, clutching his nose.

At once Bobby, the tender-hearted, dropped down beside him.

'I didn't really hurt you, did I, Uncle Jimmy?' he asked anxiously.

Jimmy wobbled his nose and spoke in a heavy nasal whine. 'I dink you spoiled by dose.'

Bobby giggled.

In falling, Jimmy had dislodged some of the presents and the two of them began to pile them up again. Corinne helped, trying not to be too conscious of the parcel with the tag that read, *To Daddy, with love from Bobby.*

'Daddy will like it, won't he, Mummy? I got it specially with my pocket money.'

'Then he'll love it, whatever it is,' she assured him. 'Aren't you going to tell me?'

Bobby shook his head very seriously. 'It's a secret between me and Daddy. You don't mind, do you?'

'No, darling, I don't mind.'

She watched how carefully he replaced the box under the tree, and her heart ached for him. Both children loved their father so much, and had been let down by him so often. And the more he failed them, the more anxiously they loved him.

But he would make up for it this time, she thought desperately. Please, don't let anything go wrong. Make him be here.

When Bobby had gone away, Jimmy murmured, 'That has to be the sweetest-tempered kid in the world.'

'Yes, and it scares me. He's wide open to be badly hurt by Alex.'

'But that won't happen, will it? Alex gave his word that he'd arrive on Christmas Eve.'

Corinne made a face. 'Yes, but a promise to us was always conditional on business.'

'But not at Christmas?' Jimmy said, shocked.

'Especially at Christmas, because that was when he could steal a march on all those wimps who spent it with their families.'

'But he promised to spend this Christmas with you and the kids.'

'No, what he promised was to arrive on Christmas Eve and leave on Christmas Day.'

'So little time? Then surely you don't have to worry about him cancelling that?'

'I wish I could believe it. Do you know? I'm not sure the children even realise that our marriage is over. They hardly see less of him now than they did then. Apart from the fact that we've moved house, not much has changed.

'I don't mind for myself, but if he disappoints Bobby and Mitzi again I'll never forgive him.'

'And you've put up with that all these years?'

'Yes,' she said, almost in a tone of surprise. 'Until the day came when I wouldn't put up with it any more. And now we're separated, soon to be divorced.'

Put like that it sounded so simple, and that was how she wanted to leave it. This wasn't the time to speak of the pain, misery and disillusionment she'd endured as she had finally given up the fight to save her marriage.

It had been twelve years, starting in unbelievable happiness. And perhaps unbelievable was the right word, because she had believed the impossible.

At eighteen you convinced yourself of whatever suited you. You thought you could marry a tough, ambitious man and not suffer for it. You told yourself that love would soften him, that he would put you first, not every time, but often enough to count.

When that didn't work you told yourself that the babies would make a difference. He was so proud of his children. Surely at least he would put *them* first?

'He can't have missed everything, surely?' Jimmy asked now.

'No, he was there for some birthdays, even some Christmases. But I always knew that if the phone rang he'd be off somewhere.'

Jimmy looked into her face, trying to see past the wry resignation to whatever she really felt. He doubted that she would let him catch a glimpse. She'd perfected that cheerful, unrevealing mask by now. That was what marriage to Alex Mead had done for her.

To Jimmy's loving eyes there was little change from the dazzling bride of twelve years ago, gloriously blonde and blue-eyed in white satin and lace, unwittingly tormenting him with the opportunity he'd missed. But opportunities sometimes came again to a man who was patient.

'By the way,' he said, 'is there somewhere I can hide my costume so that the kids don't find it?'

He was playing Santa at Hawksmere Hospital that evening, roped in by Corinne, a member of the 'Friends of Hawksmere Hospital.'

'It means going round the wards, ho-ho-ho-ing,'

she'd said. 'And then you settle down in the grotto for the children who can walk out of the ward, or who happen to be in the hospital visiting someone.'

And Jimmy, good-natured as always, had agreed, just to please her.

'You can put it in the boot of my car,' she said now. 'I'll be leaving at five to take Bobby and Mitzi to a kids' party. When I've dropped them off I'll come back for you at six, and deliver you to the hospital by seven.'

'Yes, *sir*!' He saluted.

'Idiot!' She laughed.

'I'm paying you a compliment. You've got this organisation thing down to a fine art,' he said admiringly.

It was true; she was good at arrangements. Years of last-minute changes of plan, because Alex had been called away, had made her an expert.

'At eight o'clock,' she resumed, 'I collect the kids and take them to the hospital, where they'll find Santa already in place. They'll never dream it's you.'

'What about coming home?'

'Easy. When Bobby and Mitzi have finished I'll take them to the "Friends" office on some errand that I'll suddenly remember, while you get changed. When we leave the office we bump into you. We'll say you've been visiting a friend.'

'By the way, Alex won't mind my staying here, will he?'

'It doesn't matter if he does,' she said firmly. 'Our marriage is over in all but name, and he has no say. Besides, you and I are related.'

Which wasn't quite fair because she knew how Jimmy had always felt about her. But that was something she wasn't ready to confront just yet.

'It could be such a happy time,' she said, 'if only that phone doesn't ring. But I'll bet you anything you like that in the next few minutes Alex will call and say, "Corinne, there's been a change of plan." And I'll be expected to be "reasonable" and not "make a fuss".'

Her voice rose sharply on the last words, making her bite it back with an alarmed look at the door in case Bobby or Mitzi could hear.

'Hey, steady.' Jimmy gently took hold of her shoulders. 'That's all over, remember?'

'It's not really over.' She sighed. 'Not while Alex and I share children who can be hurt by him.'

'In the end they'll see him for what he is.'

'But that's just it. I don't want them to see him for what he is. I want them to go on believing in him as the most wonderful, glorious father there ever was, because that's what they need.'

'Just don't let *yourself* be hurt by him.'

'No, that can't happen any more.'

'I wish I believed that.'

'Believe it. I'm completely immune. Whatever was between Alex and me was over a long time ago.' She gave him a bright smile. 'Honestly.'

'*Mummy!*' came a shriek from the garden. '*Uncle Jimmy! Come and look. It's going to be a white Christmas.*'

It wasn't merely snowing; it was coming down in drifts, huge, thick snowflakes that settled and piled up. Jimmy immediately bounded out into the garden to join the children in a game. Corinne stood in the window, watching them jumping about and laughing. Dusk was falling and the only light came from the house. Through the driving snow she could only just make out the fast moving figures. They could have been anyone.

They could have been the newly-weds, blissful in their first Christmas, hurrying together through the snow to the shabby little flat that had been their first home.

And the happiest, she recalled now.

The next one had still been happy, but they had already been in their first proper house, with Alex promising her 'a palace by next year'. She hadn't wanted a palace. All she had asked was for her joy to last, but the first cracks were already appearing.

Even so, she hadn't realised yet that she had a rival, a beloved mistress called Mead Consolidated. And, as years had passed, the rival had grown all-consuming. How wearily used she had grown to the phone calls, and Alex's voice saying, 'There's been a change of plan.'

But not this year, she thought desperately. I don't mind for myself, but don't let him disappoint the children.

The phone rang.

For a moment she couldn't move. Then, in a burst of anger, she snatched up the phone, and snapped, 'Alex, is that you?'

'Yes, it's me. Look, Corinne, there's been a change of plan—'

On the last lap of the journey the snow began to come down even harder. Alex cursed and set his windscreen wipers to go fast.

It had been an awkward sort of day, with people forcing him to change course at the last moment, which he disliked. First Craddock and his mad Caribbean party, then, just as he was reaching out to call Corinne, the phone had rung.

It had been Craddock's secretary to say that her boss had been rushed to hospital with suspected appendicitis. The whole trip was off. The signing would have to be done later.

The upside was that he could call Corinne and say he would be there a day earlier.

'Alex, that's wonderful. The children will be thrilled.'

'OK, I'll be there tonight, but I'm not sure when. The traffic's difficult.'

'We're going out, but I'll leave the key in a little box in the porch. Maybe you'll be there when we get back.'

'Fine. I'll see you.'

The snow was coming down harder, and his car began to slide over the road. He slowed, but then more snow seemed to collect on his windscreen.

Why had she insisted on moving out to the very edge of London instead of staying in the mansion he'd bought her? It was a beautiful house, full of everything a wife could possibly want, but she had fled it without a backward glance.

And where had she chosen instead? A dump. A cottage. He knew he was exaggerating because it was a five-bedroom detached house, far better than where they'd lived when they were first married, but nothing compared to what he'd given her later.

It still hurt when he thought of the home he'd provided for her. The price had been extortionate, but he'd paid it willingly, thinking how thrilled Corinne would be.

It had had everything, including a paddock for the pony he intended to buy as soon as Bobby had learned to ride. Those riding lessons had been a kind of eldorado in his mind. How he would have loved them in his own childhood! And how different the reality had been!

But, for Bobby, everything would be perfect.

As always, he felt something melt inside him when he thought of his children, Mitzi, wide-eyed and appealingly cheeky. Bobby, quiet, self-assured even at nine, rapidly growing up to be a companion to his father.

And then Corinne had blown the whole dream apart. He'd come home one day to find the beautiful house empty and his family gone.

When he'd seen her again she'd talked about divorce, which he didn't understand. There was nobody else for either of them, so who needed divorce? He'd refused even to consider it.

He had thought his firmness would make her see sense and come home, but she had quietly refused to budge. She would wait out the divorce, if necessary.

She didn't actually say that the important thing was to be away from him, but the implication hung in the air.

He was nearing his destination now. He had never been there before, and darkness and snow made it hard to find the way. It was this road—no, the next!

Relieved, he swung the car into the turning and immediately saw a man crossing in front of him, moving slowly.

What happened next was too fast to follow, although later his mind replayed it in slow motion. The man saw him and began to run, and at the exact same moment he slammed on the brakes. The sudden sharp movement made the car skid over the ice that lay on the road beneath the snow.

It was the merest bad luck that the car went in the same direction as the man. Whether he, too, slithered on the ice or the car actually touched him nobody could ever be sure. But the next moment he was lying on the ground, groaning.

Alex brought the car to a cautious halt and got out. By now a woman had appeared from a house and hurried over to the victim. She was wrapped up in a thick jacket whose hood concealed everything about her head.

'Jimmy? Oh, God, Jimmy, what happened?'

'That idiot was going too fast. Hell, my shoulder!'

He winced and, clutching his neck, gasped with pain.

'Corinne, can you give me your arm?'

'Corinne?'

Alex drew back the side of the hood to her indignation.

'Hey, what are you—? Alex! Did you do this?'

'He slipped on the ice.'

'Which I wouldn't have done,' Jimmy said, 'if you hadn't been going too fast to stop.'

'I was barely doing—'

'Shut up both of you,' she said fiercely. 'This isn't the time.'

'Right. I'll call an ambulance.'

'No need,' Jimmy groaned. 'We were on our way to the hospital anyway. Corinne, let's just go. I'm sure it's only a sprain and they can patch me up before I do my stuff.'

He climbed slowly to his feet, holding on to Corinne and refusing all offers of help from Alex. But when Corinne touched his arm he yelled with pain.

'Be sensible,' said Alex, tight-lipped. 'If you don't want an ambulance I'll take you. Wait here!'

He strode off to where he'd parked. Jimmy, clinging to Corinne, gasped, 'Corinne, please, anybody's car but Alex's.'

'Fine. Mine's just here.'

In a moment she'd opened the door and eased him into the passenger seat. She was starting the engine when Alex drew up beside her.

'I said I'd take him,' he yelled.

'You don't know the way. Wait for us in the house, Alex.'

She pulled away without waiting for his answer. Muttering angrily, Alex swung around to follow her. He'd just about recognised Jimmy from their wedding. As Corinne's sole relative he had given her away, but his languishing looks had suggested that he would rather have been the groom.

Soon the main entrance of Hawksmere Hospital came into view. He followed Corinne and drew up behind her as she was opening the passenger door.

From the way Jimmy moved he was more badly hurt than had appeared at first. Alex marched ahead into the hospital and up to the reception desk, emerging a few moments later with an orderly and a wheelchair.

'He's right, Jimmy,' Corinne said. 'Let them take you in.'

Jimmy muttered something that Alex didn't catch, which made Corinne exclaim, 'To blazes with Santa Claus! It's you that matters.'

They made a little procession into the hospital, the orderly wheeling Jimmy, Corinne beside them, and Alex bringing up the rear.

Once inside, Jimmy was whisked away to an examination cubicle. Now, Alex thought, he would get the chance to talk to Corinne, but she insisted on going too. There was nothing for him to do but sit down and wait, which he found the hardest thing in the world to do.

Relief came ten minutes later with the whirlwind arrival of an elderly lady of military aspect and forthright manner.

'Where is he? I was told he'd arrived and we're waiting for him.'

'Who?' asked Alex.

'Santa Claus. Jimmy. Corinne promised he'd do it, but where is he?'

'In a cubicle, having his shoulder examined,' Alex said. 'He met with an accident.'

'Oh, dear! I do hope it isn't serious. That would be most inconvenient.'

'I dare say he'd find it inconvenient as well,' Alex said sardonically.

She whirled on him like an avenging fury.

'It's easy for you to sit there and mock, but you don't have a crowd of children who are expecting Santa to arrive with his sack and give out presents, and you've got to tell them that he isn't coming.'

Alex was saved from having to answer this by the arrival of Corinne.

'Mrs Bradon, I'm so sorry,' she said at once. 'Jimmy's got a broken collar-bone and a cracked rib. I'm afraid he can't be Santa.'

'But can't he be Santa with a broken collar-bone?' Mrs Bradon asked wildly. 'The children won't mind.'

'It's being set now. He's in a lot of pain,' Corinne explained.

'Well, they can give him something for that.'

'They *are* giving him something, and it's going to send him to sleep.'

'Oh, really! That's very tiresome!'

Alex's lips twitched. He couldn't help it. Mrs Bradon's single-mindedness would have been admirable in a boardroom, but here it was out of place.

'There must be a way around the problem,' he said.

'Like what?' Corinne confronted him, eyes flashing. 'This is your fault. You ran Jimmy down, driving like a maniac.'

'I was doing ten miles an hour, if that. He slipped on the ice. He always was a slowcoach.'

'Well, he can't be Santa, whatever the reason, and it was your car.'

The sheer injustice of this took his breath away.

'What does it matter whose car it was if I didn't hit him?'

'Jimmy says you did.'

'And I say I didn't.'

'Will you two stop making a fuss about things that don't matter?' Mrs Bradon said crossly. 'We have a crisis on our hands.'

'Surely not,' Alex said, exasperated. 'How hard can it be to play Santa? A bit of swagger, a ho-ho-ho or two—anyone can do it.'

'Fine!' said Corinne. 'You do it!'

'I didn't mean—'

'What a wonderful idea!' Mrs Bradon cut across him. 'You're about the same height so the costume will fit you. You have got it?' This was to Corinne.

'Yes, it's in the car. And you're right, the size is fine.'

'I'm sure you don't need me,' Alex said defensively. 'This is a hospital. There must be a dozen men around—'

'There are a hundred,' said Mrs Bradon firmly. 'But they are doctors, nurses, ward orderlies. Which one of them do you suggest should be taken off his duties to save you from having to do *your* duty?'

'It's hardly my—'

'You deprived us of our Santa Claus,' said Mrs Bradon implacably. 'It's your job to take his place!'

'Look, ladies—'

Alex met Corinne's eyes, seeking her support. But she was looking at him angrily.

'After all,' she echoed him, 'how hard can it be? A bit of swagger and a ho-ho-ho or two.'

'All right, all right,' he snapped.

'Splendid!' Mrs Bradon hooted triumphantly. 'You'd better get to work right away. Corinne will show you what to do. Hurry up!'

She bustled away.

'You're finding this very funny, aren't you?' Alex growled.

'It has its moments. When was the last time someone spoke to you like that without you flattening them in return?'

'I can't remember,' he admitted.

'I'll get the costume and you can get to work.'

'Corinne, wait.' He detained her with a hand on her arm. 'Must I really do this? Surely—'

'Aha! Backing out!' She began to cluck like a hen.

'I am not chicken,' he said furiously.

'Sez who?' she jeered. 'You're just afraid you're not up to it. That's the first time I've heard you admit that there is something you can't do better than the next man.'

'I didn't mean that.'

'No, you meant that it's beneath you.'

'I just think that there has to be another way.'

'Of course there is. All you have to do is find a replacement who can do this in exactly ten minutes' time.'

He ground his teeth.

'All right. Get the costume and let's get this over with.'

'I'd rather you came out to the car with me. I don't want to let you out of my sight.'

'Dammit, Corinne!' Alex said furiously. 'Why must you overreact to everything? I've said I'll do it, and I'll do it. After all, how hard can it be?'

She fetched the costume and took him into a small kitchen where Jimmy had planned to change. As Alex dressed she explained his duties.

'You have to go around both the children's wards with your sack, giving out presents.'

'How will I know who to give what?'

'Leave that to me. I'll be there. I'll tell you who everyone is and hand you the right present. After that you go and sit by the big tree in the hall and you'll get some children who are in here visiting people. Then I'll have to leave you for a few minutes to collect Bobby and Mitzi.'

'Did you tell them I called? That I was coming a day early?'

'No, I thought I'd let it come as a nice surprise when you turned up.'

'You mean you thought I'd let you down?' he asked wryly.

'Well, if I did I was wrong,' she conceded. 'Maybe I've done you an injustice. When I heard your voice I thought you were going to cry off again. But you didn't, and that's wonderful. It'll be the best Christmas ever.'

Remembering how close he'd come to cancelling, he had the grace to feel awkward and was glad that fiddling with his beard gave him an excuse not to look at her.

'Here,' she said, laughing. 'Let me fix that.'

'There's an awful lot of stuff to put on,' Alex said. 'I thought it would just be a white thing with hooks over the ears.'

'Well, there are hooks, but there's also glue so that it fits your mouth and stays in place. Jimmy believes in doing things properly. He got this from a theatrical costumier, and he chose the best.'

'Jimmy?'

'Jimmy is spending Christmas with us—or he was before he was knocked down by some maniac driver.'

'I did not knock him down,' Alex said through gritted teeth. 'He fell.'

'Whatever. He chose the costume, and it's a good one.'

Alex had to admit that it was the best. The beard was soft and silky, gleaming white, with a huge moustache that flowed down into the beard itself. When it was fixed in place it covered his mouth almost completely.

But there was something else.

'A wig?' he protested.

'Of course. How can you be convincing with a white beard and brown hair?'

'Won't my hair be covered by a hood?'

'Even with a hood they'd notice. Children notice everything these days. They see wonderful special effects on films and television, and when they get close up to reality they expect it to be just as convincing.'

He grumbled some more, but when the wig was on he had to admit that it looked impressive. Long, thick and flowing, it streamed down over his shoulders, mingling with the beard, which was also long and flowing.

He looked nothing like himself, and that was some consolation, he reflected. At least nobody would be able to identify him.

He was beginning to get into the part now, driven by the instinct that governed his life—to be the best at whatever he undertook.

If you weren't the best there was no point in doing it. Right?

In some respects he had the physique, being over six foot. But there was one flaw.

'I'm too thin,' he objected. 'This suit was made for someone a lot bigger.'

'There's some padding,' Corinne said, diving back into the bag.

With the padding in place he had a satisfactory paunch.

'Will I do?' he demanded.

'Your cheeks need to be rosier.'

'Get off! What are you doing?'

'Just a little red to make you convincing.'

'I won't even ask what you've just put on my face.' He groaned. 'I don't want to know.'

'You look great. Completely convincing. Now, let's have a ho-ho-ho!'

'Ho-ho-ho!' he intoned.

'No, you need to be more full and rounded. Try it again, and make it boom this time.'

'*Ho-ho-ho!*'

To her surprise, he made a good job of it.

'Well done,' she said. 'That was really convincing.'

'You thought I couldn't be?'

'Jimmy never manages it that way. He tries but it comes out sounding reedy.'

'What about my eyebrows?' Alex asked. 'Are they white enough?'

He was right. His dark brown eyebrows now looked odd against the gleaming white hair and whiskers.

'There aren't any false eyebrows,' she said, inspecting the bag. 'You'll have to go as you are.'

'No way. We'll do this properly. This is a kitchen, right? Won't there be some flour?'

'The kitchen's just for making tea,' Corinne objected, opening cupboard doors.

But, against all odds, she found a small bag of flour with some left inside.

'Fancy you thinking of that,' she said, rubbing it into his eyebrows until the natural colour faded.

'When I was a kid I wanted to be an actor,' he said.

'You never told me that before.'

'I was never trapped under half a ton of gum and whiskers before.'

She stood back and regarded him.

'You look great,' she said. 'Here's your sack of toys, all labelled. Are you ready?'

'Let's go!'

CHAPTER TWO

ELEPHANT WARD had been designed and decorated for children. Streams of cheerful-looking cartoon elephants walked around the walls and played games with their trunks.

Alex stood in the doorway and boomed, '*Ho-ho-ho!*' to an accompaniment of shrieks from the rows of beds. When it quietened, Corinne murmured, 'First bed on the right, Tommy Arkright, broken pelvis. Fascinated by ghosts.'

Whoever had planned this had done it well, Alex realised as soon as he began talking to Tommy. The name, the ailment and the interest were all accurate, and when Tommy unwrapped his gift, which turned out to be a book of ghost stories, it was a triumphant moment.

It was the same with the next child, and the next. From being self-conscious, Alex began to relax, and even to enjoy himself. In part this was due to the knowledge that he was unrecognisable. Not that people here would have known him anyway, but the total anonymity still made him feel easier.

He was in a good temper when he came to the end of the ward and turned in the doorway for a final wave and a cry of, 'Goodbye, everyone.'

'*Goodbye, Santa!*' came the answering roar.

'I'll say this for that Bradon woman,' he growled as they headed down the corridor towards Butterfly Ward. 'She prepared the ground properly.'

'What do you mean?'

'Every detail was right. Good preparation is the secret.'

'I agree. But why do you give the credit to her?'

'Didn't she organise all this?'

'No, *I* did, you rotten so-and-so,' she said indignantly. 'I personally went round every child, asking questions, trying not to be too obvious about it.'

'You?' His surprise was unflattering but she told herself she was past being bothered by him now.

'Yes, me,' she said lightly. 'Feather-brained Corinne who can just about manage a shopping list, remember? I prepared the ground, gathered intelligence, surveyed the prospects—er—' She clutched her forehead, trying to think of other businesslike expressions.

'Appraised the situation?' He helped her out. 'You did a great job.'

'So did you.'

'Much to your amazement,' he said with a grin that she could just detect behind the beard.

'You see over there—' she said, not answering directly '—the Christmas tree in the corner?'

'Yes.'

'When you've finished on Butterfly Ward that's

where you go and sit. I'm off to collect Bobby and Mitzi, and I'll be back as soon as possible.'

'Are you going to tell them it's me?'

'No, I think it will be nicer not to. Let's see if they guess.'

'Of course they'll guess. I'm their father.'

She did not reply.

On Butterfly Ward it was the same as before, except that now he was full of confidence and performed his part with a touch of swagger that went down well.

Corinne stayed long enough to see him settle in before leaning down to murmur, 'I'm off now. Back soon.'

It was only a few minutes' drive to the house where the party was being held. Bobby and Mitzi piled into the car, wearing party hats, clutching gifts and giggling.

'No need to ask if you had a good time,' Corinne said.

'And now we're going to see Father Christmas,' Mitzi yelled gleefully.

Bobby touched Corinne's arm and spoke quietly. 'Is Daddy still coming?'

'Yes, darling, he's still coming.'

'He didn't cancel while we were at the party?'

'No, he didn't.'

He searched her face.

'Are you *sure*?'

Until then Corinne had been feeling in charity with Alex, but at the sight of Bobby's painful anxiety she discovered that she could hate him again. No man had the right to do that to a child, to destroy his sense of security in his parents, so that every moment of happiness had to be checked and rechecked to discover the catch.

'Darling, I give you my word. Daddy has not cancelled and he isn't going to.'

He settled into the car, apparently satisfied.

'By the way—' she said as she drove to the hospital '—Uncle Jimmy had an accident. He fell over on the icy road and broke his collar-bone.'

They were loud in their cries of dismay.

'Will Uncle Jimmy be in hospital for Christmas?' Bobby asked.

'I don't know. They're putting him in plaster now. When I've delivered you to Santa I'll go up to see him.'

At the hospital she took them straight to where Alex should be sitting by the tree, only half expecting him to be there.

But of course he was there! Alex had run his pride up this flagpole and it was really no surprise that he was doing well. He had one child on his knee and another standing beside him, while their mother looked on, smiling. There were three others waiting.

Corinne inched forward carefully, keeping her

eyes on Bobby and Mitzi, waiting for the moment of recognition.

It didn't come.

Of course it was the beard and hair, she realised. The disguise was magnificent. It would be different when they were closer.

At that moment Alex looked up. His eyes went first to Corinne, then to the children, then back to Corinne, while his eyebrows signalled a question. Almost imperceptibly she shook her head.

She took them to the end of the little queue, said something to them and walked away.

Alex was glad that he'd bothered to dress up properly when he heard one child mutter, just audibly, 'He looks like a real Santa, Mummy.'

At last his own two children stood before him, Mitzi keeping back a little. It was weeks since he'd seen her, and he'd forgotten how fast children grew. Her hair, which had been short, was now long enough to wear in bunches which stood out from her head, giving her the appearance of a cheeky elf. He couldn't help grinning at the picture she presented.

But right now she was solemn and seemed unwilling to come forward.

'Go on,' Bobby urged her.

But she shook her head.

'She's a bit shy,' Bobby confided to Santa.

'But I'm—' He checked himself, and amended

the words to, 'But I'm Santa Claus. Nobody is shy of me.'

He waited for one of them to say, Daddy! But neither of them did.

Of course, he thought. They were pretending not to know, enjoying the joke.

He leaned down to Mitzi. 'Aren't you going to tell me what you want for Christmas?' Big mistake. Mitzi was surveying him, wide-eyed with astonishment.

'But I already told you. I put it in my letter. Didn't you get it?'

'Of course I did,' he improvised hastily.

Over her head his frantic eyes met Bobby's. The boy mouthed 'Marianne doll set.'

Since he'd never heard of this, Alex had to signal bafflement with his eyebrows. Bobby mouthed it again, more emphatically, and this time Alex understood. 'Ah, now I remember. You want a Marianne doll set,' he echoed, and saw his daughter's eyes light up.

'The one in the riding habit,' his son mouthed at him.

'The one in the riding habit,' Alex repeated.

Mitzi's beaming smile told him he'd got it right.

'But is that all?' he asked. 'Isn't there anything else you've thought of since?'

Mitzi hesitated until her brother nudged her gently and whispered, 'Go on.'

Emboldened, the little girl reached up to say, 'And can I have a necklace?'

'Of course you can,' Alex said.

Suddenly the little girl hugged him. He tensed, thinking of the beard that might be dislodged. But it held, and he became aware of her arms, holding him without restraint.

She had hugged him before, but not like that. Now he knew what he had always sensed in her embraces. It had been caution. And it wasn't there now.

Before he had time to take in the implications, she had released him and moved aside, making room for her brother, who came in close.

But before addressing Santa he wagged a finger at his sister.

'Don't wander off,' he told her severely.

She stuck out her tongue.

'Does she give you much trouble?' Alex asked with a grin.

'She's OK most of the time,' Bobby said seriously. 'But sometimes she won't do as I say 'cos I'm not very much older than her.'

It was a three-year difference, but a sudden inspiration made Alex say, 'About five years?'

Bobby looked pleased. 'Not quite as much as that,' he admitted. 'But almost. And it's a great responsibility being the man of the family.'

'The man of—? Don't you have a father?'

Bobby made a face. 'Sort of.'

Alex felt an uneasy stillness settle over him.

'What do you mean, sort of?'

'Well, I don't really know him very well,' Bobby said. 'He's not around much.'

'I expect he's busy,' Alex said.

'Oh, yes, he's always very busy. Too busy for us. He and Mummy aren't together any more.'

'Do you know why that is?' Alex asked carefully.

Bobby gave a shrug.

'They were always rowing, and Mummy cried a lot.'

A strange feeling went through Alex. Corinne had never let him see her cry. Not for a long time.

'Did she tell you why she cried?' he asked.

Bobby shook his head.

'She doesn't know I've seen her and I have to pretend not to, because she doesn't like anyone to know.'

'So you don't know why?'

Bobby shook his head.

'Perhaps she misses your dad?' Alex ventured.

'I don't think so. He's nasty to her.'

'How?' Alex asked, a touch more sharply than he'd meant to.

'I don't know, but when they talk on the phone she cries after she's hung up. But he doesn't *mean* to be nasty,' Bobby added quickly. 'He just doesn't know how people feel about things.'

Alex hesitated for a while before saying, 'So maybe it's better that they're not together?'

'Oh, no,' Bobby said, shaking his head vigorously. 'He's coming home for Christmas and it's going to be brilliant—that is—if he really comes.'

'Has he said he will?'

'Yes, but—' Bobby's shrug was more eloquent than a thousand words.

Alex could not speak. There were too many thoughts swirling around in his head, and they were all of the kind he found hard to cope with. The best he could manage was to put his arm around Bobby's shoulders and squeeze.

'You think he'll back out?' he asked at last.

'I keep telling myself he'll be there,' Bobby said. 'It isn't for long. Just Christmas Eve until Christmas Day. He could spare us that, couldn't he?'

'I should think he could spare you more than that,' Alex managed to say in a voice that he hoped didn't shake too much.

'Could you fix it?' Bobby asked.

'You want me to arrange for him to stick around for longer than that?'

'Oh, no,' Bobby disclaimed quickly, as though saying that nobody should ask for the impossible. 'Just make sure he's there for when he said he'd be.'

'All right. It's a promise.'

Bobby searched his face anxiously. 'You really mean it?'

'You think I can't do it?'

Bobby shook his head, his eyes fixed on Santa with a look in them that was almost fierce.

'You can do anything,' he said, 'if you really want to.'

The air seemed to be singing in Alex's ears. He wondered if he'd imagined the emphasis in the last words.

'Then I promise,' he said.

'Honestly? Dad will be here until Christmas Day, and he won't leave early?'

Alex was swept by a mood of recklessness. 'I can do better than that,' he said. 'He'll arrive early, and he'll stay longer than Christmas Day.'

He waited for the effusion of joy. It did not come. If anything, the fierce scrutiny on the child's face intensified.

'Really and truly?' he asked. 'Cut your throat and hope to die?'

'Of course. When I give my word, I keep it.'

'That's what *he* says,' insisted Bobby. And suddenly it was a child's voice again, forlorn and almost on the edge of tears.

Alex put his hands on both Bobby's shoulders.

'He will be there tonight,' he said. 'You have my solemn promise. Word of a Santa!'

Bobby nodded, as though satisfied.

'Now,' Alex said, 'tell me what you want for Christmas.'

'But I just did,' Bobby said.

'That's it? Nothing else?'

'That's the thing that matters. And you said I could have it. You promised.'

'Yes, I did. So you just go on home and see what happens.'

Bobby smiled, and for the first time it was the happy, natural smile of a child. It made Alex feel as though he had been punched in the stomach.

'All right, you two?' It was Corinne, appearing suddenly. 'Move along. Father Christmas still has customers.'

Another three children had joined the little queue, and Bobby and Mitzi moved off to join their mother.

'How's Uncle Jimmy?' Bobby asked. 'Can he come home?'

'We might get him home tomorrow. We'll have to wait and see. Come on, let's be off home. Goodbye, Santa.'

'Goodbye, Santa,' they chorused.

Alex raised a hand in a gesture of farewell and turned back to his next 'customer' with reluctance.

He wasn't sure how he got through the next few minutes. His mind followed Corinne and the children out of the hospital and into her car, watching them talking, wondering what they were saying.

At last it was over and he was free to go. To his

relief, Mrs Bradon joined him in the kitchen just as he finished changing. He would not have thought it possible that he could have been glad to see her.

'What about the costume?' he asked.

'Just take it with you. Corinne will know what to do with it.'

He packed up the costume into its bag and tossed it into the back of his car. On the journey, he wondered how much Corinne would have told the children after they left.

When he reached the house he intended to go straight in. Instead, he found himself sitting in the silent car, trying to psyche himself into taking the next step.

It should be his great moment. He would burst through the front door, keeping Santa's promise and enjoying the look on his children's faces.

Without warning, his courage failed. He didn't know why. His son had spoken like a child who loved his father and looked forward to seeing him. Yet he had said, 'It isn't for long, just Christmas Eve until Christmas Day. He could spare us that, couldn't he?'

Something about those words haunted Alex painfully.

He could spare us that, couldn't he?

Was that how Bobby saw his father? Doling out his time in small, begrudged amounts?

He did not want to go inside the house.

Cowardice. The weakness he had always despised most.

With sudden decision, he got out of the car. In the porch he hunted for the key that Corinne had left out for him, hearing sounds inside the house. There was her voice.

'Bobby, what are you doing in the hall?'

'Nothing, Mummy.'

'Come and have an iced bun.' That was Mitzi, a little more distant, sounding as if her mouth was full.

'In a minute,' Bobby replied. His voice still came from the hall.

Then Corinne's voice.

'Darling, why are you watching the front door?'

Suddenly, as though a spotlight had come on inside him, he saw his son's face, staring at the front door with painful intensity, not daring to believe.

He didn't know where that light had come from, except that it had something to do with his talk with Bobby. It lit all the world from a new angle, showing what had always been there, but which he'd never noticed.

He turned the key.

'Daddy!'

The ear-splitting shriek came from Mitzi. Corinne was standing by the kitchen door, watching his arrival with pleasure. Only Bobby did not react. He stood completely still, his face a mask of total and utter disbelief.

Alex wanted to cry out, But I promised you. You knew I was coming. Instead, he concentrated on hugging his daughter, who was almost strangling him with the exuberance of her embrace.

'Hello, darling,' he said.

'Daddy, Daddy,' she carolled.

'Hey, don't choke me,' he said, laughing. 'How's my girl?'

She gave him a smacking kiss, which he returned. Then it was time to face his son.

Bobby was strangely pale. 'Hello, Daddy,' he said.

'Hello, son.'

To his dismay, Bobby held out his hand politely, almost as though meeting a stranger. Or a ghost.

'Hello, Daddy.'

Then he broke suddenly, as belief came rushing through, and flung himself against his father, burying his face against him.

Alex's arms closed protectively about his son as he felt the storm of emotion go through the child. He didn't know what to do except stay as he was, trying to understand but feeling helpless.

Looking up, he found Corinne's eyes on him. Her expression was gentle but he had the feeling that she was conveying a warning.

Bobby drew back to look at his father. His face bore the marks of tears, which he rubbed aside hastily. Alex brushed some of them away with his own fingertips.

'It's all right, son,' he said quietly. 'I'm home.'

Bobby sniffed. 'Hello, Daddy.'

'Hey, is that any way to greet your old man? Crying? Shall I go away again?'

It was a feeble joke and a badly misjudged one. Bobby clung to him, his eyes full of sudden dread, and Alex drew in his breath. He was floundering badly.

'You're not getting rid of me that easily,' he backtracked, saying anything that came into his head. 'I'm here now and I'm staying. You've got me for Christmas, whether you like it or not.'

Mitzi began hopping about, yelling, 'Yippee, Yippee!' Bobby, the thoughtful one, smiled.

'Come on, kids,' said Corinne. 'Let Daddy come in and get his breath back.'

Alex straightened up and kissed her cheek. Corinne did the same, smiling to present a show of cordiality for the children.

'You said you weren't coming until tomorrow,' Mitzi reminded him.

'Well, I got away early and thought it would be nice to see a bit more of you.' He tweaked her hair. 'You don't mind, do you?'

She shook her head ecstatically and pointed to the centre of her mouth. 'I lost a tooth,' she informed him proudly.

He studied the gap with great interest. 'That's very impressive. When did that happen?'

'Last week,' she said.

'I'm sorry I missed that.'

'I saved it for you,' she reassured him.

'Then I'll look forward to seeing it,' he said gamely.

Mitzi promptly pulled it out of her pocket. Alex heard Corinne give a soft choke of laughter.

'How about selling it to me?' he said. 'I'll bid you a pound.'

Mitzi made a face.

'One pound fifty?'

She finally got him up to two pounds and the deal was struck. Mitzi pocketed her profit and went off to explain to Bobby how to do business.

'A chip off the old block,' Corinne said when Alex joined her in the kitchen.

'Better,' he agreed. 'At her age I'd have settled for fifty pence.'

'Ah, but don't forget inflation,' she said, teasing. 'I'll say this for you—you coped very well with that tooth. I thought it was going to faze you.'

'Nothing fazes me,' he insisted. Then he looked at the tooth in his hand. 'What am I supposed to do with this?'

'Treasure it.' She laughed. 'You just paid a high price for it. I expect you're ready for something to eat.'

'I don't know when I last ate,' he admitted.

'I do,' she said, giving him a friendly smile. 'Breakfast was a cup of black coffee. You meant to catch up at lunchtime, but you were caught between meetings so you made do with a sandwich.'

'Am I that predictable?'

'Yes.'

'I had a roll in the car on my way here.'

'Oh, well, then. You don't need the steak I got for you.'

Suddenly he was ravenous. 'Just try me.'

She poured him some tea, very strong and heavily sugared, as he liked it, and he wandered into the next room. Like the rest of the house, it was decorated with paper chains and tinsel.

It was an old house, full of a kind of shambling charm. The original fireplace was still there, although only a vase of artificial flowers adorned it now, and, out of sight, the chimney was blocked to keep out draughts.

Beside it stood the tree. It was smaller and less impressive than the one in his office, and the fairy on the top looked wonky, as though she were clinging on for dear life. But the parcels around the base were all addressed to people and, when picked up, rattled reassuringly.

Alex stood looking at it and suddenly the inner light shone again, showing him that this was a real tree, with real presents, for real people.

He looked at some of the labels. There were gifts from Corinne to the children and from them to her, gifts from Jimmy to all of them, and from them to him. It occurred to him how often Jimmy's name appeared.

'Time for bed, kids,' Corinne called. 'There's lots to do tomorrow.'

'I want Daddy to put me to bed,' Mitzi said at once.

'All right,' Alex said. To Bobby he added, 'What do you want?'

'I put myself to bed,' the child said gruffly. 'But you can look in, if you want.'

'Fine.'

His daughter bounded all over him and rode on his back down the hall to her bedroom, which turned out to be a shrine to horses. Horse pictures adorned the walls; horses leapt all over her duvet cover. Her slippers were shaped like horses and picture books about horses filled her shelves.

Alex spoke without thinking. 'Now I understand.'

He meant the Marianne doll in the riding habit that she had mentioned to Santa earlier. With his little girl's eyes on him he remembered, too late, that he was supposed to know nothing.

'Now I understand what you've been doing recently,' he improvised. 'We'll have lots to talk about tomorrow. Goodnight, pet.'

He kissed her and departed hastily before he could make any more slips.

Bobby's bedroom was curiously unrevealing. There were no pictures on the wall, or books, beyond a few school books. Alex flicked through one of these.

'Good marks,' he observed. 'You're working hard, then?'

Bobby nodded.

'That's good. Good.' He was floundering. 'Are you all right, son? All right here, I mean?'

'Yes, it's nice.'

'Don't you miss your old home?'

Bobby hunted for the right words. 'Places don't really matter.'

'No. People matter. Right?'

'Right.'

'Well, I'm here now.'

'Yes.'

Alex searched his face. 'You are glad, aren't you?'

'Yes, of course I am.'

He would have doubted it if it hadn't been for their memory of the earlier conversation. How could all that have gone?

Because now he knows it's me.

'Tomorrow's a big day,' he said cheerfully.

'Yes.'

It was becoming a disaster. He had resolved to

act on what he'd learned from Bobby that evening,
and use it to make this visit a triumph. That was the
secret of success—good intelligence and knowing
how to use it. But all his gains were slipping away.

'Daddy—'

'What is it?' His voice betrayed his eagerness.

'Tomorrow, will you ask Mitzi about the school
play? She was ever so good in it.'

The school play? The school play? His mind fran-
tically tried to grapple with this. When had it been?
Why hadn't he known?

'It was a pantomime—' Bobby said, reading his
face without trouble '—and Mitzi was an elf. She
had two lines.'

'Er—?'

'It was last week. You were abroad.'

'Of course—yes—otherwise I'd have—'

'Yeah, sure. You will remember to ask her, won't
you?'

'Of course I will. Goodnight, son.'

Corinne said her goodnights after him. As they
passed in the corridor she said, 'I've put you in that
room at the end. Your things are in there.'

He looked in before going downstairs. It was a
small, neat room with a narrow bed.

Alex thought about the other rooms. Presumably
Corinne had the big room on the corner of the house,
but where, he wondered, had she put Jimmy?

CHAPTER THREE

HE CAME down the stairs so quietly that Corinne didn't hear him, and he had a moment to stand watching her as she worked in the kitchen.

The steak smelled good, and suddenly he was transported back to the early days of their marriage, when steak had been a luxury. But somehow she had managed to wring the price out of the meagre housekeeping money they had.

They had been partners—laughing at poverty, competing with each other in loving generosity, squabbling to give each other the last titbit. But that was long ago.

The years had barely touched her, he thought. The slim, graceful figure that had once enchanted him was the same, two children later.

She had been gorgeous at eighteen—beautiful, sexy, witty, knowing her own power over young men and enjoying it. They had all competed for her, but Alex had made sure that he was the one who won her.

Her face had changed little, except that it was thinner, and the ready laughter no longer sprang to her eyes. They were still large, beautiful eyes but there was a sad caution there now.

'It's ready,' she called, seeing him.

Like every meal she had ever cooked him it was excellent—the wine perfectly chosen, the salad exactly as it should be.

Their last meeting had been three months ago, and it had ended in a fierce quarrel. Since then there had been communication between lawyers, and the odd phone call that had left each of them resolved that it should be the last. Her invitation for Christmas had been delivered through a letter addressed to his office.

'Thank you for letting me come,' he said quietly.

'I didn't think you would. I was amazed that you actually turned up early. What happened? Did something more important fall through?'

He winced.

'I'm sorry,' she said at once. 'I didn't mean it like that.'

'There's nothing more important than being with my family,' he said emphatically.

'It means the world to the children.'

'What about you, Corinne?'

'Never mind about me. This is their time.'

'But I do mind about you. It's ours too, isn't it?'

'Well, it's a chance for us to be civilized with each other. We haven't done much of that lately.'

'And that's all?'

'Yes, that's all. I'm not your wife any more—'

'The hell you aren't!' he said with the swift anger

that sometimes overtook him these days. 'We're not divorced yet, and maybe we never will be.'

She regarded him with a quizzical air that was new to him. 'You have to win every negotiation, don't you? But you won't win this one, Alex. So why don't we just leave it there? I don't want to spoil this holiday.'

'Is there someone else?'

The question jerked out of him abruptly, without finesse, tact or subtlety.

She sat silent.

'Tell me,' he insisted.

'No, there's nobody else. I don't want anyone else. That's not why I left you.'

'Just to get away from me, huh?'

'If you care to put it that way—yes. But why must we put it that way or any way? It's Christmas, Alex. Let it go.'

'All right,' he said hastily.

As she set coffee before him she said, 'How about you?'

'I beg your pardon?'

'Do *you* have someone else?'

'Do you care?' he growled.

'If you can ask, so can I,' she said lightly.

'Except that you broke up this marriage. That hardly gives you a stake in the answer.'

She shrugged. 'You're right. Do you want a drop of brandy in that?'

'Thanks.'

As she was pouring the brandy he said, 'The answer's no.'

She didn't answer directly, but she took his cup and carried it and her own into the next room, where the tree glowed.

'Sit down and relax,' she said. 'You look dead on your feet.'

He leaned back in an armchair, closing his eyes, desperately tired in a way that had nothing to do with work. Mercifully he felt the strain begin to drain away, leaving him as close to being relaxed as he ever came.

'How did it go after I left the hospital?' Corinne asked. 'Did the children recognise you?'

'No,' he said slowly. 'At least, they didn't show it if they did.'

'Mitzi would have shown it,' Corinne said at once. 'She's got no subtlety, that little one. Her riding instructor says she has no nerves, but lots of nerve.'

'Riding instructor?' Alex queried. 'She's learning to ride too?'

Corinne shook her head. 'Just her. Bobby gave it up.'

'Don't tell me he was afraid?' Alex said sharply.

'No, not afraid. Bored. It just didn't interest him, and there are other things he wants to do. But Mitzi is crazy about horses, so she does it instead.'

He was silent, swallowing his disappointment. Corinne eyed him sympathetically.

'Come out of the nineteenth century,' she chided.

'What do you mean by that?'

'In those days you could have told Bobby what he had to be interested in, but not now. He doesn't have to ride a horse just because you wanted to and couldn't.'

Alex's father had mucked out stables for a racehorse trainer. Alex had grown up surrounded by beautiful animals, none of which he had been allowed to touch.

'And it has to be your son who carries on your dream, doesn't it?' Corinne pursued. 'Somehow a daughter isn't the same. Pure nineteenth century.'

'That's nonsense,' he growled.

'No, it isn't. It's the way your mind works. But you ought to go and see Mitzi ride, see how good she is.'

'All right, I will.'

'You'd be proud of Mitzi. She's a real natural. In fact, I think you ought to learn yourself.'

'Me? Take riding lessons?'

'Why not? You used to tell me how it was your dream when you were a boy. What's the point of making all that money if you don't spend some of it making your dreams come true?'

It flashed across his mind that he was too busy earning it to enjoy spending it, but all he said was,

'Sure, and let my six-year-old daughter make rings round me!'

'Well, she's bound to at first, because she's had some practice and you're just a beginner,' Corinne said, 'but I'm sure she'd make allowances for you.'

He gave a reluctant grin at her teasing. Suddenly he remembered, 'She says she wants a Marianne doll set, the one in the riding suit. What's she talking about?'

'"Marianne" is the latest craze. It's a doll that comes with its own lifestyle—ballgown, ballet tutu, riding habit.'

'Where do I get one?'

To his bewilderment Corinne rocked with laughter.

'You don't think I left it to the last minute, do you? It's Christmas Eve tomorrow. People have been trampling each other to death in toy shops for the last two months. Don't worry, I've got one tucked safely away. You can give it to her, if you like.'

'Do you think I haven't bought her a present?'

'No, I think you've probably got her something very expensive. But what she wants is that doll, and if you give it to her you'll be her hero.'

'Thanks,' he said gruffly. 'I'd like that. And she also wants a necklace.'

'I've got that too,' she assured him.

'Like I said earlier, you're really well organised. I could do with a few like you in the firm.'

'Funny, Jimmy says the same.' Corinne laughed. 'Only he says they need me in the army. It makes me wonder how the country has muddled along without me for so long.'

Alex scowled. He didn't want to talk, or even think, about Jimmy.

'Anyway, Mitzi's easy to understand,' Corinne went on. 'Bobby is more complicated, and it's much harder to know what he's thinking. Did he recognise you?'

'I don't know,' Alex said slowly. 'I honestly don't know. He didn't say anything, but—Corinne he was just a few inches away from me. Surely he *must* have recognised his own father?'

'It was a very complete disguise,' she reminded him. 'The wig and the hair and the padding. And he wasn't expecting you to arrive today.'

The words, And he hasn't seen you for weeks, hung in the air.

'Did he tell you what he wanted?' Corinne asked. 'I think I've got that covered too, but I'd be glad of any "insider tips" you picked up.'

Oh sure, he thought, *my son said he wanted me home for Christmas, like it was an impossible fantasy. He reckons he has a 'sort of' father, and he's bracing himself for when I let him down.*

'Hey, there!' Corinne was waving. 'Anybody home?'

'Sorry!' he said, forcing himself to smile. 'No, I didn't get any inside information. You'll have to tell me. What's his big interest?'

'Drawing, painting—anything to do with art.'

'Doesn't he like soccer or any sports?'

'He watches them on television, but his interests are the quiet ones.'

'Corinne, are you sure? He's never said anything about drawing to me.'

'Of course not. He knows you wouldn't like it. But he's passionate about drawing and painting since he discovered that he has a talent for it. He's just getting deep into water-colours now, and if you gave him something connected with that he'd be thrilled. But I'll bet you've bought him a pair of riding boots.'

'Among other things,' Alex growled. 'I suppose you don't want me to give them to him?'

'That's up to you.'

'Sure!' he snapped. 'Like I'm going to dig my own grave by giving him something he doesn't want, thus proving I'm the useless father that you claim! You'd like that, wouldn't you?'

Once in a blue moon Corinne lost her temper. She did so now—big time!

'Don't be *stupid,* Alex! I know it's hard, but try not to be laughably, moronically stupid. If that's what I wanted I wouldn't be warning you now, would I?'

'No,' he said hastily. 'Sorry. I didn't—I just fly off the handle sometimes. I don't mean to. I shouldn't have said it.'

'It doesn't matter. It's the children who matter. Just try to see Bobby as he is, and not as "Alex Mead's son." How I've come to hate "Alex Mead's son"!'

'What the devil do you mean by that?'

'He's a character who's hung around our home ever since Bobby was born. He has plenty of "boy's interests." He likes the "manly" sports and anything that involves getting dirty. He's got no time for art or music or thinking, and he's the opposite to Bobby.

'That boy has spent his life so far pretending to care for things that bore him rigid because that was the only way to get your attention. He knew ages ago that he didn't fit the picture of your ideal son. In fact, the only person I know who does fit it is Mitzi.'

He was silent, too shocked to speak.

At last she got up and brought him another brandy.

'Thanks. I need it.'

When he'd revived his courage a little he managed to ask, 'If I'm so hateful why does he bother to pretend?'

'Because he *adores* you,' Corinne said. 'He worships you. He'd go through fire and water for you. Haven't you got that through your thick skull yet?'

She broke off and gave a sigh of frustration. 'We're quarrelling again.'

'Yeah, well—' He shrugged, sharing her frustration.

He was saved from needing to say any more by the sound of his cellphone coming from the hall. He answered it with relief.

It was Mark Dunsford, his assistant, as zealous about business as he was himself. Mark was jealous of Kath, who had been with Alex longer and had his total trust. He tried to compensate by giving himself to the job, body and soul, twenty-four hours a day, and making sure that his employer knew it.

'I just wondered if you had any final instructions for me,' he said now.

'No way. It's Christmas. Get off home to your family.'

'I don't have a family.'

'Well, get off home, anyway. Or wherever you get off to.'

'Wherever I am, I'll be keeping an eye on things. I thought that you would be, too.'

'Mark, lighten up. It's Christmas. There's nothing to keep an eye on.'

'All right, but perhaps you'd better give me a contact number where you are. I know I can call the cellphone, but another number is always useful.'

He hesitated. Nothing was likely to happen, but it was as well to be prepared.

'OK. The phone number of this house is—'

He stopped. Corinne had wandered out into the hall and was looking at him, her head on one side.

'No,' he said. 'This is a private number. I can't give it out and I'd rather you didn't contact me at all. In an emergency, use the cellphone, but it had better be life or death or there'll be trouble. I'll call you when I'm ready.'

'But—'

'Goodbye, Mark.'

He hung up and looked at Corinne with a touch of defiance.

'Thank you,' she said warmly.

He put out his hand and she took it between both of hers. 'I'm glad you came,' she said. 'It's going to be a great Christmas.'

Her eyes were as warm as her voice and he tightened his hand. But the next moment she stepped back, smiling and saying, 'It's time for bed. I'll see you in the morning. Goodnight.'

Next morning the snow lay thick on the ground as they had Christmas Eve breakfast.

'Are we going to see Uncle Jimmy?' Mitzi asked.

'No need,' Corinne said. 'I've already called the

hospital and he can come home. I'm going to fetch him later. You three can go shopping.'

The children cheered, but a few minutes later Alex took her aside.

'It's a bit soon for him to be leaving hospital, isn't it?'

'Hospitals don't encourage people to stay over Christmas, and it's only a collar-bone. I can look after him here. Jimmy's been kind to me.'

She saw him scowl and said firmly, 'Alex, I am not leaving him to spend Christmas in hospital. Besides, you'll be the gainer.'

'How?'

'I'll be spending a lot of time with Jimmy, leaving you with the children. So, you make the most of it.'

For a man who wanted to be with his children it was a good bargain. But 'I'll be spending a lot of time with Jimmy' had a melancholy sound.

Alex became aware that Bobby was signalling to him, and remembered.

'So, tell me how the school play went,' he said, tweaking Mitzi's hair. 'I want to know all about it.'

She produced her photo album so fast that it was clear she'd had it ready, and they began turning the pages together. There she was in a green hat and green costume with bells, giving the world her wide, gap-toothed grin.

Alex gave her an answering grin, but it was too

late to smile back at her. It was only a week ago but that mischievous imp was already gone for ever.

Along with many other things.

After that he made a good job of it, showing an enthusiasm that Mitzi, the unsubtle, accepted at face value. When she'd gone away happy he met Bobby's eyes, silently asking the child if he'd done all right. And his nine-year-old son nodded in approval.

They split into two parties. Corinne headed for the hospital, while Mitzi and Bobby piled into Alex's car and directed him to the shopping precinct.

It was quieter than Alex had expected, with most shoppers having finished the day before. On the lower floor an amateur brass band played carols, with spectators joining in. Bobby and Mitzi enthusiastically sang 'While Shepherds Watched their Flocks' while Alex, suddenly inspired, sang 'While Shepherds Washed their Socks,' at the top of his voice, until compelled to desist by the glares of a large woman shaking a collecting box.

Under her reproving gaze he put a very large donation into the box and scurried away, his children clinging to his hands and rocking with laughter.

'Oh, Daddy, you are funny.' Mitzi giggled.

'I used to sing that at school,' he remembered. 'It got me into trouble then, too.'

Strolling around later, Mitzi noticed something that made her gasp with joy.

'Daddy, look! Santa Claus!'

The precinct's Santa was just embarking on his last stint, complete with grotto and tree. Mitzi looked up at her father eagerly, but Bobby touched her arm and shook his head.

'We already saw Santa,' he urged. 'Yesterday.'

'We saw him last week too,' she pointed out, 'and the week before.'

Alex watched to see if his son would be stuck for an answer. But he wasn't.

'They were just pretend Santas,' he said. 'The one we saw last night was the *real* Santa.'

'How do you know?' she demanded rebelliously.

'I just do.'

'How?'

'I *do*.'

Mitzi subsided, apparently satisfied with this brand of logic. Bobby looked up at his father and received a wink, which he returned.

'Why don't we go in there?' Alex said, pointing quickly at a store that sold books, CDs and various related items.

As soon as they were inside he struck lucky, coming across a display of 'Marianne' picture books, with one prominently displayed featuring Marianne as a rider.

'Has she got that?' Alex muttered to Bobby.

'No.'

'Here.' He shoved some notes into Bobby's hands. 'You get it while I distract her.'

The teamwork went like clockwork. In a short time Bobby was back with a parcel wrapped in anonymous brown paper.

'What's that?' Mitzi demanded.

'What?' Bobby looked innocently around.

'That!'

'I don't see anything. Do you, Dad?'

'Not a thing.'

Making a covert purchase for Bobby was harder, because he couldn't use Mitzi as an agent. But he struck lucky, noticing a series of video cassettes titled 'Water-colour Technique'. Managing to catch the assistant's eye, he mouthed, 'How much?' pointing at Bobby to explain the reason for silence.

She indicated the price and Alex produced his card. The videos vanished and reappeared safely wrapped.

Luckily, Bobby had started bickering with Mitzi and noticed nothing.

'How about something to eat?' Alex asked. All this undercover work was exhausting.

They found a café and Alex studied the menu, but the other two knew what they wanted.

'Cocoa and cream buns,' Mitzi said blissfully.

'Yes, please,' Bobby chimed in at once.

'But what about your lunch?' Alex objected. 'If I

take you home already full your mother will kill me.'

'It's real cream,' Bobby pointed out.

'Lots and lots of it,' Mitzi said ecstatically.

'Does Mummy allow you to eat cream buns before lunch?'

They considered.

'No,' Bobby said regretfully.

'No,' Mitzi agreed.

'Well, then!'

Bobby regarded him innocently. 'But Mummy isn't here.'

Alex made the mistake of engaging him in debate.

'But aren't you equally bound by her rules even when she's absent?'

'No,' Bobby explained. 'Because it's Christmas, so she might have changed her mind, just this once. We don't know, do we?'

'I suppose we don't,' Alex said, eyeing his son with new respect. 'Mind you, I've got my phone. We could call and ask her.'

'That wouldn't be fair,' Bobby said quickly. 'Mummy's very busy, doing last-minute things. We shouldn't interrupt her.'

'Ah!' Alex gave this idea his full attention. 'You think we could simply assume her agreement—out of consideration for her?'

'Yes,' Bobby said firmly.

They shook hands.

'When you want a job,' Alex told him, 'come to your old man. The thought of you arguing on the other side scares me stiff. You've got every trick.'

'I learned them from my dad.'

'Oh, no, you don't!' Alex said at once. 'I'm not taking the blame for your devious mind.'

Bobby grinned.

They each had three cream buns and two cups of cocoa, and Alex thought he'd never tasted anything so delicious. Then they went home to confess to Corinne. But she wasn't fazed.

'Fine. It'll save me cooking a big lunch. Uncle Jimmy's here, kids.'

Overjoyed, they dashed into the next room where Jimmy, swathed in plaster, was reclining on the sofa. Alex followed and was in time to see them climbing up beside him, moving carefully, not to hurt him.

Mitzi was on his uninjured side and put her arms about him. 'Poor Uncle Jimmy,' she said. 'Is it very bad?'

'Not really,' he said cheerfully.

'What did you do?'

'Fell in the road,' he said at once. 'Silly me.'

Alex regarded him with mixed feelings. It was decent of Jimmy not to have blamed him. On the other hand he couldn't like him, especially as Mitzi was greeting him with real affection. Bobby was less effusive, but he was on Jimmy's injured side.

'Tea up!' Corinne called, entering with a cup.

She handed it gently to Jimmy, who smiled, receiving it, while Mitzi solicitously plumped up his cushions.

A shiver went through Alex. It was absurd, of course, but for a moment they had looked like a family.

The stockings and socks were in place, hanging from the mantelpiece. Jimmy, clowning, had produced one full of holes, which had reduced the children to fits of laughter.

'Right now, you two,' Corinne said. 'Bed.'

'Mummy, we haven't left things for Santa,' Mitzi urged. 'In case he gets hungry and thirsty.'

'What do you want to leave, pet?'

'Jam tarts and milk,' Mitzi said at once.

'Ginger biscuits,' Bobby said. 'And some beer.'

'You can't leave beer,' Mitzi said, scandalised.

'Why not? He'd hardly be drunk in charge of a reindeer after just one beer!' Bobby said.

'But it won't be just one,' Mitzi pointed out. ''Cos he'll have been to lots of other people first, and drunk what they left, and—'

'Well, they won't all have left beer,' Bobby argued.

'Will.'

'Won't.'

'Will.'

'Won't.'

'Will.'

'Won't.'

Corinne tore her hair. 'Break it up, you two. Peace on earth, goodwill to all men.'

'And all women?' Jimmy suggested.

'Especially all the women,' Corinne clowned. 'They're so busy cooking for everyone.'

'I'd do it for you if I had more than one arm.'

'Yeah, sure you would,' she jeered.

'You're a hard woman.'

They grinned at each other. Alex tried to tell himself that they were like brother and sister, but there was something about the cheerful ease of their relationship, the way they shared the same sense of humour, that troubled him.

'Anyway, I vote for jam tarts and milk,' Jimmy insisted.

'I vote for ginger biscuits and beer,' Alex said at once. 'I think Santa gets left a lot of milk, and beer will come as a nice change for him.'

In the end they compromised, which meant that Bobby left out a can of beer and some biscuits, while Mitzi stubbornly left out a carton of milk, jam tarts, and two glasses.

'Why two?' Bobby demanded.

'So that he doesn't have to drink milk and beer out of the same glass,' she riposted.

'He won't drink the milk at all.'

'He will.'

'He won't.'

'Will.'

'Won't.'

'That's enough!' Corinne roared. 'Get to bed, both of you.'

They vanished.

'I think I'll go up too,' Jimmy said.

'You look all in,' Corinne agreed. 'Have you had your pills?'

She fussed over him until he'd taken his medication and at last, to Alex's relief, Jimmy took himself off to bed.

'That's it!' Corinne brushed the hair back from her brow. 'I'm bushed.'

'It's been a great day,' Alex said.

'Yes, it has. You've been terrific.'

'Have I?'

'The kids are so happy. Haven't you seen?'

But it wasn't quite what he wanted to hear.

'What about you?' he insisted.

'It's not about me. It's about you and them. Alex, I've never seen them so much at ease with you. And Bobby—surely you've noticed how he—?'

He kissed her.

He did it so fast that she had no time to resist. Surprise had always brought him results in business, and for a moment he thought it was working here. Corinne didn't try to push him away, but neither did she embrace him back. Instead, she remained so still that it finally got through to him.

'Corinne—'

'Alex, please don't. It's been so lovely. Don't spoil it.'

'Is it spoiling it to say that you're still my wife and I still love you?'

'Don't talk like that,' she begged.

'Corinne, what is it? I thought that when we'd been apart for a while—'

'I'd "see sense"? That's how you think of it, isn't it? You think I had to be crazy to leave you, and that I'll realise I made a mistake.'

'Are you going to say you didn't?'

'Yes, I am saying that. I wanted a home, husband and children, and all I got was the children. They're lovely kids, but I wanted a husband as well.'

'And you couldn't love me?'

'You weren't there. You haven't been there for years.'

His eyes kindled. 'Tell me about this man you want to love. He wouldn't be called Jimmy by any chance?'

'Don't be ridiculous.'

'Is it? I can see that he's a lot of things I'm not— things you might want.'

'Yes, he is. He's kind and dependable, and I always know where I am with him, but—'

Corinne checked herself, on the verge of saying, But he's not you.

It had been a risk, asking Alex to stay for Christmas, but she'd told herself that she must take it for the children's sake. Now she knew it had been a mistake. Her love was not sufficiently buried, or perhaps not sufficiently dead. It threatened her too often and too piercingly.

Alex watched her, willing her to say something that would ease his heart.

'But?' he urged. 'But you haven't forgotten "us." Have you?'

'No,' she admitted unwillingly. 'I can't forget that. I'm not sorry we married. We were very happy back then, and I'll never regret it.'

'If we had the time over again—you'd still marry me?'

'Oh, yes. Even knowing how it would end, I'd still do it.'

'It hasn't ended yet. We don't know how it's going to end.'

'Alex—'

He took hold of her shoulders, very gently. 'It's too soon to say,' he told her. 'Don't let's rush to part, Corinne.'

She gave a wry smile. 'I thought we *had* parted. I should have remembered that no position is ever final until you've agreed to it.'

'Tell me that you don't love me any more,' he said insistently.

'And you're an ace negotiator, always knowing the other side's weak spot.'

'Then you do love me.'

'I don't know.' She sighed. 'I'm trying not to.' She added reluctantly, 'But it's hard.'

He drew her against him, not kissing her this time but wrapping his arms about her body and holding her close while he rested his cheek on her head.

After a while he felt her arms slowly go around him, and they stayed there peacefully together for a long time.

CHAPTER FOUR

WHEN his tiny illuminated clock showed midnight, Bobby slid out of bed and went quietly into the hall. The house was completely silent and almost dark, except for a faint glow he could see downstairs.

Moving noiselessly, he crept down the stairs and into the room where the tree glowed. On the threshold he stopped and an expression of relief crossed his face.

'I knew you'd be here,' he whispered.

The red-clad figure by the tree turned and smiled at him through his huge white beard.

'Come in,' he said.

Bobby moved closer. In dim light, and on his feet, Santa looked bigger than ever.

'Did you have trouble with the chimney?' he asked. 'I was afraid it might not be big enough.'

Santa looked down at his wide girth. 'You mean with there being so much of me?'

'I wasn't being rude.'

Santa laughed, not a *ho-ho-ho,* but a kindly, understanding sound.

'It's not as bad as some places I've tried,' he said.

'What about when there's no fireplace?' Bobby asked. 'How do you get in then?'

Santa tapped the side of his nose and winked. 'Trade secret,' he said.

He sat down in the armchair, put down the can of beer he was holding and signalled for Bobby to sit. Bobby plonked himself down on the floor.

'You know how I got so fat?' Santa asked.

Bobby shook his head.

'In their kindness, people leave more out for me than I can possibly eat.' He indicated the hearth. 'How about you have the milk and we'll split the tarts and biscuits? I've had most of the beer and it was great. Whoever left that was a genius.'

'It was my idea,' Bobby said eagerly. 'Mitzi insisted on putting out a glass for you as well. I said you wouldn't be bothered, but you know what girls are.'

'Actually, Mitzi was right,' Santa confided, holding up a glass with beer in it. 'Drinking from the can is awkward when you've got a beard.'

He poured milk from the carton into the other glass and the two of them sat sipping and sharing tarts.

'So what happened?' he asked. 'Did your dad show up?'

'Yes, just like you said. A day early. How did you know?'

Santa hesitated. 'Inside information.'

'Do you know everything?'

'No,' Santa replied at once.

'So you can't tell me how long he's going to stay?'

'I already did, when we talked yesterday. Longer than tomorrow.'

'But after that?'

'What do you really want him to do?' Santa asked thoughtfully

'Stay as long as possible.'

Santa looked at him keenly. 'Are you hoping I'll wave a magic wand?'

But his thoughtful son shook his head. 'No,' he said. 'He has to want to, or there's no point.'

'That's right,' Santa agreed. 'You can't make people choose what you'd like them to.'

'You mean he doesn't really want to stay with us?'

'Oh, yes, he does. You're his family, and he loves you all more than anything else on earth, even if he doesn't always show it very cleverly. But he got confused and other things got in the way. Now he's trying to find the way back to the place where he took the wrong turning, but it isn't easy. The road seems different when you're looking backwards. But you could help him.'

'How?'

'I can't tell you that. You have to sense it for yourself. But you will. Don't worry.'

Santa indicated the tree.

'Have you got your presents sorted out?'

'Yes. I got a scarf for Mum and a picture book for Mitzi.'

'And your dad?'

'Well—I got him a pair of cufflinks.'

'It sounds like a good choice, so what's the problem?' Bobby's voice had hinted that all was not well.

'I got him something else too, but I'm not sure if I should give it to him.'

'If it's from you, he'll love it,' Santa said without hesitation. 'You can rely on that.'

'Can I show it to you?'

'That would be really nice.'

'It's upstairs.' Bobby went to the door, then hesitated. 'You won't go away?'

'Cross my heart and hope to die.'

Bobby vanished and reappeared a moment later with a large, flat object that he put into Santa's hands, switching on a side lamp so that he could see.

It was a picture of a family sitting under the trees by water, evidently having a picnic. There was a man in a red shirt, a woman in a green and white dress, a small boy of about five and a toddler in a pink dress. It had been painted in water-colours by an inexperienced but talented hand.

'Did you paint this?' Santa asked in a strange voice.

Bobby nodded. His eyes were on Santa's face.

'I think you should definitely give it to him,' Santa said at last.

'You think he'll understand?'

'You put a lot of work into it, and he'll think it's wonderful that you took so much trouble to please him.'

'But will he *understand*?' Bobby asked with a touch of desperation.

'Yes,' Santa said decisively. 'He will.'

'Everything?'

Santa put his hand on the child's shoulder. 'He'll understand everything that you want him to understand,' he said. 'I promise you.'

A smile of pure, blinding relief broke over Bobby's face.

'You'd better go and wrap it now,' Santa said. 'I have a lot of other houses to visit.'

'Goodnight.'

'Goodnight.'

At the door Bobby paused and looked back. 'I didn't used to believe in you. But I do now.'

He vanished quickly.

The brilliant sunlight flashed and glinted off the water and bathed the river-bank with warmth. The man and the woman picnicking under the trees leaned back in the welcome shade and smiled at each other with secret knowledge.

'That was good,' he said. 'The best I ever tasted. Happy birthday, darling.'

She didn't answer in words, but she blew him a kiss. Her arms were curled around the two-year-old girl sleeping in her arms, but her eyes, full of love, were on the man.

'It's not much of a birthday for you, though,' he mused, 'having to do the catering for a picnic.'

'You helped.'

'Did I? Oh, you mean when I dropped the butter?'

They laughed together.

'Wouldn't you rather have had a big night out?' he asked. 'Fancy restaurant, champagne, everything of the best?'

She looked down at the little girl sleeping in her arms. 'You've already given me the best,' she said.

He nodded. 'Yes, this is as good as it gets.'

Suddenly she chuckled.

'What?' he demanded, looking around. 'What?'

'It's that bright red shirt you're wearing. It's so un-you. You're usually so sober-suited.'

'On the contrary, this is the real me. The suit is a uniform, although sometimes it gets to feel like a second skin.'

'So the truth is that you're a bit of a devil?' she teased.

He winked. 'You know more about that than anyone.'

He shifted position to get closer to her, but then

something that came into view made him leap to his feet.

'*Bobby*, not so near the water. Come back here.'

He dashed over and scooped up the five-year-old child, who chuckled with delight as his father carried him back to the picnic.

'Whadaya mean by giving your old man a heart attack, eh?' he demanded as he sat down beside his wife. 'What's the big idea?'

As he joked he buried his face against the child, who screamed with laughter.

'Don't scare him,' the woman protested.

'He's not scared of me. He's my boy. Aren't you?'

'Yes,' said the little boy firmly, putting his arms around his father's neck.

The man turned his head to smile at the woman. 'Do you have any idea how much I love you?' he whispered.

She gave a soft laugh. 'Not a clue. You'll have to tell me.'

He leaned sideways to kiss her, and she leaned towards him. It was awkward because they were each holding a child, but they managed somehow between love and laughter. And the little boy in his father's arms went contentedly to sleep.

Alex awoke with a start and found that he was already sitting up. The dream had been so clear, like being taken back four years to relive the moment.

He'd seen it all again—the trees, the water, the sun. More than that, he'd felt again the blissful contentment of that day.

This is as good as it gets.

That had been his feeling. When had he known it since?

He'd thought of it as something between himself and Corinne. Who would have imagined the little boy was imprinting it all on his mind, to carry there for years until his hands had the skill to reproduce it, like a silent reproach to the adults who had let the happiness slip through their fingers?

He discovered that he was shaking and pulled himself together. He'd been lucky. He'd remembered in time.

Bobby looked in. 'C'mon Daddy. We're opening presents!'

He pretended to lie down again. 'Already? I was hoping for a lie-in.'

'Daddy!'

He grinned and allowed himself to be hauled downstairs in pyjamas and dressing-gown. 'Sorry about this,' he told Corinne. 'I wasn't given any choice.'

'You and me both,' she said, laughing. She'd managed to dress, but only in hastily flung on jeans and sweater, before getting to work in the kitchen.

'Mummy, can we open the presents now?' Mitzi cried.

'Just a moment, pet. Let Uncle Jimmy come downstairs.'

When Jimmy had come cautiously down and settled on the sofa it was time to start. The children first, tearing off gaily coloured paper with excited screams.

Alex held his breath as Bobby opened the water-colour videos and then became totally still, so that Alex feared the whole thing had misfired. But then Bobby looked at him with eyes so full of incredulous joy and relief that Alex's own eyes blurred suddenly.

With Mitzi he scored a double hit, giving her not only the Marianne book but a pair of riding boots. They were too large, but Alex immediately clutched his head, swore he couldn't understand how the mistake had happened, and offered to change them as soon as the holiday was over, and Mitzi was happy.

'Brilliant,' Corinne murmured appreciatively when she had him alone for a moment.

'Even those of us who are moronically stupid have our clever moments,' he riposted.

'Oh, don't be smug.'

His gift to her was a small bottle of expensive perfume, one he'd bought for her in the past. He had thought it a safe present, but suddenly it seemed intimate enough to draw down her disapproval. But she only thanked him with an impersonal smile and said nothing more. He found himself strangely relieved, almost as though he'd been afraid.

Her gift to him had been as impersonal as her smile—a scarf of very fine cashmere, beautiful but meaningless. It told him nothing beyond the fact that she wanted the children to see them being friendly.

The present-giving was nearly over and there were only a few small items left around the base of the tree.

Alex found himself studying them in hope, but none seemed exactly right. The severity of his disappointment shocked him. He was grown up, for Pete's sake! Grown-ups didn't get upset because the right gift wasn't under the tree.

Yet for a moment he was a child again, fighting back the tears because Mum had bought the wrong book and shrugged the mistake aside with, 'Oh, well, it's the same thing, really, isn't it?' And he couldn't explain that it wasn't the same thing at all because she had more important things to worry about than his feelings.

Then he saw his son gradually easing something out from behind an armchair, and relief swept him.

'This is yours,' Bobby said, holding out the brightly wrapped parcel.

'Thank you, son.'

Alex unwrapped it slowly, revealing the picture inside—a water-colour of the happy family sitting

by the river. As he gazed at it he became aware of
his son watching him, full of tension, waiting for
what he would say.

'It's beautiful, son. Did you do it?'

'Yes, I painted it myself.'

'But how do you recall that day? You were only
five years old.'

'You remember, Daddy?' Bobby asked breathlessly.

'Sure I do. It was Mummy's birthday, and we
went out for a picnic. You wandered too near the
water and I had to run and grab you. That was a
great day, wasn't it?'

Bobby nodded. Corinne's eyes were on Alex.

'Do you remember?' Alex asked her.

'Oh, yes, it was lovely.'

'You've even got the details right,' Alex said, returning to the picture. 'Right down to that red shirt.'

'Mummy still has it,' Bobby said.

'Really? Well, that's lucky.'

Corinne was suddenly doing something else. Alex
couldn't even be sure she'd heard the words, although they seemed to sing in his own ears.

Mummy still has it.

It changed everything. Suddenly he was no longer
fighting darkness.

He put a hand on Bobby's shoulder. 'Thank you,'
he said quietly.

The rest of the day was standard-issue

Christmas—turkey, plum pudding, crackers filled with silly jokes and funny hats, Christmas cake, more crackers. Alex faded contentedly into the background, doing nothing that might spoil the atmosphere.

There was the odd awkward moment. From somewhere Jimmy produced a sprig of mistletoe and wandered into the kitchen where Corinne was cooking. Alex heard a giggle, then a silence that tested his control to the utmost. But he forced himself to stay where he was.

And nothing could really spoil the one blazingly beautiful gift that had been given to him unexpectedly.

Corinne had kept the red shirt. He could live on that for a while.

Alex insisted on helping with the washing-up.

'You can't ask the kids and spoil Christmas for them,' he explained. 'And poor Jimmy isn't up to it.'

'Poor Jimmy!' she exclaimed indignantly. 'You're a smug hypocrite, you know that?'

He grinned. 'It's what I'm good at.'

She gave a reluctant laugh and accepted his help.

'I'll wash,' he said. 'I don't know where to put things. Pinny?'

'The only one I have,' she said defiantly, 'has flowers on it.'

'I'll be brave.'

He looked so ridiculous in the flowered apron, with a garish paper hat still on his head, that Corinne's heart melted. He did a good job too, washing and rinsing properly, and it reminded her of how domesticated he was. He'd always done his share in the old days.

'What made you pick this house?' he asked. 'You could have had something better.'

'You mean more expensive? I don't think it comes any better than this. It has a big garden, is full of atmosphere, and the kids love it because it's a house where they can be untidy.'

Bobby appeared in the doorway.

'What is it, darling?' Corinne asked.

'Nothing.'

'Did you want something?'

The boy shook his head. His eyes were fixed on Alex.

Suddenly the little kitchen clock gave three clear chimes, and Alex understood.

Three o'clock. The time when he had originally meant to leave. Bobby was watching him intently.

'It's all right,' he said. 'I'm not going anywhere.'

It was a pleasure to see the smile that came over Bobby's face, but in the very same moment Alex's cellphone rang in the hall. Without a word, Bobby went and fetched it, handing it to his father, his face a careful blank.

The screen was showing Mark Dunsford's number, and for a moment Alex hesitated, tempted to shut it off without answering. But he didn't.

'Mark,' he said in his most discouraging voice.

'Simply checking to see if you need me,' came his assistant's tinny voice.

'For pity's sake, it's Christmas Day!'

'I just thought you'd like to know that I'm on the ball.'

Alex ground his teeth. 'Go and eat some Christmas cake, Mark, and don't call me back unless it's a real crisis.'

He hung up. Bobby's eyes were shining, but all he said was, 'Are you coming back soon, Dad? We haven't used up all the crackers.'

'I'll be there in a moment, son. Put this back for me, will you?'

He handed him the cellphone and Bobby disappeared.

'I'm glad you got rid of that man,' Corinne said. 'I don't like him.'

'Have you met Mark? Oh, yes, he came to the house once.'

'Horrible man.'

'I suppose he reminds you of me,' Alex said wryly.

'Not really. You were always full of fire and enthusiasm. It lit you up inside, and it was exciting. I remember once you got out of bed at one in the

morning to work out some brilliant idea. Your eyes
were shining and your voice had an edge, as though
you'd seen a vision. I never knew what you were
going to do next. But Mark Dunsford is a robot. He
never had an original thought in his life, and he's
trying to make his name by standing on your shoulders. You should watch out for him.'

The same thought had occasionally occurred to
him. Now he marvelled at the shrewdness that had
shown Corinne so much in one brief meeting.

'That must be the first time you've said anything
good about me and the business,' he observed.

'I grew to hate it because it always came first—
before me, before the kids.'

'You never understood how driven I felt.'

'You're wrong. I saw you being driven all the
time. At first, like I say, it was exciting, but later I
saw what it did to you. I used to dream that there'd
come a time when you could ease up, but of course
there never did, and it went on and on, getting worse
and worse.'

He gave a mirthless grunt of laughter.

'Funny! I thought of it as getting better and better,
because I could provide for you properly. A nice
house, holidays—'

'Half of which we ended up taking alone,' she
reminded him. 'Where's the fun in that?'

'But can't you—?'

She stopped him hurriedly. 'Alex, it's all right.

It's finished. It doesn't matter any more. Let's leave it.'

The washing-up was done. Alex looked up at the sprig of mistletoe that Jimmy had fixed overhead.

'Do I get a Christmas kiss?' he asked, speaking lightly to take the sting out of the refusal he expected.

'Of course,' she said.

Moving quickly, she reached up and kissed him on the cheek. He had a brief sensation of her sweetness, the faint tang of the perfume he'd bought her, the warmth of her breath against his face. Then she was gone before he could catch her.

At the end of the day the last cracker had been cracked, the last silly joke read out, the last paper hat reduced to a crumpled wreck. Jimmy opted for an early night. Mitzi, already asleep, was carried to bed, and Bobby went without protest.

'I'm going up now,' Corinne said to Alex, who was drying a cup in the kitchen.

'I'll stay down for a little,' he said. 'There's a late film I want to see.'

'Goodnight, then.'

'Goodnight.'

He kissed her cheek and she put her arms gently around his neck, resting her head on his shoulder. He held her close, swaying back and forth a little in a gentle rhythm.

'It's been a lovely day,' she whispered.

'Yes,' he said. 'Thank you for everything, Corinne. Thank you for making it possible, and not driving me away.'

'I could never want to do that,' she said, raising her head and looking into his face.

It was once more the face she loved, not distorted by anger or masked against her as it had been in the worst days of their failing marriage. For a moment she saw again the vulnerability that had always been there beneath the arrogance, and which had touched her heart.

It touched her now and she turned away quickly.

'What is it?' he asked.

'Nothing.'

He brushed his fingertips across her eyelashes and found them wet.

'Sometimes I feel like doing that,' he said. A tremor went through him. 'I miss you so much.'

'I miss you too. The love doesn't just switch off.'

'Even though you're trying to make it?' he asked.

'I'm working on it. I don't pretend it's easy.'

He kissed the top of her head.

'Goodnight,' he whispered.

She went upstairs and he was left alone.

Midnight. The clock in the kitchen chimed. The room was in darkness except for the tree lights that still glowed and flickered.

Santa smiled at the figure in the doorway. 'Have you come to say goodbye?'

'I wasn't sure if you'd be here,' Bobby said. 'You're supposed to have gone back to the North Pole by now.'

'That's one of the advantages of being the boss. You can change the rules to suit yourself. I thought I'd pop back to see how it was going.'

'It's been brilliant.' Bobby sighed happily. 'He's still here. He liked the picture and everything. He even remembered what it was.'

'Did you think he wouldn't? Yes, well, I suppose you couldn't be blamed for thinking that.' Santa's voice was gentle as he added, 'Let's face it, he's not much of a father.'

'Yes, he is,' Bobby said instantly. 'He's the best.'

'Doesn't spend as much time with you as he should, though, does he?'

'He's very busy. He has lots of other things to think of. But he always comes back to us, because he loves us best in all the world.'

For a moment Santa seemed lost for words. At last he said, 'I know he does.'

'Did he tell you?'

'I just know. He loves his family so much that it hurts, but he's not good at saying things.'

'And we love him best in all the world too,' Bobby said firmly. 'I do, and Mitzi does, and Mum does.'

'Well, I don't know—'

'She does. I know she does.'

There was a silence before Santa said, 'Never mind that. Tell me about Mitzi. Did she have a good day?'

'Oh, yes. Dad gave her that Marianne doll with the riding habit—the one she asked you about the other day. You must have told him.'

Santa grinned. 'Let's just say that I can give him a nudge in the right direction. That's not always easy, because he's a stubborn fellow who doesn't listen as often as he ought.' Seeing Bobby about to flare up, he added quickly, 'Now, be fair; you know that's true.'

'Sometimes,' Bobby conceded.

'Always,' Santa insisted.

'Now and then.'

'All right, I'll settle for now and then. You're quite a negotiator.'

Bobby giggled. 'That's what Daddy says. He says he wants me working for him when I grow up.'

'I thought you wanted to be an artist?'

'Couldn't I be both?'

'You could. But it's better to be what you really want. Your way might be better.'

'Will you be back again, after tonight?'

'I don't know,' Santa said. 'Christmas is passing.'

'But it's not gone yet. Tomorrow's still sort of Christmas. Dad won't leave tomorrow, will he?'

'No, he won't. And if you have him, you don't need me.'

'It's different. I can talk to you.'

'And not to him?'

'Not about everything. He minds too much, you see, and I don't want to hurt him.'

Santa spoke gruffly. 'How do you know he minds so much?'

'Because he tries so hard to pretend that he doesn't,' Bobby said simply.

Santa turned away. 'Goodnight,' he said huskily. 'Go to bed now. Wait for what tomorrow may bring.'

Bobby moved towards the door. As he reached the hall he paused a moment, wondering if he really had heard a noise. But all was dark and quiet. After a moment he sped upstairs.

Alone by the tree, Santa did not move but stood with his head bent, as though trying to bear up under a heavy load.

'Are you all right?'

He turned quickly. Corinne was standing there.

'Of course I am.' He added feebly, 'Ho-ho-ho!'

'You seemed a bit tired.'

He shrugged. 'It's a great responsibility being Father Christmas. It's scary.'

'It must be.' She hesitated. 'I'm glad you came back. He needed to talk to you again.'

Abruptly Santa asked, 'Did you know he was protecting his father?'

'Yes. He always talks about him protectively. Nothing is ever Daddy's fault. If he ever lost that faith it would hurt him more than he could bear.'

'Actually not discussing things in case his father can't cope? This is a nine-year-old child.'

'Nobody really knows what Bobby is thinking,' Corinne said. 'Except maybe you. He tells you things he can't tell anyone else.'

'Not even you?'

'He's protecting me too. Santa Claus can help because he's not involved. And my husband—'

'Your husband's a thick-head, and don't let him tell you any different.'

'He's not that bad.'

'Yes, he is. Take my word.'

Corinne smiled. 'Well, he may have a thick head but he has a thin skin. Only he doesn't know it.'

Santa made a sound like a snort.

'It sounds to me as though you're protecting him too. I'll bet he doesn't know that, either.'

'I don't think it's ever occurred to him.'

'You invited him here for Christmas for his sake as much as the children's, didn't you?'

'You're very astute.'

'Well, maybe a little more than I was,' Santa said gruffly.

'He's lost so much already,' Corinne said. 'I don't

want him to lose any more, otherwise it'll soon be too late.'

Santa stared into the fireplace. 'I think he knows that. Tell me something. Do you know why Bobby chose that picnic to paint?'

'I think it was the last completely happy time we had together. Alex's business was building up fast, but we were still a family. When the picnic was over we went home and put the children to bed. And then we made love—' her voice softened '—and it was the most beautiful thing that had ever happened. He told me over and over how much he loved me and how our love would fill his heart and his life until his very last moment.'

'Is that why you kept the shirt?'

'Yes,' she said softly. 'That's why I kept it.'

'Perhaps you should have thrown it out of your life, along with him.'

'I haven't thrown him out of my life. I never could. It was really the other way around. The day after that picnic he got a call that changed everything. Suddenly it was "big time," and he was never really ours after that. That's why I was surprised he recognised the moment. I should think it feels like another life to him by now.'

'Maybe it does,' Santa said wistfully. 'Another sweeter life that he lost somewhere along the way.' He gave a brief laugh. 'He's not a very clever fellow, is he?'

'Cleverer than I thought,' she murmured.

'I think you should go now,' he said abruptly.

'Can't I stay? I could get you a beer and—'

'Go,' he said with soft vehemence. 'It's better, believe me.'

'Yes,' she said with a sigh. 'I suppose it is.'

When she'd gone Santa stood looking at the doorway, as though hoping she would return. When she didn't, he switched out the tree lights and sat for a long time in the darkness.

CHAPTER FIVE

ALEX could still remember the first Christmas of his marriage, when he and Corinne had gone out early on December the twenty-sixth, and dived into the sales. She had an eye for a bargain, and they had triumphantly carried back home several pieces of household equipment at rock-bottom prices.

As they'd prospered they hadn't needed the sales and Alex, who had been able to buy her anything she wanted, had been bemused by her continued enthusiasm. So it hardly came as a surprise that she was set on attending this year.

He came downstairs to find several newspapers spread out on the kitchen table with four eagerly debating heads leaning over them.

'Washing machine!' Jimmy was making a list.

'Shoes,' Corinne added. 'And a lawnmower—'

They went on compiling the list and Alex, who had learned wisdom, stayed in the background.

At last Mitzi looked up and noticed him, giving him a hug and offering to make him some tea—an offer her mother hastily overruled.

'I'll do it, darling.'

'Morning, Jimmy,' Alex said affably. 'How are

340

you feeling today? You're not looking so good. I expect yesterday took it out of you.'

'It did a bit,' Jimmy admitted. 'But, heck, I wouldn't miss it for anything. I can be ill later.'

'Uncle Jimmy's a soldier,' Bobby said in explanation of this reckless heroism.

'And a good soldier doesn't give in,' Alex agreed, straight-faced. 'But you're looking a bit seedy now. Are you taking your medication?'

'Well, I skipped a bit,' Jimmy conceded. 'You can't drink if you're taking the pills, and it is Christmas—'

'Of course,' Alex agreed. 'But now it's time you took proper care of yourself.'

Corinne turned around, her jaw dropping with indignation at what she could clearly see him up to. But she was pulled up short by the sight of Jimmy's face. He really was pale and strained.

'Oh, Jimmy, you are an idiot.' She sighed affectionately. 'You should have said—or I should have noticed. Stay in bed today.'

'No way. There's masses of sport on television. But I wouldn't mind staying in and watching it with my feet up. You won't mind if I don't come out with you?'

'We'll bear up,' Alex assured him.

He sauntered innocently out into the hall, looking back to catch Bobby's eye and send him a signal. Bobby glanced at Mitzi and Alex nodded.

Message received and understood.

After a moment the two children followed him out.

'Listen, kids,' Alex said hurriedly. 'You're fond of your Uncle Jimmy, aren't you?'

'Yes,' said Mitzi.

Bobby nodded, alert, ready to tune in to his father's signal.

'Well, you wouldn't want to leave him all on his own at Christmas, would you?' Alex asked. 'It wouldn't be a very kind thing to do. Why don't you both stay here with him?'

'What's it worth?' Bobby asked.

'What—? You're my son.'

'And I'm up to every trick. You said so.'

'But, like any skill, it should be used wisely,' Alex said. 'There's a time for using it and a time for not using it.'

'This is a time for using it,' Bobby said firmly.

Alex eyed him with respect mixed with caution.

'I want to come to the shops,' Mitzi said. 'Mummy said she'd get me a doll's house.'

'It's in Bellam's Toys,' Bobby explained. 'There's a big range, and number four is going cheap now because they've just brought out number five. So Mum promised her number four.'

His eyes met Alex's. 'Of course, Mitzi would really prefer number five.'

'Mummy said it would cost too much.' Mitzi sighed.

'But we're holding all the cards,' her brother told her.

'You are, aren't you?' Alex said in appreciation of these tactics. 'Number five it is, on condition you stay at home.'

Mitzi scampered off to tell Jimmy, whose head was aching, that he was going to have the pleasure of her company and they could talk and talk and talk.

'What about you?' Alex asked his son. 'What's your price?'

'Nothing,' Bobby told him.

'But you just said—'

'I always meant to stay at home anyway.'

Alex looked at him with sheer admiration, although he felt compelled to point out, 'But, like you said, you have all the cards. I'd have paid. You missed a trick there, son.'

Bobby shook his head. 'No, I didn't,' he said earnestly. 'Don't you see? I didn't really.'

Alex's amused irony faded and he took Bobby's hand. 'Yes, I do see,' he said seriously.

'Good luck, Dad.'

He knew everything, of course, Alex thought.

'I'll do my best,' he promised his son.

The road to the shopping centre lay through open country. The snow had stopped falling and now lay settled thickly on the ground, the perfect picture of a white Christmas.

They went in Corinne's car, which was larger than Alex's sleek vehicle, made to accommodate children and big enough for the mountain of things she was planning to buy.

'I haven't seen this before,' he observed as they climbed in.

'I got it a month ago.'

Third-hand, from the look of it, he thought. He was wise enough, now, not to say he could have bought her something better, but it flashed through his mind that this was one more thing she'd done without him.

How many other things, now and in the future?

Corinne had on a thick sheepskin jacket and jeans which showed off her long, slim legs, and seemed in high spirits this morning.

'You were rotten to poor old Jimmy,' she chided Alex.

'I advised him to rest and take care of himself, and he was only too glad to accept. He really is feeling poorly, so how can you blame me?'

'Very clever! You know, if there was one thing about you that got up my nose more than any other it was your way of making your most self-interested actions seem perfectly virtuous.'

'But what possible ulterior motive could I have

for wanting Jimmy to stay at home?' he asked innocently. 'You're not suggesting that I was scheming to be alone with you?'

A sideways glance showed her that he was grinning.

'If I wasn't driving I'd thump you,' she said, falling in with his humorous mood. It was hard to be anything but cheerful in the brilliant white scenery around them.

She reckoned that must be the reason for her new sensation of well-being this morning. It was strange how she had awoken full of contentment, almost happiness, and the feeling had lasted so that now she felt oddly light-hearted, like a teenager again.

The shabby old car saw them safely through the treacherous conditions and into the shopping centre car park. They went from store to store, bagging the washing machine first and then working their way down the list.

'Doll's house!' Alex said, seeing Bellam's. 'Quick, before they sell out of number five.'

'Number four,' Corinne objected. 'That's what I promised her.'

'That's a little out of date,' Alex said cautiously. 'What have you been up to?'

'Who? Me?' Under her suspicious gaze he confessed, 'Mitzi and I discussed it and came to a joint decision that number five was a better choice.'

'You mean you bribed her?'

'Bribed is a harsh word.'

'But true.'

'Let's hurry,' he said diplomatically.

Just inside the shop they found a counter with a sale of tiny Christmas trinkets that nobody had bought. To Corinne's surprise Alex lingered there a surprisingly long time, but she didn't see whether he bought anything because an assistant asked her if he could be of help and she hurried to claim the doll's house.

Alex secured the last number five available and bore it out of the shop in triumph, refusing the shop's suggestion of delivery.

'Next Monday?' Alex echoed, aghast. 'If I don't take it home now I won't live that long.'

The box was so big that it blocked his view, and Corinne had to guide him into the elevator, then out and to the car.

'A bit to the left—bit more—stop.'

'Corinne, I can't see a thing,' came a muffled voice from behind the box.

'It's all right, trust me. Take two steps forward. Oh, dear!'

'What does "Oh, dear!" mean?' came a plaintive cry.

'There are some steps just ahead. Go slowly. That's it. Put your foot down very carefully.'

'I didn't need telling that!'

'Now another one—and another—just one more. Now you're on land again. Walk forward.'

'Will you please stop laughing?'

'Who's laughing?' she chuckled, opening the back of the car so that he could edge the box through and finally release it.

'I need something to eat after that,' he said.

They found a café and tucked into fish and chips.

'That'll teach me to make rash promises,' he said, grinning. ''She never warned me it was almost as big as a real house.''

'Alex,' she said abruptly, 'how long can you stay?'

'That's up to you.'

'As long as you like. I have to return to work on Monday, but there's no reason for you to go.'

'Work?'

'Yes, I've got a job.'

'Don't I give you enough to live on? You should have said—'

'You give me far more than I need. That's why I can afford to work part-time. I get the kids off to school first, then I go in to work. In the afternoon my neighbour collects them and they stay with her until I come home. Don't pull a face. They like going there. She's got a dog they can play with.'

'Where do you work?'

'A lawyer's office. It's really interesting. Eventually I thought I could train and get some qualifications.'

'Be a lawyer, you mean?'

'Yes. Not just yet. In five or six years, when the children are more independent. For the moment I just do part-time secretarial work to get the feel of it. I took a computer course and my boss says I'm the best in the office.'

'How long will your training take?'

'About four years to pass all the exams. I reckon I'll be qualified about ten years from now.'

He was silent for so long that Corinne thought he was about to fight her on this, and braced herself to stand up to him. She didn't want to fight, but nor was she going to yield.

But all he said was, 'You must be brilliant if you did that computer course so quickly.'

'I started doing it six months ago. I used the computer you bought for Bobby.'

'Six months? While we were together?'

'Uh-huh!'

It was painful, like discovering that she'd had a secret life—which, in a way, he supposed she had.

'And you made sure you didn't tell me?'

'No, Alex, I didn't ''make sure'' of not telling you. I'd gladly have told you if you'd shown any interest, or even been there. But you were such an absentee that I could have got away with murder. I could have had a dozen lovers and you'd never have suspected.'

'Very funny.'

'Don't glare at me. Many men who live for their work secretly know that their wives are getting up to every kind of mischief behind their backs. But my furtive trysts were with a computer. My "clandestine mail" came from a correspondence course, and you never surprised my guilty secret because it never occurred to you that I was interesting enough to have one.

'Well, I had, and I passed with very high marks. My boss is very glad to have me around. They've just had a load of state-of-the-art machines delivered and I'm the only one who knows what to do with them. I can't tell you how—' She stopped suddenly.

'How proud that made you?' he suggested.

'No, how sad it made me. There was nobody to tell.'

He nodded. 'And you need someone to tell your triumphs to or they don't amount to much. I always told things to you. Nobody else's opinion ever mattered as much as yours.'

'I'd have loved to tell you, but I knew it would look very trivial to the boss of Mead Consolidated.'

After a moment he asked, 'Does Jimmy know?'

'Only since he came here last week.'

'And I suppose he's rooting for you?'

'Yes, he thinks it's great.'

Alex was silent. He was afraid to ask any more about Jimmy. Instead he said, 'You've got the rest of your life pretty well mapped out, haven't you?'

'It's good to have a goal.'

'Yes, I see that. Ten years—heck! I don't know anyone who plans that far ahead.'

'I must. I'm thirty already. I have to make the most of my time.'

'Where do I come into your plans?'

'You're still the children's father.'

'I'm still your husband, and I want to go on being your husband.'

'Alex, nothing's going to change. You are as you are. What's the point of saying all this? I tried to explain when we broke up, and you weren't listening then, either.'

Alex sighed. 'Yes, I was. I know it didn't seem like it, but I heard. You were saying you were better off without me.'

Dumbly she shook her head. It was less a denial than an attempt to fend off confusion.

'I never said that,' she said at last. 'And I never, never will. Not with all the things I remember.'

'What do you remember?' he asked gruffly.

'You, as you were when I met you,' she said wistfully. 'You were wonderful—the most wonderful, generous, loving man in the world.'

Her words hurt him unbearably. 'I'm still the same—' he pointed to himself '—in here.'

'I wouldn't know,' she said sadly. 'It's a long time since I've known what was happening in there.'

'Nothing's changed. Not towards you. Tell me it's the same with you. Or can't you say it?' His voice was ragged.

'Yes.' She sighed. 'I can say it. But we're not youngsters now, and it's not enough.'

'Are you happy?' he asked abruptly.

'I don't know,' she said slowly. 'I'm not sure it really matters.'

He realised that she had altered in some indefinable way. There was a calm about her now, as though she had settled something that had long been troubling her.

'Alex,' she said suddenly, 'will you tell me something honestly?'

'Fire away.'

'But I mean honestly. No polite lies. No gilding the lily. The unvarnished truth.'

'All right.'

'Why did you arrive here early and stay late?'

He hesitated, knowing that he was going to confirm her worst suspicions. Yet she'd asked for honesty and he could give her no less.

'Something fell through,' he said reluctantly. 'Craddock set up a party in the Caribbean, to settle the contract. Then he got ill.'

She faced him. 'And if he hadn't got ill?'

It was the question that he'd dreaded, but he said, 'Then I wouldn't have come at all.'

She didn't seem to react, only nodded slightly, as though something had been confirmed.

It made him burst out, 'But I did come, and I found myself talking to my son, who didn't know it was me. And I found out a lot of things I didn't know before. Maybe it's my fault that I didn't, but I know them now. It makes everything different.'

'Between you and the children. Not between you and me.'

'But it can if we let it. Corinne, come home. I want to try again. Don't you want that too, in your heart?'

'I can't come back to that soulless place, Alex. I hated it. My home is here.'

'Then I'll come here.'

'Here? You mean move into where I'm living now?'

'It doesn't matter as long as we're together. If we stay here you'll still have your job and—'

'Wait, Alex, please. I know you when you've set your heart on something. You go bull-headed for it without thinking it through. How long would it be before things went wrong again? I know you've understood things these last few days, but that isn't the complete answer you seem to think.'

'But if we still love each other—'

'I do still love you, but—'

'But you think I'm beyond redemption,' he said wryly.

'You don't need redemption. I think you might need a different kind of wife—one who can enjoy the entertaining you want, and wear glamorous clothes, and be a credit to you.'

'To blazes with that!' he said impatiently. 'None of that stuff matters. I want you, and the children. My God!' He was growing angry. 'You've not only mapped out your own life but mine too. I'm headed for a trophy wife, am I? You'd better tell me her name now, because I'm sure you've picked her out.'

'Calm down!'

'I'm damned if I will! What do you suggest—a luscious little blonde with a cleavage, or a busty brunette who'll marry me for my gold card? Do you think I want anyone like that after being married to *you,* or is that all you think I'm worth?'

'I'm sorry,' she said in anguish. 'I didn't mean to hurt you.'

He didn't say any more. But he took her hand and laid it against his cheek, closing his eyes.

'Alex—'

'Hush,' he said. 'Don't say anything.'

She nodded and lifted her other hand to touch his face gently.

'There won't be anyone,' he said in a voice that was both fierce and quiet. 'It's just you. Nobody else. Sometimes I wish that wasn't true. Hang it,

Corinne, I'd like to be able to forget you and pass on to something new as easily as you've done. But I can't. If that's inconvenient, I'm sorry, but I always was an awkward cuss, and I haven't changed in that way either.'

She wanted to tell him that it was all an illusion. She hadn't passed on to something new because he still haunted her and always would. But those would be dangerous words to say to him.

Suddenly he seemed to pull himself together.

'Come on,' he said. 'It's time we got back to work. There's a lot still on that list.'

He rose abruptly, leaving her no choice but to do the same. The subject was closed, she thought. He had simply put it behind him.

It was two hours before they had completed the list and were able to start the journey home. By that time the temperature had fallen sharply and Corinne drove in silence, concentrating on the road, which had become treacherous.

When they left the town and reached the country stretch they slowed.

'It looks like it snowed here in the last half-hour,' he said, 'and there hasn't been much traffic, so it's probably icy—'

The words were barely out of his mouth when the car began to make choking noises.

'What's that?' Alex asked.

'Nothing,' she said quickly. 'It's done it before.

It doesn't mean anything. It'll go back to normal in a moment.'

But instead of going back to normal the vehicle choked some more, slowed, and then quietly died in the middle of the road.

'Oh, heck!' she said wretchedly. 'Is anything coming?'

'No, but let's get this to the side before anything does.'

Together they set their shoulders to the rear and pushed the car until it glided on to the grass verge, where it settled, out of danger but totally useless.

Alex pulled his cellphone out of his pocket and called the rescue service. As he'd expected, he was at the end of a long line.

'An hour, minimum,' he groaned as he hung up.

'We have to stay here for an hour?' she asked, horrified.

'Not necessarily here. If we take a walk through those trees I think there are some buildings on the other side. There might be a pub where we could get a sandwich.'

'Can I borrow your phone?'

She called home and was answered by Bobby.

'Everything's fine, Mum. Mitzi's looking through her books and Uncle Jimmy's watching telly.'

'Can I talk to him?'

Jimmy assured her that all was well and there

would be no trouble about her being late. Corinne hung up, satisfied.

'Let's see where the trees lead,' she said to Alex.

He took her hand and kept hold of it as they wandered beneath the great oaks. The sun was beginning to set, sending golden beams slanting through the branches and on to the snowy ground, and for a while they walked in silence.

It was magic, Corinne thought; the kind best enjoyed in silence. But when she looked at Alex she saw that he was walking with his head down, scowling with tension. His misery reached her almost tangibly, defeating her resolve to keep her distance.

'Alex—' She stopped and turned him to face her, and at once it seemed natural to put her arms about him and pull his head on her shoulders. Hang good resolutions, she thought. He was in pain, and she could no more refuse to comfort him than refuse to breathe.

'Corinne, I'm afraid,' he whispered.

'Afraid of what, my dearest?'

'Everything. Going back to that empty house, that empty life, knowing it's all I'm fit for now. I'm losing everything I care about, and I don't know how to stop it.'

Her heart ached for him. She longed to say, Come home. Everything is all right again, and see the happiness return to his face.

But she knew she mustn't say it. Everything was

still not right. Perhaps it would never be right. She shared his sense of helplessness. It was too soon to think that a reconciliation could be easy, or even possible. Until she could see the way ahead she could say nothing to comfort him.

This visit wasn't working out as she'd expected. She had sent the invitation to the brusque, hard-faced man he had been at the end. But the man who'd arrived had been closer to the old Alex, reminding her of the unexpected touch of defence-lessness that he'd always tried so hard to disguise, and had succeeded with everyone but her.

She'd vowed to keep her heart to herself in future, but he'd exerted his dangerous spell on it again, filling her with confusion.

'Don't be afraid,' she said. 'You're the man who's never afraid, remember?'

'That's all a con,' he admitted. 'Underneath, my knees were always knocking. Except with you. They never really stopped. Hold on to me.'

She did so, feeling him clinging to her in return, holding her as tightly as a drowning man might clutch a lifeline.

'I love you so much,' he said huskily.

'I love you,' she told him truthfully.

Let's try again.

The words trembled on her tongue, but somehow they couldn't be spoken, although she could sense the longing to hear them in every tremor of his body.

Instead she raised her face to him and felt his lips cover hers.

He had kissed her before, on Christmas Eve, but that had been different. That kiss had lacked the driving intensity of this one. Last time he'd been overconfident and it had made her freeze. Now he kissed her like a man who feared he might never be able to do so again, with a dread and desperation that made it impossible for her to hold out against him.

His lips still had the skill to excite her, carrying the reminder of a thousand other times when a kiss had been the prelude to lying naked in his arms and being taken to another world that they made themselves out of love and desire. The memories crowded in on her now, making her ache with longing for what she had renounced.

She was kissing him back. She didn't mean to, but she couldn't help herself, for she too thought this might be the last time, and there was so much that she wanted to remember.

Alex, the generous lover, seeking her delight before his own, as subtle in his lovemaking as he was unsubtle in his daily life—the man who could be hurt by a word or a look, and who would move heaven and earth to hide it. He had been hers, she had let him go, and soon she would send him away for good.

'Corinne—Corinne—'

Just that. Just her name, spoken in a voice of racking anguish. It tormented her, but she would stay firm somehow.

'Don't cry,' he whispered.

She hadn't known that she was crying, but she knew why she couldn't help it. She was saying a final goodbye to the only man she could love, and though it broke his heart, and her own, she was resolved on doing it.

'*Excuse me!*'

It took a long moment for them to return to reality enough to realise that a man was trying to attract their attention.

'*Are you the gentleman who sent for a tow?*'

'Yes,' Alex said raggedly. 'I am.'

'I know we said an hour, but I managed to get here a bit early,' the man called. 'Right, let's get to work. Can I have the keys?'

Alex was pale and his hands shook, but he had regained command of himself. He stood aside as Corinne handed over the keys to the car, then they all walked back through the trees in the setting sun.

CHAPTER SIX

ALEX supposed it was natural for reaction to set in as Christmas passed. That was the only reason he could think of for the weight that suddenly seemed to descend on Bobby. He had always been a thoughtful child, but now he was more silent than usual, as though burdened by some extra care.

'Do you know what ails him?' Alex muttered to Corinne, joining her in the kitchen on the morning of the twenty-seventh.

'No, all I know is that it happened suddenly, some time yesterday evening. But if I ask him about it he swears nothing's wrong. It's best to leave him alone, then maybe he'll tell us.'

Alex nodded and tried to do as she said, but it was hard to realise that the newly established trust between himself and his son was melting away, and be unable to understand. It was also painful to see the forced brightness that Bobby sometimes remembered to assume.

To divert him, he started a snowball fight in the garden, with Mitzi joining in and Jimmy cheering from the sidelines. When they had got each other wet they dashed back into the house, dried off hastily and continued the fight with cushions.

To Alex's pleasure, Bobby became caught up in what he was doing and laid about him vigorously with a big soft cushion, yodelling with glee.

Totally absorbed in the tussle, Alex failed to hear the front doorbell, or observe Corinne go to answer it. It was taking all his attention to deal with Bobby, who wielded the big cushion expertly until suddenly it collided with Alex's shoulder and split. A cloud of little feathers flew up to the ceiling and settled back over Alex, who had fallen on to the sofa in a paroxysm of laughter.

He was madly blowing feathers away when a figure he recognised walked into the room.

'Mark!' he exclaimed.

Mark Dunsford regarded his employer with something close to disapproval in his eyes.

'I've been trying to get hold of you since yesterday,' he said. 'It's very urgent.'

Out of the corner of his eye he saw Corinne grow very still. Little Mitzi did the same. But the stillest of all was Bobby.

'It can't be that urgent,' he said. 'You could have called me.'

'I tried. Your cellphone is switched off.'

'No way,' Alex said at once. 'I never switch it off.'

'I assure you, it's switched off now.'

Frowning, Alex rose and went out into the hall

where his coat hung, plunged his hand into the pocket and pulled out the phone. It was off.

'But how did—?'

Alex checked himself. The air was singing about his ears, and suddenly he knew that what he said next was going to be critical.

'Well—' he said at last '—so I switched it off and forgot. Is that so strange at Christmas?'

'What is strange is that it seems to have been switched off after I made a call,' Mark observed.

'That's impossible. You must be mistaken.'

'It definitely rang several times, long enough for my identity to be displayed on the screen. Then it was turned off. I was curious, as you've never done such a thing before.'

Alex shrugged. 'There's a first time for everything. I must have been overcome by the Christmas spirit.'

'But to do it now, when such an important deal is hanging in the balance!' Mark sounded aghast at the thought that his idol might have feet of clay. 'That's simply not like you.'

The next moment he had another shock. Alex's voice was cool as he asked, 'What was so urgent that it couldn't wait?'

'I called you to let you know of the change of plan. It seems that Craddock's illness was a false alarm—just indigestion—so the Caribbean is on again. The flight leaves this afternoon. You've just about got time.'

'Time for what?' Alex asked blankly.

'Time to catch the plane. I went to the office first, and collected your passport and ticket. Luckily your address book was there and I was able to discover where your wife was living.'

'But how did you know I'd be here?' Alex asked quietly. 'I didn't tell you.'

'It was a reasonable supposition, and luckily correct, otherwise I wouldn't have known where to find you at all.'

'I see. Well, I would rather you hadn't done that. Please remember for the future.'

'But to put yourself completely out of touch when—well, I've found you now. You'll have to hurry.'

Alex rubbed his eyes. 'I'm sorry, I'm afraid I'm not quite with you. I'm not going anywhere, Mark.'

'You don't understand. The contract—'

'I understand all right. Old man Craddock thinks he can snap his fingers and everyone will jump.'

'He knows we need that contract—'

'No, we don't need it,' Alex interrupted him firmly. 'We want it, but we don't need it. He won't find another firm that'll do the job as well for such a reasonable price, and he knows it. *He* needs *us*, and I'm not cutting short the best Christmas of my life just to dance to his tune.'

'But—'

'Mark, do you know why he wanted to gather us all round him on the other side of the world? Because he's a lonely old man with no family. He has no children and both his wives left him. I'm sorry for him, but I'm damned if I'm going to end up like him.'

Mark was aghast at this heresy.

'But somebody ought to be there, representing the firm. If you won't go, then let me.'

Alex shrugged. 'OK, you can do it if you like. I'm sure you've got your passport, because I always used to carry mine, and you strike me as frighteningly like myself as I was in those days.'

'Frighteningly?'

'Terrifyingly. Appallingly. You've got that look in your eyes. It's like talking to a ghost of myself.'

Mark looked indignant.

'I'm not ashamed of following your lead. And if, as you say, I can go—'

'You can if you want to, but if you've got any sense you won't. I know you have no family, but isn't there a girlfriend you ought to be with?'

'I do have a girlfriend, and I've spent some time with her this Christmas—'

'*Some* time? God help you!'

'But she understands that I need to seize every opportunity—'

'Spare me the speech.' Alex was talking to Mark,

but he was aware of Corinne, watching him, holding her breath. 'I wrote that speech myself, long ago. Now I'm tearing it up. Catch the plane if you want to, Mark, tell Craddock I've got a bug or something, and you're fully empowered to sign for me. Otherwise tell him I'll be back in the office next Monday, ready to do business. It's up to you, but try to be wiser than I was.'

Mark was stiff with outrage.

'Then, with your permission, I'll go to the Caribbean and watch over your interests there.' His tone implied that somebody needed to mind the shop until his employer recovered his senses.

'Fine, I'll see you when you get back and knock some sense into you then.' Alex grinned. 'We'll have cocoa and cream cakes in my office.'

At this, Mark's hair practically stood on end. 'Cocoa and—?'

'Never tried it? You haven't lived. You'd better be off if you're going to catch that plane.'

When Mark had left nobody spoke for a while. For the first time Alex realised that he was still covered with feathers. No wonder Mark had thought he was crazy.

He caught Corinne's eye and realised that she'd had the same thought. She was smiling at him, but not just in amusement. There was a warmth and tenderness in her eyes that he had not seen there for a long time.

She came forward, hands outstretched to him.

'You really did that?' she asked eagerly. 'You really switched the phone off and blocked his call?'

For a moment the temptation to say yes was overwhelming, but with her candid eyes on him he had to say, 'No, I didn't do that. I don't know how it happened. I'm glad of it, but it's a mystery to me.'

'It was me.'

For a moment they had forgotten Bobby standing there, silently watching everything. Now they saw his face, white and determined.

'It was me,' he said again.

'What do you mean, son?' Alex went and sat on the sofa, taking Bobby's hands in his.

'I was in the hall last night, and I heard your cellphone ringing,' Bobby said. 'I took it out of your coat pocket. I was going to take it to you, but—then I didn't.'

'Why not?' Alex asked gently.

'Because I knew it was that man,' Bobby said desperately. 'It was displayed on the screen, the same as last time he called. I knew he'd want to take you away, and I didn't want you to go, so I switched it off and put it back in your pocket, and I never told you.'

'Oh, darling,' Corinne said quickly, fearful of Alex's anger at this interference and wanting to protect the child from it. 'I know why you did it, but you really shouldn't have—'

She broke off. Alex's hand was suddenly raised to silence her. He was looking intently at his son and there was no anger in his face.

'Were you going to tell me about it?' he asked gently.

'Yes, but only when it was too late,' Bobby blurted out with such fierce resolve that Alex's lips twitched. 'I knew you'd be angry but I didn't want you to go. It's been brilliant this Christmas—the best ever. You've really *been* here, *really* been here, not just pretending like other times, but talking and—and *listening,* and being interested, and I didn't want it to end. I wanted you to stay and stay for ever, but he'd have made you go away and—and—'

'Hey, steady on, calm down,' Alex said softly, brushing back a lock of tousled hair from his son's forehead. 'You wanted me that much?'

Bobby nodded vigorously.

'Well—' Alex had to stop for a moment to control his voice, which was beginning to shake. 'I can't be angry at you for wanting me, can I?'

'I'm sorry, Daddy.'

'Sorry for what?'

'Your trip—and your contract.'

'I didn't want the trip, and I haven't missed the contract. Or, if I have, I'm well rid of it if that was the only way I could have it.'

Bobby looked at him uncertainly. 'Really?'

'Let me tell you something, son. What you did was completely unnecessary. If I'd spoken to Mark last night I'd have said the same as you heard me say today.'

Bobby didn't reply. He was gazing at his father, as though longing to believe what he'd just heard, if only—

Alex spoke again, in a rallying tone. 'You don't think I'd want to go away from all of you, do you?'

Bobby shook his head.

'Well, then!' Alex smiled at his son. 'I tell you what, it proves what a great team we make. You did exactly what I'd do, just as though you'd read my mind.'

Those words brought forth Bobby's own beaming grin, full of joy and relief. The next moment he was in his father's arms.

With Bobby encircled by one arm and Mitzi by the other, he looked up at Corinne. She was not smiling, as he'd hoped, but looking at him with a kind of satisfaction, as though he'd just confirmed something that she'd known in her heart all the time.

'This is our last meeting,' Santa said. 'I don't usually stick around this long, but I did this time, just for you.' He leaned down to look at the boy. 'Do you think you'll manage?'

'Oh, yes,' Bobby said simply. 'It's all right now.

But you will come back next year, won't you?' he added anxiously.

'Yes, I'll be back. In the meantime, keep this to remember me by.'

He handed Bobby a small object that he took from his pocket—a medallion made of wood, with the head of Santa Claus in relief. It was a trivial thing, such as anyone might have bought cheap in the sales now that the season was over. But to Bobby it was a precious talisman.

'For you,' said Santa. 'Until we meet again.'

'Goodbye,' Bobby whispered. 'Until we meet again.'

When he'd gone Santa stayed there a while, wondering. He'd almost given up when another figure appeared in the doorway.

'You're a wise man,' she said. 'Tell me what I should do.'

'It depends whether you're thinking of him or yourself,' Santa told her. 'For your own sake you should send him on his way and marry Jimmy.'

'That's your advice?'

'It's what's best for you.'

'Would it be best for him?'

Santa shook his head. 'It would finish him. He couldn't cope. He told you about going home to an empty place, but he didn't say how bad it is without you—how he makes excuses to work extra late so that he doesn't have to go back and face the emptiness, or how he jumps whenever the phone rings in case it's you, and curses when it isn't.

'I know he's a difficult man, but he understands things now that he didn't understand before. Doesn't he deserve a chance to show you? I'm not saying it'll be easy. He's still going to get it wrong a lot of the time, maybe most of the time. But he loves you and he needs you, and without you he's going to turn into a mean, miserable old man. Are you simply going to abandon him to that fate?'

'But you just told me that I ought to marry Jimmy.'

'He's steady and reliable, and he'll give you no trouble.' Santa couldn't resist adding, with a marked lack of Christmas spirit, 'He'll also bore the socks off you.'

'That's true. And maybe I feel I could cope with a little trouble.'

He looked at her uncertainly, as though not sure that he'd heard correctly.

'So—what are you going to tell him?' he asked cautiously.

'Nothing.' She gave Santa the smile of a conspirator. 'You're such a great ambassador. Why don't you tell him?'

'Tell him what?'

'Whatever you think he most wants to hear.'

She kissed him on the cheek. Then she was gone.

*　　*　　*

Jimmy was up early the next morning, packing his suitcase with one inexpert hand.

'Will you be all right for the journey?' Corinne asked, coming to help him. 'You surely don't have to go yet?'

'Yes, I do,' he said sadly. 'I'm a soldier, remember? I know when I'm beaten.'

She didn't ask what that meant.

Alex drove him to the station, and they parted on reasonably cordial terms, considering. Alex was feeling cordial to the whole world this morning, although there was still a touch of anxiety in his manner when he returned and went to find Corinne. He found her upstairs in her bedroom, pushing clothes aside in the wardrobe.

'It's still a bit cramped,' she said. 'But your things can overflow into the guest room now Jimmy's gone.'

'Are you sure?' he asked quietly. 'There's still time to send me away.'

She smiled. 'Is there? Would you go if I told you to?'

'Nope.' He took her into his arms. 'This is home now.'

'You don't mind moving in here?'

'I wouldn't have it any other way. This is the home where we became a family, and where we'll stay a family.'

'Suddenly you're very wise,' she said.

'I've been taking advice from a mysterious friend. He's a very old man who knows a lot because people tell him things. He says the problems won't simply vanish, but if the love is there we should never give up on it.'

'And the love *is* there,' she said.

'Yes. Always.' He took her face between his hands. 'I love you, Corinne, with everything in me. Promise me that you'll remember that when I act like a jerk.'

'Are you likely to do that?'

He nodded wryly. 'Oh, yes.'

'Me, too.'

'We've just taken the first step,' he said seriously. 'I don't know where the other steps will lead, but if you're with me I'll follow the path in any direction.'

'It may lead to some strange places,' she reminded him.

'Just keep tight hold of my hand.'

He drew her close and kissed her. If their last kiss had been one of farewell, this was one of greeting, neither quite knowing who the other was any more, but glad to be introduced.

They didn't see the door open and two heads look in, then withdraw silently.

'Told you,' Bobby said triumphantly. 'I *said* Dad would come back for good.'

'You were just guessing,' Mitzi accused.

'I wasn't.'

'Was.'

'Wasn't.'

'Was.'

'I knew he was coming back. I had—' Bobby looked around significantly '—inside information.'

'Go on! Who?'

'Santa Claus.'

Mitzi looked at him with six-year-old sisterly scorn. 'You're batty, you are!' she announced. 'There is no Santa Claus.'

'There is.'

'Isn't.'

'Is.'

'Isn't.

'Is. What's more, I talked to him.'

'Batty!' she said again. 'Batty, batty, batty!'

She ran off down the stairs, yodelling the word happily.

Bobby was not upset by this reaction. At six, Mitzi still had a lot to learn about life, and people, and Santa.

'Santa Claus,' he said. 'Santa Claus—Father Christmas.'

He took the little wooden medallion from his pocket and turned it over in his fingers, still murmuring softly. 'Father Christmas, Father Christmas—'

He smiled to himself with secret contentment.

'*Father.*'

EPILOGUE

One year later

'YOU see, I kept my word,' Santa said.

Bobby nodded, slipping into the room and regarding his friend with shining eyes.

A year had made him two inches taller, and the shape of his face was a little different. His eyes were, perhaps, a little too wise for his age, but that was his nature. The tension and sadness were gone.

'I knew you'd come because you said you would,' he said.

Santa looked around him at the room. 'I hardly recognise this place.'

Bobby nodded. 'We've been redecorating. Dad tried to do this room himself, only he's rotten at it, and Mum said he should chuck the paintbrush away and she'd get a firm in to do it, and anyway they had better things to do, now that I'm going to have a baby brother or sister.'

He turned to look at a small figure who had appeared in the doorway.

'Come in. I told you he'd be here.'

Mitzi came further into the room, eyeing Santa

with a touch of suspicion, then coming close and poking him in the stomach.

'Ow!' he remembered to say.

'You see, I'm not batty,' Bobby told her.

'Yes, you are,' she said firmly.

'Aren't!'

'Are!'

'Aren't!'

'Are!'

'That's enough, the pair of you,' Corinne said, coming in. 'Go to bed, now. Santa still has a full night's work to do.'

He leaned down to them. 'That's right. I'll say goodbye now. I won't be back tomorrow, like I was last time.'

'And next year?' Bobby asked.

'We'll see.' Santa added thoughtfully, 'Most boys of your age don't believe in Santa Claus.'

Bobby regarded him with a faint quizzical smile. 'I believe in *you*,' he said.

Mitzi nodded. Then she put her arms around his huge girth as far as they would go, which wasn't far. Santa leaned down and she vanished into his white hair.

'Goodnight, both of you,' he said huskily.

When the children were gone Corinne looked at Santa's belly, then at her own, which was about the same size.

'I wouldn't have much luck cuddling you, either,'

she said, chuckling. 'Cross fingers that we'll make it through Christmas.'

'Well, if not, that husband of yours. is here.' Beneath his beard Santa paled slightly. 'He may not be much use, but he's here.'

'Don't you say a word against my husband. The clinic said he was doing the breathing exercises very well. Better than me.'

He grinned, but then the grin faded. 'Are you going to be all right?' he asked seriously.

She smiled. '*We're* going to be all right. All of us.'

'Sure?'

'I'm like Bobby. I believe in *you*. Happy Christmas, Santa. Now and always.'

SPOTLIGHT

Every month we'll spotlight original stories from Harlequin and Silhouette Books' Shining Stars!

Fantastic authors, including:
- Debra Webb
- Julie Elizabeth Leto
- Merline Lovelace
- Rhonda Nelson

Plus, value-added Bonus Features are coming soon to a book near you!

- Author Interviews
- Bonus Reads
- The Writing Life
- Character Profiles

SIGNATURE SELECT SPOTLIGHT
On sale January 2005

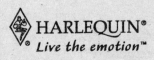

HARLEQUIN®
Live the emotion™

Silhouette®
Where love comes alive™

Escape with a courageous woman's story of motherhood, determination...and true love!

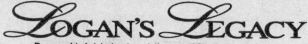

ᒪOGAN'S ᒪEGACY

Because birthright has its privileges and family ties run deep.

Coming in December...

CHILD OF HER HEART

by

CHERYL ST.JOHN

After enduring years of tragedy, new single mother Meredith Malone escaped with her new baby daughter to the country—and into the arms of Justin Weber. The sexy attorney seemed perfect...but was he hiding something?

Where love comes alive™

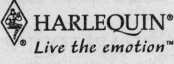

Bachelors of Shotgun Ridge returns with a
new story of dramatic passion and suspense...

Award-winning author

MINDY NEFF

When Abbe Shea's fiancé is killed by the mob, she
flees to Shotgun Ridge, Montana...and to the safety
of Grant Callahan's breeding ranch. Grant knows
she's in trouble...and he's determined to protect her.

"Mindy Neff is top-notch!"–author Charlotte Maclay

**Look for SHOTGUN RIDGE,
coming in September 2004.**

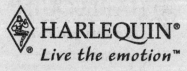

HARLEQUIN®
Live the emotion™

www.eHarlequin.com

PHSR

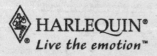